CONRaD'S
FATE

THE WORLDS
✷OF CHRESTOMANCI✷

Book 1: CHARMED LIFE
"An outstandingly inventive and entertaining novel.
Altogether a delightful book."—*Times Literary Supplement*

Book 2: THE LIVES OF CHRISTOPHER CHANT
✷ "A cracking good story."—ALA *Booklist,* starred review

Book 3: THE MAGICIANS OF CAPRONA
"Chalk up another triumph for Jones, who is as gifted
at spellbinding as any of her characters."—*Publishers Weekly*

Book 4: WITCH WEEK
"Entertaining and often hilariously funny."—*The Horn Book*

Book 5: CONRAD'S FATE
"*Conrad's Fate* is quintessential Chrestomanci—funny, smart,
twisty, exciting, tricky, delightful, and always perfectly magical."
—Neil Gaiman

MIXED MAGICS: FOUR TALES OF CHRESTOMANCI
"A new addition to the Chrestomanci canon is cause for celebration."
—*The Horn Book*

✷✷✷

THE CHRONICLES OF CHRESTOMANCI, VOLUME I
(Contains Books 1 and 2)

THE CHRONICLES OF CHRESTOMANCI, VOLUME II
(Contains Books 3 and 4)

DIANA WYNNE JONES

CONRAD'S FATE

A CHRESTOMANCI BOOK

GREENWILLOW BOOKS

An Imprint of HarperCollins*Publishers*

Conrad's Fate
Copyright © 2005 by Diana Wynne Jones
All rights reserved. No part of this book may be used or reproduced in any manner whatsoever without written permission except in the case of brief quotations embodied in critical articles and reviews. Printed in the United States of America. For information address HarperCollins Children's Books, a division of HarperCollins Publishers, 1350 Avenue of the Americas, New York, NY 10019.

www.harperchildrens.com

The right of Diana Wynne Jones to be identified as the author of this work has been asserted by her.

The text of this book is set in Granjon.
Book design by Chad W. Beckerman

Library of Congress Cataloging-in-Publication Data
Jones, Diana Wynne.
Conrad's fate/ by Diana Wynne Jones.
p. cm.
"Greenwillow Books."
Summary: When his uncle sends him to work at the mysterious Stallery Mansion, twelve-year-old Conrad Tesdinic must overcome his bad karma and discover the source of the magic that threatens to pull his world into one of the eleven other parallel universes.
ISBN 0-06-074743-9 (trade).
ISBN 0-06-074744-7 (lib. bdg.)
[1. Magic—Fiction. 2. Witchcraft—Fiction.
3. Fantasy.] I. Title.
PZ7.J684Co 2005 [Fic]—dc22   2004042462

First Edition 10 9 8 7 6 5 4 3 2 1

Greenwillow Books

For Stella

One

When I was small, I always thought Stallery Mansion was some kind of fairy-tale castle. I could see it from my bedroom window, high in the mountains above Stallchester, flashing with glass and gold when the sun struck it. When I got to the place at last, it wasn't exactly like a fairy tale.

Stallchester, where we had our shop, is quite high in the mountains, too. There are a lot of mountains here in Series Seven, and Stallchester is in the English Alps. Most people thought this was the reason why you could only receive television at one end of the town, but my uncle told me it was Stallery doing it.

"It's the protections they put round the place to stop anyone investigating them," he said. "The magic blanks out the signal."

My Uncle Alfred was a magician in his spare time, so he knew this sort of thing. Most of the time he made a living for us all by keeping the bookshop at the cathedral end of town. He was a skinny, worrity little man with a bald patch under his curls, and he was my mother's half brother. It always seemed a great burden to him, having to look after me and my mother and my sister, Anthea. He rushed about muttering, "And how do I find the *money*, Conrad, with the book trade so slow!"

The bookshop was in our name, too—it said GRANT AND TESDINIC in faded gold letters over the bow windows and the dark green door—but Uncle Alfred explained that it belonged to him now. He and my father had started the shop together. Then, just after I was born and a little before he died, my father had needed a lot of money suddenly, Uncle Alfred told me, and he sold his half of the bookshop to Uncle Alfred. Then my father died, and Uncle Alfred had to support us.

"And so he should do," my mother said in her vague way. "We're the only family he's got."

My sister, Anthea, said she wanted to know what my father had needed the money for, but she never could find out. Uncle Alfred said he didn't know.

"And you never get any sense out of Mother," Anthea said to me. "She just says things like 'Life is always a lottery' and 'Your father was usually hard up'—so all I can think is that it must have been gambling debts. The casino's only just up the road, after all."

I rather liked the idea of my father gambling half a bookshop away. I used to like taking risks myself. When I was eight, I borrowed some skis and went down all the steepest and iciest ski runs, and in the summer I went rock climbing. I felt I was really following in my father's footsteps. Unfortunately, someone saw me halfway up Stall Crag and told my uncle.

"Ah, no, Conrad," he said, wagging a worried, wrinkled finger at me. "I can't have you taking these risks."

"My dad did," I said, "betting all that money."

"He *lost* it," said my uncle, "and that's a different matter. I never knew much about his affairs, but I have an idea—a very shrewd idea—that he was robbed by those crooked aristocrats up at Stallery."

"What?" I said. "You mean Count Rudolf came with a gun and held him up?"

My uncle laughed and rubbed my head. "Nothing so dramatic, Con. They do things quietly and mannerly up at Stallery. They pull the possibilities like gentlemen."

"How do you mean?" I said.

"I'll explain when you're old enough to understand the magic of high finance," my uncle replied. "Meanwhile . . . " His face went all withered and serious. "Meanwhile, you can't afford to go risking your neck on Stall Crag, you really can't, Con, not with the bad karma you carry."

"What's karma?" I asked.

"That's another thing I'll explain when you're older," my uncle said. "Just don't let me catch you going rock climbing again, that's all."

I sighed. Karma was obviously something very heavy, I thought, if it stopped you climbing rocks. I went to ask my sister, Anthea, about it. Anthea is nearly ten years older than me, and she was very learned even then. She was sitting over a line of open books on the kitchen table, with her long black hair trailing over the page she was writing notes on. "Don't bother me now, Con," she said without looking up.

She's growing up just like Mum! I thought. "But I need to know what karma is."

"Karma?" Anthea looked up. She has huge dark eyes. She opened them wide to stare at me, wonderingly. "Karma's sort of like Fate, except it's to do with what you did in a former life. Suppose that in a life you had before this one you did something bad, or *didn't* do something good, then Fate is supposed to catch up with you in *this* life, unless you put it right by being extra good, of course. Understand?"

"Yes," I said, though I didn't really. "*Do* people live more than once, then?"

"The magicians say you do," Anthea answered. "I'm not sure I believe it myself. I mean, how can you *check* that you had a life before this one? Where did you hear about karma?"

Not wanting to tell her about Stall Crag, I said vaguely, "Oh, I read it somewhere. And what's pulling the possibilities? That's another thing I read."

"It's something that would take *ages* to explain, and I haven't time," Anthea said, bending over her notes again. "You don't seem to understand that I'm working for an exam that could change my entire life!"

"When are you going to get lunch, then?" I asked.

"Isn't that just my life in a *nutshell*!" Anthea burst out. "I do all the work round here *and* help in the shop twice a week, and nobody even *considers* that I might want to do something different! Go away!"

You didn't mess with Anthea when she got this fierce. I went away and tried to ask Mum instead. I might have known that would be no good.

Mum has this little bare room with creaking floor-boards half a floor down from my bedroom, with nothing in it much except dust and stacks of paper. She sits there at a wobbly table, hammering away at her old typewriter, writing books and magazine articles about women's rights. Uncle Alfred had all sorts of smooth new computers down in the back room where Miss Silex works, and he was always on at Mum to change to one as well. But nothing will persuade Mum to change. She says her old machine is much more reliable. This is true. The shop computers went down at least once a week—this, Uncle Alfred said, was because of the activities up at Stallery—but the sound of Mum's typewriter is a constant hammering, through all four floors of the house.

She looked up as I came in and pushed back a swatch of dark gray hair. Old photos show her looking rather like Anthea, except that her eyes are a light yellow-brown, like mine, but you would never think her anything like Anthea now. She is sort of faded, and she always wears what Anthea calls "that horrible mustard-colored suit" and forgets to do her hair. I like that. She's always the same, like the cathedral, and she always looks over her glasses at me the same way. "Is lunch ready?" she asked me.

"No," I said. "Anthea's not even started it."

"Then come back when it's ready," she said, bending to look at the paper sticking up from her typewriter.

"I'll go when you tell me what pulling the possibilities means," I said.

"Don't bother me with things like that," she said, winding the paper up so that she could read her latest line. "Ask your uncle. It's only some sort of magicians' stuff. What do you think of 'disempowered broodmares' as a description? Good, eh?"

"Great," I said. Mum's books are full of things like that. I'm never sure what they mean. That time I thought a disempowered broodmare was some sort of weak nightmare, and I went away thinking of all her other books, called things like *Exploited for Dreams* and *Disabled Eunuchs*. Uncle Alfred had a whole table of them down in the shop. One of my jobs was to dust them, but he almost never sold any, no matter how enticingly I piled them up.

I did lots of jobs in the shop, unpacking books, arranging them, dusting them, and cleaning the floor on the days Mrs. Potts's nerves wouldn't let her come. Mrs. Potts's nerves were always bad on the days after she had tried to tidy Uncle Alfred's workroom. The shop, and the whole house, used to echo then with shouts of "I told you just the *floor*, woman! You've *ruined* that experiment! *And* you're lucky not to be a goldfish! Touch it again and you'll *be* a goldfish!"

But Mrs. Potts, at least once a month, just could not resist stacking everything in neat piles and dusting the chalk marks off the workbench. Then Uncle Alfred would rush up the stairs shouting and the next day Mrs. Potts's nerves kept her at home and I would have to clean the shop floor. As a reward for this, I was allowed to read any books I wanted from the children's shelves.

To be brutally frank with you—which is Uncle Alfred's favorite phrase—this reward meant nothing to me until about the time I heard about karma and Fate and started wondering what pulling the possibilities meant. Up to then I preferred doing risky things. Or I mostly wanted to go and see friends in the part of town where televisions worked. Reading was even harder work than cleaning the floor. But suddenly one day I discovered the Peter Jenkins books. You *must* know them: *Peter Jenkins and the Thin Teacher, Peter Jenkins and the Headmaster's Secret*, and all the others. They're great. Our shop had a whole row of them, at least twenty, and I set out to read them all.

Well, I had already read about six, and those all kept harking back to another one called *Peter Jenkins and the Football Formula* that sounded really exciting. So that was the one I wanted to read next.

I finished the floor as quickly as I could. Then, on my way to dust Mum's books, I stopped by the children's shelves and looked urgently along the row of shiny red and brown Peter Jenkins books for *Peter Jenkins and the Football Formula*. The trouble is, all those books look the same. I ran my finger along the row, thinking I'd find the book about seventh along. I knew I'd seen it there. But it wasn't. The one in about the right place was called *Peter Jenkins and the Magic Golfer*. I ran my finger right along to the end, and it still wasn't there, and *The Headmaster's Secret* didn't seem to be there either. Instead, there were three copies of one called *Peter Jenkins and the Hidden Horror*, which I'd never seen before. I took one of those out and flipped through it, and it was almost the same as *The Headmaster's Secret*, but not *quite*—vampire bats instead of a zombie in the cupboard, things like that—and I put it back feeling puzzled and really frustrated.

In the end I took one at random before I went on to dust Mum's books. And Mum's books were different—just slightly—too. They *looked* the same, with FRANCONIA GRANT in big yellow letters on them, but some of the titles were different. The fat one that used to be called *Women in Crisis* was still fat, but it was now called *The Case for Females*, and the thin, floppy one was called *Mother Wit*, instead of *Do We Use Intuition?* like I remembered.

Just then I heard Uncle Alfred galloping downstairs, whistling, on his way to open the shop. "Hey, Uncle Alfred!" I called out. "Have you sold all the *Peter Jenkins and the Football Formula*s?"

"I don't think so," he said, rushing into the shop with his worried look. He hurried along to the children's shelves, muttering about having to reorder as he changed his glasses over. He peered through them at the row of Peter Jenkins books. He bent to look at the books below and stood on tiptoe to look at the shelves above. Then he backed away looking so angry that I thought Mrs. Potts must have tidied the books, too. "Would you look at that!" he said disgustedly. "That's a third of them different! It's criminal. They went for a big working without even *considering* the side effects! Go outside and see if the street's still the same, Conrad."

I went to the shop door, but as far as I could see, nothing . . . Oh! The postbox down the road was now bright blue.

"You *see*!" said my uncle when I told him. "You see what they're like! All sorts of details will be different now—*valuable* details—but what do *they* care? All *they* think of is money!"

"Who?" I asked. I couldn't see how anyone could make money by changing books.

He pointed up and sideways with his thumb. "Them. Those bent aristocrats up at Stallery, to be brutally frank with you, Con. They make their money by pulling the possibilities about. They look, and if they see they could get a bigger profit from one of their companies if just one or two things were a *little* different, then they twist and twitch and *pull* those one or two things. It doesn't matter to them that *other* things change as well. Oh no. And this time they've overdone it. Greedy. Wicked. People are going to notice and object if they go on doing this." He took his glasses off and cleaned them. Beads of angry sweat stood on his forehead. "There'll be trouble," he said. "Or so I hope."

So this was what pulling the possibilities meant. "*How* do they change things?" I asked.

"By very powerful magic," said my uncle. "More powerful than you or I can imagine, Conrad. Make no mistake, Count Rudolf and his family are very dangerous people."

When I finally went up to my room to read my Peter Jenkins book, I looked out of my window first. Because I was at the very top of our house, I could see Stallery as just a glint and a flashing in the place where green hills folded into rocky mountain. I found it hard to believe that anyone in that high, twinkling place could have the power to change a lot of books and the color of the postboxes down here in Stallchester. I still didn't understand why anyone should want to.

"It's because if you change to a new set of things that might be going to happen," Anthea explained, looking up from her books, "you change *everything* just a little. This time," she added, ruefully turning the pages of her notes, "they seem to have done a big jump and made a big difference. I've got notes here on two books that don't seem to exist any-more. No wonder Uncle Alfred's annoyed."

We got used to the changes by next day. Sometimes it was hard to remember that postboxes used to be red. Uncle Alfred said that we only remembered anyway because we lived in that part of Stallchester. "To be brutally frank with you," he said, "half Stallchester thinks postboxes were always blue. So does the rest of the country. The King probably calls them royal blue. Mind games, that's what it is. Diabolical greed."

This happened in the glad old days when Anthea was at home. I think Mum and Uncle Alfred thought Anthea would always be at home. That summer Mum said as usual, "Anthea, don't forget that Conrad needs new school clothes for next term," and Uncle Alfred was full of plans for expanding the shop once Anthea had left school and could work there full time.

"If I clear out the boxroom opposite my work-room," he would say, "we can put the office in there. Then we can put books where the office is—maybe build out into the yard."

∗ ∗ ∗

Anthea never said much in reply to these plans. She was very quiet and tense for the next month or so. Then she seemed to cheer up. She worked in the shop quite happily all the rest of the summer, and in the early autumn she took me to buy new clothes just as she had done last year, except that she bought things for herself at the same time. Then, after I had been back at school a month, she left.

She came down to breakfast carrying a small suitcase. "I'm off," she said. "I start at university tomorrow. I'm catching the nine-twenty to Ludwich, so I'll say good-bye now and get something to eat on the train."

"*University!*" Mum exclaimed. "But you're not clever enough!"

"You can't," said Uncle Alfred. "There's the shop—and you don't have any money."

"I took an exam," Anthea said, "and I won a scholarship. That gives me enough money if I'm careful."

"But you *can't!*" they both said together. Mum added, "Who's going to look after Conrad?" and Uncle Alfred said, "Look here, my girl, I was *relying* on you for the shop."

"Working for nothing. I know," Anthea said.

"Well, I'm sorry to spoil your plans for me, but I do have a life of my own, you know, and I've made arrangements for myself because I knew you'd both stop me if I told you. I've looked after all three of you for years. But now Conrad's old enough to look after himself, I'm going to go and get a life."

And she went, leaving us all staring. She didn't come back. She knew Uncle Alfred, you see. Uncle Alfred spent a lot of time in his workroom setting up spells to make sure that when Anthea came home at the end of the university semester she would find herself having to stay with us for good. Anthea guessed he would. She simply sent a postcard to say she was staying with friends and never came near us. She sent me cards and presents for my birthdays, but she never came back to Stallchester for years.

Two

Anthea's going made a dreadful difference, far worse than any change made by Count Rudolf up at Stallery. Mum was in a bad mood for weeks. I'm not sure she ever forgave Anthea.

"So sly!" she kept saying. "So mean and secretive. Don't you ever be like that, Conrad, and it's no use expecting me to run after you. I have my work to do."

Uncle Alfred was tetchy and grumpy for a long time, too, but he cheered up after he had set the spells that were supposed to fix Anthea at home once she came back. He took to patting me on the shoulder and saying, "*You're* not going to let me down like that, are you, Con?"

Sometimes I answered, "No fear!" but mostly I wriggled a bit and didn't answer. I missed Anthea horribly for ages. She had been the person I could go to when I had a question to ask or to get cheered up. If I fell down or cut myself, she had been the one with sticking plaster and soothing words. She used to suggest things for me to do if I was bored. I felt quite lost now she was gone.

I hadn't realized how many things Anthea did in the house. Luckily I knew how to work the washing machine, but I was always forgetting to run it and finding I'd no clothes to go to school in. I got into trouble for wearing dirty clothes until I got used to remembering. Mum just went on piling her clothes into the laundry basket as she always had, but Uncle Alfred was particular about his shirts. He had to pay Mrs. Potts to iron them for him, and he grumbled a lot about how much she charged.

"The ingredients for my experiments cost the earth these days," he kept saying. "Where do I find the *money*?"

Anthea had done all the shopping and cooking, too, and this was where we all suffered most. For the week after she left we lived on cornflakes, until they ran out. Then Mum tried to solve the problem by ordering two hundred frozen quiches and cramming these into the freezer. You can't believe how quickly you get tired of eating quiche. And none of us remembered to fetch the next quiche out to thaw. Uncle Alfred was always having to unfreeze them by magic, and this made them soggy and seemed to affect the taste.

"Is there anything else we can eat that might be less squishy and more satisfying?" he asked pathetically. "Think, Fran. You used to cook once."

"That was when I was being exploited as a female," Mum retorted. "The quiche people do frozen pizzas, too, but you have to order them by the thousand."

Uncle Alfred shuddered. "I'd rather eat bacon and eggs," he said sadly.

"Then go out and buy some," said my mother.

In the end we settled that Uncle Alfred did the shopping and I tried to cook what he bought. I fetched books called *Simple Cookery* and *Easy Eating* up out of the shop and did my best to do what they told me. I was never very good at it. The food always seemed to turn black and stick to the bottom of the pan, but I usually had enough on top to get by with. We ate a lot of bread, though only Mum got noticeably fatter. Uncle Alfred was naturally skinny, and I kept growing. Mum had to take me shopping for new clothes several times a year from then on. It always seemed to happen when she was very busy finishing a book, and this made her so unhappy that I tried to make my clothes last as long as I could. I got into trouble at school once or twice for looking like a scarecrow.

We got used to coping by next summer. I suppose that was when it finally became obvious that Anthea was not coming back. I had worked out by Christmas that she had left for good, but it took Mum and Uncle Alfred most of a year.

"She'll *have* to come home this summer," Mum was still saying hopefully in May. "All the universities shut for months over the summer."

"Not she," said Uncle Alfred. "She's shaken the dust of Stallchester off her feet. And to be brutally frank with you, Fran, I'm not sure I *want* her back now. Someone that ungrateful would only be a disturbing factor."

He sighed, dismantled his spell to keep Anthea at home, and hired a girl called Daisy Bolger to help in the shop. After that, he was always worrying about how much he had to pay Daisy in order to stop her going to work at the china shop by the cathedral instead. Daisy knew how to get money out of Uncle Alfred much better than I did. Talk about sly! And

Daisy always seemed to think I was going to mess up the books when I was in the shop. Once or twice Count Rudolf up at Stallery worked another big change, and each time Daisy was sure it was me messing the books about. Luckily Uncle Alfred never believed her.

Uncle Alfred was sorry for me. He would look at me over his glasses in his most worried way and shake his head sadly. "I reckon Anthea's going has hit you hardest of all, Con," he took to saying sadly. "To be brutally frank, I suspect it was your bad karma that caused her to leave."

"What did I *do* in my past life?" I asked anxiously.

Uncle Alfred always shook his head at that. "I don't know *what* you did, Con. The Lords of Karma alone know that. You could have been a crooked policeman, or a judge that took bribes, or a soldier that ran away, or maybe a traitor to the country—anything! All I know is that you either *didn't* do something you *should* have done, or you did something you *shouldn't*. And because of that, a bad Fate is going to keep dogging you." Then he would hurry away, muttering, "Unless we find a way you could expiate your misdeed, I suppose."

I always felt horrible after these conversations.

Something bad almost always happened to me just afterward. Once I slipped when I was quite high up climbing Stall Crag and scraped the whole front of me raw. Another time I fell downstairs and twisted my ankle, and one other time I cut myself quite badly in the kitchen—blood all over the onions—but the truly nasty part was that each time I thought, I *deserve* this! This is because of my crime in my past life. And I felt horribly guilty and sinful until the scrapes or the ankle or the cut had healed. Then I remembered Anthea saying she didn't believe people had more than one life, and after that I would feel better.

"Can't you find out who I was and what I did?" I asked Uncle Alfred, one time after I had been told off by the headmistress because my clothes were too small. She sent a note home with me about it, but I threw it away because Mum had just started a new book, and anyway, I knew I *deserved* to be in trouble. "If I knew, I could do something about it."

"To be brutally frank," said my uncle, "I fancy you have to be a grown man before you could change your Fate. But I'll try to find out. I'll try, Con."

He did experiments in his workroom to find out, but he never seemed to make much headway.

About a year after Anthea left, I got really annoyed with Daisy Bolger when she tried to stop me looking at the newest Peter Jenkins book. I told her my uncle had said I could, but she just kept saying, "Put it *back*! You'll crease it, and then I'll be blamed."

"Oh, why don't you go away and work in that china shop!" I said in the end.

She tossed her head angrily. "Fat lot *you* know! I wouldn't *dream* of it. It's *boring*. I only say I will to get a decent wage out of your uncle—and he doesn't pay me half what he could afford, even now."

"He does," I said. "He's always worrying how much you cost."

"That," said Daisy, "is because he's stingy, not because he hasn't got it. He must be rich as the Count up at Stallery almost. This bookshop's coining money."

"*Is* it?" I said.

"I keep the till. I know," Daisy said. "We're at the picturesque end of town, and we get *all* the tourists, winter *and* summer. Ask Miss Silex if you don't believe me. She does the accounts."

I was so astonished to hear this that I forgot to

be angry and forgot the Peter Jenkins book, too. That was no doubt what Daisy intended. She was a very cunning person. But I couldn't believe she was right, not when Uncle Alfred was always so worried. I began counting the people who came into the shop.

And Daisy was right. Stallchester is a famous beauty spot, full of historic buildings and surrounded in mountains. In summer, we got people to look at the town and play the casino and hikers who walked in the mountains. In winter, people came to ski. But because we are so high up, we get rain and mist in summer, and in winter there are always times when the snow is not deep enough, or too soft, or coming down in a blizzard, and those are the days when tourists come into the shop by their hundreds. They buy everything, from dictionaries to help with crosswords to deep books of philosophy, detective stories, biographies, adventure stories, and cookery books for self-catering. Some even buy Mum's books. It only took a few months for me to realize that Uncle Alfred was indeed coining money.

"What does he spend it all on?" I asked Daisy.

"Goodness knows," she said. "That workroom

of his is pretty expensive. And he always buys best vintage port for his Magicians' Circle. All his clothes are handmade, too, you know."

I almost didn't believe that either. But when I thought about it, one of the magicians who came to Uncle Alfred's Magicians' Circle every Wednesday was Mr. Hawkins, the tailor, and he often came early with a package of clothes. And I'd helped carry dusty old bottles of port wine upstairs for the meeting, often and often. I just hadn't realized the stuff was expensive. I was annoyed with Daisy for noticing so much more than I did. But then, she was a really cunning person.

You would not believe how artfully Daisy went to work when she wanted more money. She often took as much as two weeks on it—ten days of sighing and grumbling and saying how overworked and hard up she was, followed by another day of saying how the nice woman in the china shop had told her she could come and work there anytime. Finally she would flare up with "That's *it*! I'm *leaving*!" And it worked every time.

Uncle Alfred hates people to leave, I thought. That's why he let Anthea go to Cathedral School, so she could stay at home and be useful here.

I couldn't threaten to leave, not yet. You have to stay at school until you are twelve in this country. But I could pretend I was not going to do any more cooking. It didn't take much pretending, really.

That first time I went even slower than Daisy. I spent over a fortnight sighing and saying I was sick to my back teeth of cooking. Finally, it was Mum who said, "Really, Conrad, to listen to you, anyone would think we exploited you."

It was wonderful. I went from simmering to boiling in one breath, and I shouted with real feeling, "You *are* exploiting me! That's *it*! I'm not doing any more cooking ever again!"

Then it was even more wonderful. Uncle Alfred hurried me away to his workroom and pleaded with me. "You know—let's be brutally frank, Con—your mother's hopeless with food, and I'm worse. But we've all got to eat, haven't we? Be a good boy and reconsider now."

I looked around at the strange-shaped glass things and shining machinery in the workroom and wondered how much it all cost. "No," I said sulkily. "Pay someone else to do it."

He winced. He almost shuddered at the idea. "Suppose I was to offer you a little something to take up as our chef again," he said cajolingly. "What could I offer you?"

I let him cajole for a while. Then I sighed and asked for a bicycle. He agreed like a shot. The bicycle was not so wonderful when it came, because Uncle Alfred only produced one that was second-hand, but it made a start. I knew how to do it now.

When winter came, I went into my act again. I refused to cook twice. First I got regular pocket money out of my uncle, and then I got skis of my own. In the spring I did it again and got modeling kits. That summer I got most things I needed. The next autumn I actually made Uncle Alfred give me a good camera. I know this was calculated cunning and quite as bad as Daisy—though I couldn't help noticing that my friends at school got skis and pocket money as if they had a right to them, and that none of them had to cook for these things either—but I told myself that my Fate had made me bad and I might as well make use of it.

I stopped the year I was going to be twelve. This was not because I was reformed. It was part of a plan. You can leave school at twelve, you see, and I knew Uncle Alfred would have thought of that. The rule is that you *can* go on to an Upper School, but only if your family pays for you. Otherwise you go and find a job. All my friends were going to Upper Schools, most of them to Cathedral like Anthea, but my best friends were going to Stall High. I thought of it as like the school in the Peter Jenkins books. Stall High cost more, but it was supposed to be a terrific place, and best of all, it taught magic. I had set my heart on learning magic with my friends. Living as I did in a house where Uncle Alfred filled the stairway with peculiar smells and the strange buzz of working spells at least once a week, I couldn't wait to do it, too. Besides, Daisy Bolger told me that Uncle Alfred had been to Stall High himself as a boy. How that girl found out these things was something I never knew.

Knowing Uncle Alfred, I knew he would try to keep me at home somehow. He might even be going to sack Daisy and make me work in the shop for nothing. So my plan was to threaten to stop cooking just near the end of my last term and get him to bribe me with Stall High. If that didn't work, I thought I would threaten to go and get a job in the lowlands and then say that I'd stay if I could go to Cathedral School instead.

I worked all this out sitting in my room staring

upward at Stallery, glimmering among the mountains. Stallery always made me wish for all the strange and exciting things that I didn't seem to have. It made me think that Anthea must have sat in *her* room making plans in much the same way—except that you couldn't see Stallery from Anthea's old room. Mum used it as a paper store now.

Stallery was in the news around then anyway. Count Rudolf died suddenly. People gossiping in the bookshop said he was quite young, really, but some diseases took no account of age, did they? "Driven to an early grave," Mrs. Potts said to me. "Mark my words. And the new Count is only twenty-one, they say. His sister's even younger. They'll be having to marry soon to preserve the family name. She'll insist on it."

Daisy was very interested in weddings. She hunted everywhere for a magazine that might have pictures of the new Count, Robert, and his sister, Lady Felice. All she found was a newspaper with the announcement of Count Robert's engagement to Lady Mary Ogworth in it. "Just plain print," she complained. "No photos."

"Daisy won't find pictures," Mrs. Potts told me. "Stallery likes its privacy, it does. They know how to keep the media out of their lives up there. I've heard there's electrical fences all round those grounds, and savage dogs patrolling inside. *She* won't want people prying, not she."

"Who's *she?*" I asked.

Mrs. Potts paused, kneeling with her back to me on the stairs. "Pass the polish," she said. "Thanks. *She*," she went on, rubbing in polish in a slow, enjoying sort of way, "is the old Countess. She's got rid of her husband—bothered and nagged him to death, I've heard—and now she won't want anyone to see while she works on the new Count. They say he's *well* under her thumb already and bound to be more so, poor boy. *She* likes all the power, all the money. *He'll* marry that girl *she's* chosen, and then she'll run the pair of them, you'll see."

"She sounds horrible," I said, fishing for more.

"Oh, she is," said Mrs. Potts. "Used to be on the stage. Caught the old Count by kicking up her legs in a chorus line, I heard. And—"

Unfortunately, Uncle Alfred came rushing upstairs at this point and upset Mrs. Potts's cleaning bucket and Mrs. Potts's nerves along with it. I never got Mrs. Potts to gossip about Stallery again. That was my Fate at work there, I thought. But I got a few more hints from Uncle Alfred himself. With his face almost withered with worry, he said to me, "What happens up in Stallery now, eh? It could be even worse. I mention no names, but someone's very power-hungry up there. I dread the next set of changes, Con."

He was so worried that he telephoned his Magicians' Circle and they actually met on a Tuesday, which was almost unheard of. After that, they met on Tuesdays *and* Wednesdays, and I helped carry up twice the number of dusty wine bottles every week.

And those weeks slowly passed, until the dread day arrived when the Headmistress came and gave everyone in the top class a School Leaver's Form. "Take this home to your parent or guardian," she said. "Tell them that if they want you to leave school at the end of this term, they must sign Section A. If they want you to go on to an Upper School, then they sign Section B. Get them to sign tonight. I want all these forms back tomorrow without fail."

I took my form home to the shop, prepared for battle and cunning. I went in through the backyard and straight upstairs to Mum. My plan was to get her to sign Section B before Uncle Alfred even knew I'd got the form.

"What's this?" Mum said vaguely as I pushed the yellow paper in front of her typewriter.

"School Leaver's Form," I explained. "If you want me to go on at school, you have to sign Section B."

She pushed her hair back distractedly. "I can't do that, Conrad, not when you've got a job already. And at Stallery of all places. I must say I'm really disappointed in you."

I felt as if the whole world had been pulled out from under me like a carpet. *"Stallery!"* I said.

"If that's what you told your uncle, yes," my mother said. And she took the form and signed Section A with her married name. F. Tesdinic. "There," she said. "I wash my hands of you, Conrad."

Three

I stood there, feeling utterly let down. I didn't know what to do or what to think. Then, when I next caught up with myself, I was racing downstairs, waving the School Leaver's Form. I rushed into the shop, where Uncle Alfred was standing behind the pay desk, and I wagged the form furiously in his face.

"What the *hell* do you mean by *this*?" I pretty well shrieked at him.

A lot of customers whirled around from the shelves and stared at me. Uncle Alfred looked at them, blinked at me, and said to Daisy, "Do you mind taking over here for a moment?" He dodged out from behind the desk and seized my elbow. "Come up to my workroom and let me explain."

He more or less dragged me from the shop. I was still flapping the form with my free hand, and I think I was shouting, too. "What do you mean— *explain?*" I screamed as we went upstairs. "You can't *do* this to me! You've no *right!*"

When we reached the workroom, Uncle Alfred shoved me inside into a strong smell of recent magic and shut the door behind both of us with a clap. He straightened his glasses, which I had knocked crooked. He was panting, and he looked more worried than I had ever seen him, but I didn't care. I opened my mouth to shout at him again.

"No, don't, Con," Uncle Alfred said earnestly. "Please. I'm doing the best I can for you. Honestly. It's your Fate—this wretched bad karma of yours— that's the problem, see."

"What's that got to do with anything?" I demanded.

"Everything," he said. "I've been doing a lot of divining about you, and it's even worse than I realized. Unless you put right what you did wrong in your previous life—and put it right *now*—you are going to be horribly and painfully *dead* before the year's out."

"*What?*" I said. "I don't believe you!"

"It's true," he assured me. "Lords of Karma will

just scrap you and let you try again when you next get reborn. They're quite ruthless, you know. But I don't ask you to believe me just like that. I'd like you to come to the Magicians' Circle this evening and see what *they* say. They don't know you, I haven't told them about you, but I'm willing to bet they'll spot this karma of yours straight off. To be brutally frank with you, it's round you in a black cloud these days, Con."

I felt terrible. My mouth went dry, and my stomach shook, in wobbly waves. "But," I said, and found my voice had gone down to a whisper, "but what's it got to do with *this*?" I tried to flourish the leaver's form at him again, but I could only manage a feeble flap. My arm had gone weak.

"Ah, I wish you'd come to me first," said my uncle. "I'd have explained. You see, I've discovered what you did wrong. There was someone in your last life Lords of Karma required you to put an end to. And you didn't. You lost your nerve and let them go free. And this person got reborn and continued his evil ways in this present life, too . . . "

"But I still don't see—" I began.

He held up a hand to stop me. It was shaking. He seemed to be shaking with worry all over. "Let me finish, Con. Let me go on. Since I discovered what caused your Fate, I've done every kind of divination to find out who this person *is* that you didn't put an end to. It's been really difficult—I don't have to tell you how the magics up at Stallery interfere with spells down here—but it was pretty definite even so. It's someone up at Stallery, Con."

"You mean it's the new Count?" I said.

"I don't know," said my uncle. "It's *one* of them up there. *Someone* up at Stallery has a lot of power and is doing something really bad, and they've got the exact pattern of this person you should have done away with last time. That's all I can find out, Con. Look on the bright side. We know where to find him or her. That's why I arranged for you to get a job up at Stallery."

"What kind of a job?" I asked.

"Domestic," said Uncle Alfred. "The kind of thing you're used to, really. The steward up there—butler, whatever—is a Mr. Amos, and he's reckoning to take on some school leavers shortly, to train up as servants to the new Count. Day after the end of term he'll be interviewing a whole bunch of you. And he'll take you, Con, never fear. I'll put a really good spell on you, so he'll have no choice. You don't need to worry about getting the job. And you'll be right in the middle of things then, cleaning boots and running errands, and you'll have *ample* opportunity to seek out the person responsible for this terrible karma you carry. . . . "

I thought, *Cleaning boots!* And nearly burst into tears. My uncle went on talking, nervously, persuasively, but I just couldn't attend anymore. It wasn't simply that my careful plan had been no use at all. It was more that I suddenly saw where the plan had been leading me. I hadn't admitted it to myself before, but I knew now—I knew very fiercely— that what I wanted was to be like Anthea, to leave the bookshop, leave Stallchester, go somewhere quite different and make a career of some kind. I hadn't actually thought *what* career, until then, but now I thought of flying an aircraft, becoming a great surgeon, being a famous scientist, or perhaps, best of all, learning to be the strongest magician in the world.

It was like peeping past a door that was just slamming in my face. I could have done so many interesting things if I had the right education. Instead, I was going to spend my life *cleaning boots*.

"I don't want to!" I blurted out. "I want to go to Stall High!"

"You haven't listened to what I've been telling you," Uncle Alfred said. "You've got to get this evil Fate of yours cleared away *first*, Con. If you don't, you die in agony before the year's out. Once you've gone up to Stallery, found out who this person is, and done away with him or her, then you can do anything you want. I'll arrange for you to go to Stall High then like a shot. Of *course* I will."

"Really?" I said.

"Really," he said.

It was like that door softly swinging open again. True, there was an ugly doorstep in the way labeled "Bad Karma, Evil Fate," but I could step over that. I found myself letting out a long, long sigh. "All right," I said.

Uncle Alfred patted my shoulder. "Good lad. I knew you'd see reason. But I don't ask you to take my word alone. Come to the Magicians' Circle tonight, and see what they have to say. All right now?" I supposed I was. I nodded. "Then *could* I get back to the shop?" he said. "Daisy hasn't the experience yet."

I nodded again. But as he pushed me out onto

the stairs, I had a thought. "Who's going to do the cooking with me gone?" I asked. I was surprised not to have thought of this before.

"Don't worry about that," my uncle said. "We'll hire Daisy's mother. Daisy's always telling me what a good cook her mum is."

I stumbled away up to my room and stared up at Stallery, twinkling out of its fold in the mountains. My mind felt like someone in the dark, stumbling about among huge pieces of furniture with sharp corners on them. I kept barking myself on the corners. No Stall High unless I went and cleaned boots in Stallery—that was one corner. The Lords of Karma scrapped you if you were no good—that was another. A person up there among those glinting windows was so wicked he had to be done away with—that was another—and I had to deal with the person now because I'd been too feeble to do it in my last life—that was yet another. Then I barked my mind on the most important corner of the lot. If I didn't do this, I'd die. It was this person or me, him or me.

Him or me, I kept saying to myself. Him or me.

Those words were going through my head while I helped Uncle Alfred carry the bottles of port up to his workroom that evening. I had to back into the room because I had two bottles in each hand.

"Dear me," someone said behind me. "What appalling karma!"

Before I could turn around, someone else said, "My dear Alfred, did you realize that your nephew carries some of the blackest Fate I've ever seen?"

All the magicians of the Circle were there, though I hadn't heard them arrive. Two of them were smoking cigars, filling the workroom with strong blue smoke, which made the place look a different shape and size somehow. Instead of the usual workbench and glass tubes and machinery, there was a circle of comfortable armchairs, each with a little table beside it. There was another table in the middle loaded with bottles, wineglasses, and several decanters.

I knew most of the people sitting in the armchairs at least by sight. The one pouring himself a glass of rich red wine was Mr. Seuly, the Mayor of Stallchester, who owned the ironworks at the other end of town. He passed the decanter along to Mr. Johnson, who owned the ski runs and the hotels. Mr. Priddy, beside him, ran the casino. One of those smoking a cigar was Mr. Hawkins, the tailor, and the other was Mr. Fellish, who owned the *Stallchester News*. Mr. Goodwin, beyond those, owned a big chain of shops in Stallchester. I wasn't quite sure what the others were called, but I knew the tall one owned all the land around here and that the fat one ran the trams and buses. And there was Mr. Loder, the butcher, helping Uncle Alfred uncork bottles and carefully pour wine into decanters. The thick nutty smell of port cut across the smell of cigars.

All these men had shrewd respectable faces and expensive clothes, which made it worse that they were all staring at me with concern. Mayor Seuly sipped at his wine and shook his head a little. "Not long for this life unless something's done soon," he said. "What's causing it? Does anyone know?"

"Something—no, *someone* he should have put down in his last life, by the looks of it," Mr. Hawkins, the tailor, said.

The tall landowning one nodded. "And the chance to cure it now, only he's not done it," he said, deep and gloomy. "Why hasn't he?"

Uncle Alfred beckoned me to stop standing staring and put the bottles on the table. "Because," he said, "to be brutally frank with you, I've only just found out who he should be dealing with. It's some-one up at Stallery."

There was a general groan at this.

"Then *send* him there," said Mr. Fellish.

"I am. He's going next week," my uncle said. "It couldn't be contrived any sooner."

"Good. Better late than never," Mayor Seuly said.

"You know," observed Mr. Priddy, "it doesn't surprise me at all that it's someone up at Stallery. That's such a strong Fate on the boy. It looks equal to the power up there, and that's so strong that it interferes with communications and stops this town thriving as it should."

"It's not just this town Stallery interferes with," Mayor Seuly said. "Their financial grip is down over the whole world, like a net. I come up against it almost every day. They have magical stoppages occurring all the time, so that they can make money and I can't. If I try to get round what they do— *bang*. I lose half my profits."

"Oh, we've all had that," agreed Mr. Goodwin. "Odd to think it's in this lad's hands to save us as well as himself."

I stood by the table, turning from one to the other as they spoke. My mouth went drier with each thing that was said. By this time I was so horrified I could hardly swallow. I tried to ask a question, but I couldn't.

My uncle seemed to realize what I wanted to know. He turned around. He was holding his glass up to the light, so that a red blob of light from it wavered on his forehead as he said, "This is all very true and tragic, but how is my nephew to know who this person *is* when he sees him? That's what you wanted to ask, wasn't it, Con?" It was, but I couldn't even nod by then.

"Simple," said Mayor Seuly. "There'll come a moment when he'll *know*. There's always a moment of recognition in cases of karma. The person he needs will say something or do something, and it will be like clicking a switch. Light will come on in the boy's head, and he'll *know*."

The rest of them nodded and made growling murmurs that they agreed, it *was* like that, and Uncle Alfred said, "Got that, Con?"

I managed to nod this time. Then Mayor Seuly said, "But he'll want to know how to deal with the person when he does know. That's quite as important. How about he uses Granek's Equation?"

"Too complicated," said Mr. Goodwin. "Try him with Beaulieu's Spell."

"I'd prefer a straight Whitewick," Mr. Loder, the butcher, said.

After that they all began suggesting things, all of which meant nothing to me, and each of them got quite heated in favor of his own suggestion. Before long, the tall landowning one was banging his wineglass on the little table beside his chair and shouting, "You've *got* to have him eliminate this person for good, quickly and simply! The only answer is a Persholt!"

"Please remember," my uncle said anxiously, "that Con's only a boy and he doesn't know any magic at all."

This caused a silence. "Ah," Mayor Seuly said at length. "Yes. Of course. Well then, I think the best plan is to enable him to summon a Walker." At this, all the others broke into rumbles of "Exactly! Of *course*! A Walker. Why didn't we think of that before?" Mayor Seuly looked around the circle of them and said, "Agreed? Good. Now what can we give him to use? It ought to be something quite plain and ordinary that no one will suspect. . . . Ah. Yes. A cork from one of those bottles will do nicely."

He held out his hand with a handsome gold ring shining on it, and Mr. Loder passed him the purple-stained cork from the bottle he had just emptied into a decanter. Mr. Seuly took it and clasped it in both hands for a moment. Then he nodded and passed it on to Mr. Johnson, who did the same. The cork slowly traveled around the entire circle, including Uncle Alfred and Mr. Loder, standing by the table, who passed it back to the Mayor.

Mayor Seuly held the cork up in his finger and thumb and beckoned me over to him. I still couldn't speak. I stood there, looking down on his wealthily clipped hair, which almost hid the thin place on top, and wondering at how rounded and rich he looked. I breathed in smells of nutty, fruity wine, smooth good cloth, and a tang of aftershave and nodded at everything he said.

"All you have to do," he said, "is first to have your moment of recognition and then to fetch out this cork. You hold it up like I'm doing, and you say, 'I summon a Walker to bring me what I need.' Have you got that?" I nodded. It sounded quite easy to remember. "You may have to wait awhile for the Walker," Mayor Seuly went on, "and you mustn't be frightened when you see the Walker coming. It may turn out bigger than you expect. When it reaches you, the Walker will give you something. I don't know what. Walkers are designed to give you exactly the tool for the job. But take my word for it, the object you get will do just what you need it to do. And you *must* give the Walker this cork in exchange. Walkers never give something for nothing. Have you got all that?" he asked. I nodded again. "Then take this cork and keep it with you all the time," he said, "but don't let anyone else see it. And I hope that when we next meet, you'll carry no karma at all."

As I took the cork, which felt like an ordinary cork to me, Mr. Johnson said, "Right. That's done. Send him off, Alfred, and let's start the meeting."

I didn't really need Uncle Alfred to jerk his head at me to go. I got out as quickly as I could and rushed upstairs to the kitchen for a drink of water. But by the time I got there, my mouth was hardly dry at all. That was odd, but it was such a relief that I hardly wondered about it at all. I wasn't even very scared anymore, and that was odd, too, but I didn't think of it at the time.

* Four *

I got much more nervous as the week marched on. The worst part was the end-of-term assembly, when I had to sit on the left side with the school leavers, while all my friends sat across the gangway because they were going to Upper Schools. I felt really left out. And while I sat there, I realized that even when I'd found the karma person and got rid of him, I'd still be a year behind my friends at Stall High. And on my side of the gangway, the boy next to me had got a job at Mayor Seuly's ironworks and the girl on the other side was going to train as a maid in Mr. Goodwin's house. I still had to get my job.

Then it suddenly hit me that I was going off on

my own to a strange place where I wouldn't know what to do or how to behave, and that was bad enough, without having to find the person causing my Evil Fate as well. I tried saying, "It's him or me," to myself, but that was no help at all. When I got home, I looked out of my window, up at Stallery, and that was terrifying. I realized that I didn't know the first thing about the place, except that it was full of powerful wizardry and that someone up there was thoroughly wicked. When Uncle Alfred came and took me to his workroom to put the spell on me that would make this Mr. Amos give me the job at Stallery, I went very slowly. My legs shook.

The workroom was back to its usual state. There was no sign of the comfortable chairs or the port wine. Uncle Alfred chalked a circle on the floor and had me stand inside it. Otherwise, the magics were just like ordinary life. I didn't feel anything particularly or notice much except a very small buzzing, right at the end. But Uncle Alfred was beaming when he had finished.

"There!" he said. "I defy anyone to refuse to employ you now, Con! It's tight as a diving suit."

I went away, shaking with nerves. I was so full of doubts and ignorance that I went and interrupted

Mum. She was sitting at her creaky table, reading great long sheets of paper, making marks in the margins of them as she read. "Say whatever it is quickly," she said, "or I'll lose my place in these blessed galleys."

Out of all the things I wanted to know, all I could think of was, "Do I need to take any clothes with me to Stallery tomorrow?"

"Ask your uncle," Mum said. "You arranged the whole caper with him. And remember to have a bath and wash your hair tonight."

So I went downstairs, where Uncle Alfred was now unpacking guidebooks out in the back, and I asked him the same question. "And can I take my camera?" I said.

He pulled his lip and thought about it. "To be frank with you, by rights you shouldn't take any-thing," he said. "It's only supposed to be an interview tomorrow. But of course, if the spell works and you do get the job, you'll probably start work there straightaway. I know they provide the uniforms. But I don't know about underclothes. Yes, perhaps you ought to take underclothes along. Only don't make it obvious you expect to be staying. They won't like that."

This made me more nervous than ever. I thought the spell had *fixed* it. After that, I had a short, blissful moment when I thought that if I was dreadfully rude to them in Stallery, they'd throw me out and not give me the job. Then I could go to Stall High next term. But of course that wouldn't work, because of my Evil Fate. I sighed and went to pack.

The tram that went up past Stallery left from the market square at midday. Uncle Alfred walked down there with me. I was in my best clothes and carrying a plastic bag that looked like my lunch. I'd arranged a packet of sandwiches and a bottle of juice artfully on top. Underneath were all my socks and pants wrapped around my camera and the latest Peter Jenkins book—I thought Uncle Alfred could spare me *one* book from the shop.

The tram was there and filling with people when we got to the square.

"You'd better get on or you won't have a seat," my uncle said. "Good luck, Con, and I'll love you and leave you. Oh, and Con," he said as I started to climb the metal steps into the tram. He beckoned and I came back down. "Something I forgot," he said. He led me a little way off across the pavement. "You're to tell Mr. Amos that your name is Grant," he said, "like mine. If you tell them a posh name like Tesdinic, they'll think you're too grand for the job. So from now on your name is Conrad Grant. Don't forget, will you?"

"All right," I said. "Grant." Somehow this made me feel a whole lot better. It was like having an alias, the way people did in the Peter Jenkins books when they lived adventurous double lives. I began to think of myself as a sort of secret agent. Grant. I grinned and waved quite cheerfully at Uncle Alfred as I climbed back on the tram and bought my ticket. He waved and went bustling off.

About half the people on the tram were girls and boys my own age. Most of them had plastic bags like mine, with lunch in. I thought it was probably an end-of-term outing to Stallstead, from one of the other schools in town. The Stallery tram was a single-line loop that went up into the mountains as far as Stallstead and then down into Stallchester again by the ironworks. Stallstead is a really pretty village right up among the green alps. People go there all summer for cream teas and outings.

Then the tram gave out a *clang* and started off with a lurch. My heart and stomach gave a lurch, too, in the opposite direction, and I stopped thinking about anything except how nervous I was. This is *it*, I thought. I'm really on my way now. I don't remember seeing the shops, or the houses, or the suburbs we went past. I only began to notice things when we reached the first of the foothills, among the woods, and the cogs underneath the tram engaged with the cogs in the roadway, *clunk*, and we went steeply up in jerks, *croink, croink, croink*.

This woke me up a bit. I stared out at the sunlight splashing on rocks and green trees and thought, in a distracted way, that it was probably quite beautiful. Then it dawned on me that there was none of the chattering and laughing and fooling about on the tram that there usually is on a school outing. All the other kids sat staring quietly out at the woods, just as I was doing.

They *can't* all be going to Stallery to be interviewed! I thought. They *can't*! But there didn't seem to be any teachers with them. I clutched at the slightly sticky cork in my pocket and wondered if I would ever get to use it to call a Walker, whatever that was. But I *had* to call one, or I would be dead. And I realized that if any of these kids got the job instead of me, it would be like a death sentence.

I was really scared. I kept thinking of the way

Uncle Alfred had told me not to be too obvious about taking clothes and then to call myself Grant, as if he wasn't too sure that his spell on me would work, and I was more frightened than I had ever been before. When the tram came out on the next level part, I stared down at the view of Stallchester nestled below, and the blue peaks where the glacier was, and at Stall Crag, and the whole lot went fuzzy with my terror.

It takes the tram well over an hour to get as high as Stallery, cogging up the steep bits, rumbling through rocky cuttings, and stopping at lonely inns and solitary pairs of houses on the heights. One or two people got on or off at every stop, but they were all adults. The other children just sat there, like me. *Let* them all be going to Stallstead! I thought. But I noticed that none of the ones with bags of lunch tried to eat any of it, as if they might be too nervous for food, just as I was. Though they *could* be saving it to eat in Stallstead, I thought. I hoped they were.

At last we were running on an almost level part, where there were clumps of trees and meadowlands and even a farm on one side. It looked almost like a lowland valley here. But on the other side of the road there was a high dark wall with spikes on top. I knew this was the wall around Stallery and that we were now really high up. I could even feel the magics here, like a very faint fizzing. My heart began banging so hard it almost hurt.

That wall seemed to run for *miles*, with the road curving alongside it. There was no kind of break in its dark surface, until the tram swung around an even bigger curve and began slowing down. There was a high turreted gateway ahead in the wall, which seemed to be some kind of a house as well— anyway, I saw windows in it—and across the road from this gateway, along the verge by the hedge, I was surprised to see some gypsies camping. I noticed a couple of tumbledown-looking caravans, an old gray horse trying to eat the hedge, and a white dog running up and down the verge. I wondered vaguely why they hadn't been moved on. It seemed unlike Stallery to allow gypsies outside their gates. But I was too nervous to wonder much.

Clang, clang, went the tram, announcing it was stopping.

A man in a brown uniform came to the gate and stood waiting. He was carrying two weird-shaped brown paper parcels. Barometers? I wondered.

Clocks? He came over as the tram stopped and handed the parcels to the driver.

"For the clock mender in Stallstead," he said. Then, as the driver unfolded the doors, the man came right up into the tram. "This is Stallery South Gate," he said loudly. "Any young persons applying for employment should alight here, please."

I jumped up. So, to my dismay, did all the other kids. We all crowded toward the door and clattered down the steps into the road, every one of us, and the gatehouse seemed to soar above us. The tram clanged again and whined away along its tracks, leaving us to our fate.

"Follow me," the man in the brown uniform said, and he turned toward the gate. It was a gateway big enough to have taken the tram, like a huge arched mouth in the towering face of the gatehouse, and it was slowly swinging open to let us through.

Everyone clustered forward then, and I was somehow at the back. My feet lagged. I couldn't help myself. Behind me, across on the other side of the road, someone called out in a strong, cheerful voice, "Bye then. Thanks for the lift."

I looked around to see a tall boy swing himself down from the middle caravan—I hadn't noticed there were three before—and come striding across the road to join the rest of us.

Anyone less likely to climb out of a shabby, broken-down caravan was hard to imagine. He was beautifully dressed in a silk shirt, a blue linen jacket, and impeccably creased fawn trousers, and his black hair was crisply cut in a way that I could see was expensive. He seemed older than the rest of us—I thought, fifteen at least—and the only gypsy things about him were the dark, dark eyes in his confident, good-looking face.

My heart sank at the sight of him. If anyone was going to get the job at Stallery, it would be this boy.

The gatekeeper came pushing past the boy and shook his fist at the gypsy encampment. "I warned you!" he shouted. "Clear off!"

Someone on the driving seat of the front caravan shouted back. "Sorry, guvnor! Just going now!"

"Then *get* going!" yelled the gatekeeper. "Go on. Hop it. Or else!"

Rather to my surprise, all five caravans moved off at once. I hadn't realized there were so many, and for another thing, I had thought the gray horse was eating the hedge and not hitched up to any of them. I dimly remembered there was a cooking fire, too, with an iron pot hanging over it. But I thought I must have been wrong about that when all six carts bumped down into the road, leaving empty grass behind, and set off, clattering away in the direction of Stallstead. The white dog, which had been sniffing at the hedge some way down the road, came pelting after them and leaped up and down behind the last caravan. A thin brown arm came out of the back of this caravan, and the dog was hauled inside with enormous scramblings. It looked as if the dog had been taken by surprise as much as I had.

The gatekeeper grunted and pushed back among us to the open gate. "Come on through," he said.

We obediently shuffled forward between the walls of the gatehouse. At the exact moment that I was level with the gate, I felt the magical defenses of Stallery cut through me like a buzz saw. It was only a thin line, luckily, but while I crossed it, it was like having my body taken over by a swarm of electric bees. I squeaked. The tall boy, walking beside me, made a small noise like "Oof!" I didn't notice if any of the others felt it because almost at once we came through under the gatehouse into a huge vista of perfect parkland. We all made little murmurs of pleasure.

There was perfect green rolling lawn wherever you looked, with a ribbon of beautifully kept driveway looping through it among clumps of graceful trees. The greenness rose into hills here and there, and the hills were either crowned with trees or they had little white-pillared summerhouses on them. And it all went on and on, into the blue distance.

"Where's the house?" one of the girls asked.

The gatekeeper laughed. "Couple of miles away. Start walking. When you come to the path that goes off to the right, take that and keep walking. When you can see the mansion, take the right-hand path again. Someone will meet you there and show you the rest of the way."

"Aren't you coming, too, then?" the girl asked.

"No," said the man. "I stay with the gate. Off you go."

We set off, trudging in a dubious little huddle along the drive, like a lost herd of sheep. We walked until the wall and the gate were out of sight behind two of the green hills, but there was still no sign of the mansion. A certain amount of sighing and shuffling began, particularly among the girls. They were all wearing the kind of shoes that hurt your feet just to look at them, and most of them had the latest fashion in dresses on, too, which held their knees together and forced them to take little tripping steps. Some of the boys had come in good suits made of thick cloth. They were far too hot, and one boy who was wearing hand-stitched boots was hobbling worse than the girls.

"I've got a blister already," one of the girls announced. "How much farther *is* it?"

"Do you think it's some kind of a test?" wondered the boy with the boots.

"Oh, it's bound to be," said the tall boy from the gypsy camp. "This drive is designed to lead us round in circles until only the fittest survive. That was a joke," he added as almost everyone let out a moan. "Why don't we all take a rest?" His bright dark eyes traveled over our various plastic bags. "Why don't we sit on this nice smooth grass and have a picnic?"

This suggestion caused instant dismay. "We *can't*!" half of them cried out. "They're expecting us!" And most of the rest said, "I can't mess up my good clothes!"

The tall boy stood with his hands in his pockets, surveying everyone's hot, anxious faces. "If they want us that badly," he said, in a testing kind of way, "they might have had the decency to send a car."

"Ooh, they wouldn't do that, not for *domestic*," one of the girls said.

The tall boy nodded. "I suppose not." I had the feeling that up until then, this boy had not the least notion why we were all here. I could see him digesting the idea. "Still," he said, "domestic or not, there's nothing to stop people taking their shoes off and walking on this nice smooth grass, is there? There's no one who could see." Faces turned to him with longing. "Go on," he said. "You can always put them on again when we sight the house."

More than half of them took his advice. Girls plucked off shoes; boys unlaced tight boots. The tall boy sauntered behind with a pleased but slightly superior smile, watching them scamper barefoot along the smooth verge. Some of the girls hauled their tight skirts up. Boys took off hot jackets.

"That's better," he said. He turned to me. "Aren't you going to?"

"Old shoes," I said, pointing down at them. "They don't hurt." His shoes looked to be handmade. I could see they fitted him like gloves. I felt very suspicious of him. "If you really thought it was a test," I said, "you've made them all fail it."

He shrugged. "It depends if Stallery wants barefoot

parlormaids and footmen with big hairy toes," he said, and I could have sworn he looked at me closely then, to see if I thought this was what we all intended to be. His piercing dark eyes traveled on down to my carrier bag. "You couldn't spare a sandwich, could you? I'm starving. The Travelers only eat when they happen to have some food, and that didn't seem to happen most of the time I was with them."

I fished him out one of my sandwiches and another for myself. "You couldn't have been with the gypsies *that* long," I said, "or your clothes would have got creased."

"You'd be surprised," he said. "It was nearly a month, actually. Thanks."

We marched along munching egg and cress, while the driveway unreeled ahead of us and more hills with trees and lacy white buildings came into view, and the other kids ran along ahead of us in a bunch. Most of them were trying to eat sandwiches, too, and hang on to coats and shoes and bags while they ate.

"What's your name?" I said at length.

"Call me Christopher," he said. "And you?"

"Conrad Te—Grant," I said, remembering my alias just in time.

"Conrad T. Grant?" he said.

"No," I said. "Just Grant."

"Very well," he said. "Grant you shall be. And you aim to be a footman and strut in Stallery in velvet hose, do you, Grant?"

Hose? I thought. I had visions of myself in a reel of rubber pipe. "I don't know what they dress you in," I said. "But I do know they can't be going to take more than one or two."

"That seems obvious," Christopher replied. "I regard you as my chief rival, Grant."

This was so exactly what I thought about him that I was rather shaken. I didn't answer, and we swung up another loop of drive to find there were now banks of flowers under some of the trees, as if we might be getting near the gardens around the house. Here a dog of some kind came lolloping from the nearest trees and put on speed toward us. It was quite a big dog. The kids on the verge instantly began milling about, yelling out that it was one of the ferocious guard dogs on the loose. A girl screamed. The boy with the hand-stitched boots swung them, ready to throw at the dog.

"Don't do that, you fool!" Christopher bellowed at him. "Do you *want* it to go for you?" He set off in

great strides up the grass toward the dog. It put on speed and came sort of snaking at him, long and low.

I'm sure the kids were right about that dog. It was snarling as if it wanted to tear Christopher's throat out, and when it got near, it bunched itself, ready to spring. A girl screamed again.

"Stop that, you fool of a dog," Christopher said. "Stop it at once."

And the dog did stop. Not only did it stop, but it wagged its tail and wagged its bunched-up hind parts and came crawling and groveling toward Christopher, where it tried to lick his beautiful shoes.

"No slobber," Christopher commanded, and the dog stopped and just groveled instead. "You've made a mistake," he told it. "No one here's a trespasser. Go away. Go back where you came from." He pointed sternly up at the trees. The dog got up and walked slowly back the way it had come, turning around hopefully every so often as it went, in case Christopher was going to let it come and grovel again. Christopher came down the hill saying, "I think it's trained to go for anyone who isn't on the path. Shoes on again, everyone, I'm afraid."

Everyone now regarded him as a sort of hero,

savior, and commander. Several girls gave him passionate looks while they put their shoes back on, and we all limped and straggled on around another curve of drive. Here there were hedges, with glimpses of flowers blazing beyond and, beyond that, a twinkle of many windows from behind the trees. A path branched off to the right. Christopher said, "This way, troops," and led everyone along it.

We went through more parkland, but it was just as well everyone had put their shoes on again, because this path was quite short and soon branched into another, among tall, shiny shrubs, where it ended in a flight of stone steps.

The boys hastily put their jackets back on. A youngish man was waiting for us at the top of these steps. He was quite skinny and only an inch or so taller than Christopher. He had a nice, snubby face. But all of us, even Christopher, stared up at him with awe because he was dressed in black velvet knee breeches, with yellow-and-brown-striped stockings below those and black buckled shoes below the stockings. He wore a matching brown-and-yellow-striped waistcoat over a white shirt above the breeches, and his fairish hair was long, tied at the back of his neck by a smooth black bow.

It was enough to make anyone stare.

Christopher dropped back beside me. "Ah," he said. "I see a footman or a lackey. But it's the breeches that seem to be velvet. The hose are striped silk."

"My name's Hugo," the young man said. He smiled at us, very pleasantly. "If you'll just follow me, I'll show you where to go. Mr. Amos is waiting to interview you in the undercroft."

Five

Everyone went quiet and nervous. Even Christopher said nothing more. We all trooped up the steps, and with the young man's buckled shoes and striped stockings flashing ahead, we followed him through confusing shrubbery paths. By now we were quite near the mansion. We kept getting glimpses of high walls and windows above the bushes, but we only got a real sight of the house when Hugo led us cornerwise to a door in a yard. Just for a moment there was a space where you could look along the front of the mansion. We all craned sideways.

The place was enormous. There were windows in rows. It seemed to have its main front door halfway up the front wall, with two big stone stairways curving up to it, and all sorts of curlicues and golden things above that, on a heavy piece of roof that hung over the door. There was a fountain jetting, down between the two stairways, and a massive circle of drive beyond that.

This was all I had time to see. Hugo led us at a brisk pace, into the yard, across it, and in through a large square doorway in the lower part of the house. In no time at all we were crowding into a big wood-lined room, where Mr. Amos was standing, waiting for us.

No one had any doubt who he was. You could tell he was a Stallery servant because he wore a striped waistcoat like Hugo's, but the rest of his clothes were black, like someone going to a funeral. He had surprisingly small feet in very shiny black shoes. He stood with his hands clasped behind his back, like something blocky that might be going to take root in the floor, his small, shiny shoes astride, his blunt, pear-shaped face forward, and he made you feel almost religious awe. The Bishop down in Stallchester was much less awe-inspiring than Mr. Amos was, although it was hard to see why. He was the most pear-shaped man I had ever seen. His striped waistcoat rounded in front, his black coat spread at the sides, and his hands had to reach a long way back in order to clasp behind him. His face was rather purple as well as pear-shaped. His lips were quite thick below his wide, flat nose. He was not much taller than me. But you felt that if Mr. Amos were to get angry and uproot his small, shiny shoes from the floor, the floor would shake and the world with it.

"Thank you, Mr. Hugo," he said. He had a deep, resounding voice. "Now I want you all standing in a line, hands by your sides, and let me look at you."

We all hastily shuffled into a row. Those of us with plastic bags tried to lean them up against the backs of our legs, out of sight. Mr. Amos uprooted himself then, and the floor did shake slightly as he paced along in front of us, looking each of us intently in the face. His eyes were quite as awesome as the rest of him, like stones in his purple face. When he came to me, I tried to stare woodenly above his smooth gray head. This seemed the right way to behave. He smelled a little like Mayor Seuly, only more strongly, of good cloth, fine wine, and cigar. When he came to Christopher at the end of the line, he seemed to stare harder at him than at anyone, which worried me quite a lot. Then he turned massively sideways and snapped his fingers.

Instantly two more youngish men dressed like Hugo came into the room and stood looking polite and willing.

"Gregor," Mr. Amos said to one, "take these two boys and this girl to be interviewed by Chef. Andrew, these boys are to see Mr. Avenloch. Take them to the conservatory, please. Mr. Hugo, all the rest of the girls will see Mrs. Baldock in the Housekeeper's Room."

All three young men nodded, murmured, "Yes, Mr. Amos," and led their batch of people away. I think most of them had to catch the next tram down into Stallchester. I never saw more than two of them again. In a matter of seconds the room was empty except for Mr. Amos, Christopher, and me. My heart began to bang again, horribly.

Mr. Amos planted himself in front of us. "You two look the most likely ones," he said. His voice boomed in the empty room. "Can I have your names, please?"

"Er," I said. "Conrad Grant."

Christopher said, with great smartness, "I'm

Christopher Smith, Mr. Amos." I bet that's a lie, I thought. He's got an alias, just like me.

Mr. Amos's stonelike eyes turned to me. "And where are you from?"

"The bookshop," I said, "down in Stallchester."

The stone eyes rolled up and down to examine me. "Then," Mr. Amos said, "I take it you'll have had no experience of domestic work."

"I clean the shop quite often," I said.

"*Not* what I had in mind," Mr. Amos said coldly. "No experience of waiting on your betters, I meant. Being polite. Guessing what they need before they ask. Being invisible until they need you. Have you?"

"No," I said.

"And you?" Mr. Amos asked, moving his stony eyes to Christopher. "You're older. You must have earned your keep, or you wouldn't have had the money for those fancy clothes."

Christopher bowed his neatly clipped dark head. "Yes, Mr. Amos. I confess I have been three years in a household of some size, though not as big as this one, of course. But, in case you get the wrong impression, I was there more as a hanger-on than precisely as part of the work force."

Mr. Amos stared intently at Christopher. "You mean, as a poor relation?" he said.

"That sort of thing, yes," Christopher agreed. I thought he sounded a little uncomfortable about it.

"So neither of you have the sort of experience I mentioned," Mr. Amos said. "Good. I like my trainees ignorant. It means they don't come to Stallery with all the wrong habits. Next big question. How do you both feel about serving as a valet, a gentleman's gentleman? This means dressing your gentleman, caring for his clothes, looking to his comfort, running errands if he asks it, even cooking for him in certain cases, and generally knowing the gentleman's secrets—but never, *ever* breathing a word of those secrets to another soul. Can you do all that?"

Christopher looked a little stunned by this. I remembered how Christopher, so oddly, had not seemed to know why he was here, and I realized that this was my best chance *ever* of making sure I got this job. "I'd like doing that a lot," I said.

"Me, too," Christopher said promptly. "Looking after clothes and keeping secrets are the two things I do best, Mr. Amos." I began to think I hated him.

"Good, good," Mr. Amos said. "I'm glad to see you both so ambitious. Because of course it will take some years of training before either of you are up to a position of such trust. But both of you seem quite promising material." He rocked back and forth on his small, shiny feet. "Let me explain," he commanded. "In a few years I shall probably be retiring. When this happens, my son, Mr. Hugo, will naturally take over my position in charge of Stallery, as I took over from *my* father here. This will leave untenanted Mr. Hugo's current post as valet to Count Robert. My aim is to train up more than one candidate for this position, so that when the time comes, Count Robert will have a choice. With this in mind, I propose to appoint the pair of you to the position of Improvers, and I expect you to regard yourselves as rivals for the honor of becoming, in time, a proper valet. I shall naturally recommend to the Count whichever of you most meets with my approval."

This was wonderful luck! I could feel my face spreading into a relieved grin. "*Thank* you!" I said, and then added, "Mr. Amos, sir," in order to start by being respectful.

Christopher seemed equally relieved but also slightly bewildered. "Er, won't you need to see any of my references, sir?" he asked. "One of them is quite glowing."

"Keep them," Mr. Amos said, "for your own encouragement. The only reference I need is my own powers of observation, honed through many years of scrutinizing young applicants. You no doubt saw the ease with which I distinguished who, among your companions, was likely to make a kitchen apprentice, who were potential maidservants, and who could only become a gardener's boy. I can do this in seconds, and I am almost never wrong. Am I, Mr. Hugo?"

"Very seldom," Hugo agreed, from the other side of the room.

Neither of us had seen him come in. We both jumped.

"Take Christopher and Conrad to their quarters, Mr. Hugo, show them the establishment, and acquaint them with their hours," Mr. Amos said. "We have our two Improvers, I am glad to say."

"Yes, sir. Where do they eat?" Hugo asked.

We could see this was an important question. Mr. Amos looked gravely at us, looked at the ceiling, and rocked on his feet. "Quite," he said. "The Middle Hall will be their station once it is in use, but since it is not . . . *Not* the Lower Hall, I fear. Young men are too prone to horseplay with the maidservants. I think we must reluctantly do as we temporarily did with the footmen and allow them to eat in the Upper Hall until the period of mourning for the late Count is past and we have Stallery full of guests again. Show them, will you. I want them present and properly dressed when I Serve Tea."

Hugo held open the door beside him and said, in his pleasant way, "If you'd come with me, then."

As I picked up my plastic bag and followed Christopher through that door, I was nervous all over again, in quite a new way. I felt as if I had accidentally entered the priesthood and wasn't cut out for it. I expected Christopher to be feeling the same, but as Hugo showed us into a slow brown lift—"Strictly for Staff," he said. "*Never* show Family or their friends to a Staff lift"—and pressed button A, for the attics, I could see Christopher was wholly delighted, bubbling over with delight, as if he had just won a game. He looked the way I felt whenever Uncle Alfred pleaded with me to go on doing the cooking.

Christopher seemed quite unable to contain his joy while the lift climbed sluggishly upward. "Tell me," he burst out at Hugo, "will Conrad and I learn your trick of entering a room through a crack in the floorboards? I once read a book where a manservant was always oozing in like some soundless liquid, but with you it was more like soundless *gas*! You were just *there*! Was it magic?"

Hugo grinned at this. Now I knew he was Mr. Amos's son, I could see the likeness. He had the big lips and the snubby nose, but in Hugo it was rather nice-looking. Otherwise, he was such a different size and shape, and seemed such a different sort of person, that it was hard to see him stepping into his father's place when Mr. Amos retired. "You'll learn how to enter a room," he said, leaning against the wall of the lift. "My father had me doing it for hours before he let me go into a room where the Family were. But the main thing you'll learn—I'm warning you—is how to be on your feet for fourteen hours at a stretch. Staff never sit down. Any more questions?"

"Hundreds," Christopher said. "So many I can't think what to ask first." This was evidently true. He had to stop and stare at the wall, trying to decide.

I seized the space to ask, "Should we call you *Mr.* Hugo?"

"Only in front of my father," Hugo said with another grin. "He's very strict about it."

"Because you're the heir to the butlership?" Christopher asked irrepressibly.

"That's right," said Hugo.

"Rather you than me!" Christopher said.

"Quite," Hugo answered, rather sadly.

Christopher looked at him shrewdly, but he said nothing else until the lift finally made it up to the attics. Then he said, "My God! A rat maze!"

Hugo and I both laughed, because it *was* like that up there. The roof was quite low, with skylights in it, so you could see narrow wooden corridors lined with doors running in all directions. It was warm and smelled of wood. I'm going to get lost up here, I thought.

"You'll be sharing a room along here," Hugo said, leading the way along a corridor that looked just like any of the rest. All the doors were painted the same dull red-brown. He opened a door like all the others. "You'll have to be careful not to make too much noise up here," he remarked. "You'll be among quite senior Staff."

Beyond the door was a fresh white room with a sloping ceiling and two narrow white beds. The little low window looked out at blue mountains, and sun streamed in. It smelled of warm whitewash. There was a carpet, a chest of drawers, and a curtained corner for hanging things in. It was rather nicer than my room at home. I looked at Christopher, expecting him to be used to much fancier bedrooms. But I'd forgotten he'd just spent a month in a gypsy caravan. He looked around with pleasure.

"Nice," he said. "Companionable. Twice as big as a caravan. Er—bathroom?"

"The end of the corridor," Hugo said. "The corner room on every passage is always a bathroom. Now come and get your uniforms. This way."

I hurriedly dumped my plastic bag on a bed, wondering if I would ever find it again, and we followed Hugo back out into the corridor.

Here Christopher said, "Just a second." He took off his narrow silk tie and wrapped it around the doorknob on the outside of the door. "Now we can find ourselves again," he said. "Or isn't it allowed?" he asked Hugo.

"I've no idea," Hugo said. "I don't think anyone's thought of doing it before."

"Then you must all have the most wonderful sense of direction," Christopher said. "Is this the bathroom?"

Hugo nodded. We both stuck our heads around the door, and Christopher nodded approvingly. "All the essentials," he said. "Far better than a tin tub or a hedge. Towels?"

"In the linen store next to the uniforms," Hugo told him. "This way."

He led us in zigzags through the narrow corridors to a place with a bigger skylight than usual. Here the doors were slatted, although they were the same red-brown as all the others. He opened the first slatted door. "Better take a towel each," he said.

We gazed at a room twice the size of the one we had been given, filled with shelves piled with folded towels, sheets, and blankets. Enough for an army, it seemed to me.

"How many Staff *are* there?" Christopher asked as we each took a big red-brown towel.

"We're down to just fifty indoors at the moment," Hugo said. "When we start entertaining again, we'll go up to nearly a hundred. But the mourning period for Count Rudolf isn't over for another fortnight, so we're very quiet until then. Plenty of time for you to find your feet. Uniforms are this way."

He led us to the next slatted door. Beyond it was an even bigger room. It had shelves like a public library, and all the shelves were stacked with clothes. There was pile after pile of pure white shirts, a wall of velvet breeches, neat towers of folded waistcoats, stack upon stack of striped stockings, rails hung with starched white neck-cloths, and more shelves devoted to yellow-striped aprons. Underneath the shelves were cardboard boxes of buckled shoes. A strong spell against moths made my eyes water. Christopher's eyes went wide, but I only dimly saw Hugo going around, checking labels, looking at us measuringly, and then taking down garments from the shelves.

We each got two shirts, two aprons, four pairs of underpants, four pairs of stockings, one waistcoat, and one pair of velvet breeches. Hugo followed those with neckcloths, carefully laid over the growing heaps in our arms, and then a striped nightshirt apiece. "Do you know your shoe sizes?" he asked.

Neither of us did. Hugo whipped up a sliding measure from among the cardboard boxes and swiftly found out. Then he fetched buckled shoes from the boxes and made us try them on, efficiently checking where our toes came to and how the heels fitted. "It's important your shoes don't hurt," he said. "You're on your feet so much." I could see he made a very good valet.

"Right," he said, dumping a gleaming pair of shoes each on top of the nightshirts. "Go and get into the uniforms and put the rest away and meet me by the lift in ten minutes." He fetched a slender gold watch out of his waistcoat pocket and looked at the time. "Make that seven minutes," he said. "Or I won't have time to show you the house. I have to start for Ludwich with Count Robert at four."

I put my chin on the shoes to hold them steady and tried to remember the way we had come here. So did Christopher. I went one way with my pile of clothes. Christopher, with a vague but purposeful look, marched off in exactly the opposite direction.

Hugo went racing after Christopher, shouting, "*Stop!* Not *there*!" He sounded so horrified that Christopher swung around in alarm.

"What's wrong?" he asked.

Hugo pointed to a wide red-brown stripe painted on the wall beside Christopher. "You mustn't *ever* go past this line," he said. "It's the women's end of the attics beyond that. You'd be sacked on the spot if you were found on the wrong side of it."

"Oh," said Christopher. "Is that *all*? From the

way you yelled, I thought there must be a hundred-foot drop along there. Which is the right way back to our room, then?"

Hugo pointed. It was in a direction that neither of us had thought of taking. We hurried off that way, feeling rather foolish, and after a while, more by luck than anything, arrived in the corridor where Christopher's tie hung on the doorknob.

"What foresight on my part!" Christopher said as we each dumped our armloads of clothing on a bed. "I don't know about you, Grant, but I know I'm going to look and feel a perfect idiot in these clothes, though not as silly as I'm going to feel in this night-shirt tonight."

"We'll get used to it," I said grumpily as I scrambled out of my own clothes. By this time Christopher's confident way of going on was annoying me.

"Do I detect," Christopher asked, climbing out of his trousers and hanging them carefully on the rail of his bed, "a certain hostility in you, Grant? Have you, by any chance, let Mr. Amos's ideas get to you? *Are* you regarding me as a rival?"

"I suppose I'm bound to," I said. I turned the black knee-length trousers around to see which was front and which was back. It wasn't easy to tell.

"Then let me set your mind at rest, Grant," Christopher said, puzzling over the breeches, too. "And hang on. I think we need to put the stockings on first. These things buckle over the stripy socks and—I hope—help to keep the wretched things up. I sincerely hope so. I hate wrinkles round my ankles. Anyway, forget Mr. Amos. I shall only be here for a short time."

"Why?" I said. "Are you sure?"

"Positive," Christopher said, wriggling a bare foot dubiously into a striped stocking. "I'm only doing this while I'm on my way to something quite different. When I find what I want, I shall leave at once."

I was at that moment standing on one foot while I tried to put a stocking on, too. It was floppy and it twisted and the top kept closing up. I was so astonished to hear that Christopher was in exactly the same position as me, that I overbalanced. After a moment or so of frantic hopping about, I sat on the floor with a crash.

"I see your feelings overwhelm you," Christopher remarked. "You really needn't worry, Grant. Regard me as a complete amateur. I shall never be a serious footman, let alone a valet or a butler."

Six

After what Christopher had said, I expected him to look all wrong in his new clothes. Not a bit of it. As soon as he had tightened the straps of his striped waistcoat, so that it sat trimly around his waist, and tied the white neckcloth under his chin, he looked a perfect, jaunty young footman. I was the one who looked wrong. I could see myself in the long stripe of mirror on the back of the door looking, ever so slightly, a mess. This was odd *and* unfair, because my hair was as black as Christopher's and I was not fat and there was nothing wrong with my face. But I looked as if I had stuffed my head through a hole on the top of a suit of clothes meant for someone else, the way you do for trick photographs.

"Seven minutes up," Christopher said, folding back the frill at the wrist of his shirt to look at his watch. "No time to admire yourself, Grant."

As we left the room, I remembered that I had left the port wine cork in the pocket of my own trousers. Mayor Seuly had said to carry it with me at all times. I had to dive back to get it and stuff it into . . . Oh. The wretched breeches turned out not to have pockets. I crammed the cork into a narrow waistcoat pocket as I followed Christopher out. I was going to tell him it was a keepsake from home, if he asked, but he never seemed to notice.

Hugo had his watch out when we found him. "You'll have to keep better time than this," he said. "My father insists on it." He put his watch away in order to tweak at my neckcloth, then at Christopher's. Everyone at Stallery was *always* trying to rearrange our neckcloths, but we didn't know that then, and we both backed away in surprise. "Follow me," Hugo said.

We didn't go down in the lift. Hugo led us down narrow, creaking stairs to the next floor. Here the ceilings were higher and the corridors wider, with matting on them, but everywhere was rather dark. "This is the nursery floor," he said. "At the moment, we use some of the rooms for the housekeepers and the sort of guests who don't eat with the Family, valets, the accountant, and so on."

On the way to the next flight of stairs, he opened a door to show us a long, dark, polished room with a rocking horse halfway down it, looking rather lonely. "Day nursery," he said.

The next flight of stairs was wider and had matting for carpet. At the bottom, the ceilings were a bit higher still, and there was carpet everywhere, new and pungent and dove gray. There were pictures on the walls. "Guest rooms?" Christopher guessed brightly.

"*Overflow* guest rooms." Hugo corrected him. "My father has his quarters on this floor," he added, taking us to the next flight of stairs. These stairs were quite broad and carpeted rather better than the best hotel in Stallchester.

Below this, it was suddenly opulent. Christopher pursed his mouth and whispered out a whistle as we stared along a wide passageway with a carpet like pale blue moss, running through a vista of gold-and-crimson archways, white statues, and golden ornaments on marble-topped tables with bent gold legs. There were vases of flowers everywhere here. The air felt thick and scented.

Hugo took us right along this passage. "You'll need to know this floor," he said, "in case you have to deliver anything to one of the Family's rooms." He pointed to each huge white double door as we came to it, saying, "Main guest room, red guest room, Count Robert's rooms, blue guest room, painted guest room. The Countess has the rose rooms, through here. This one is the white guest room, and Lady Felice has the rooms on this corner. Round beyond there are the lilac room and the yellow room. We don't use these so often, but you'd better know. Have you got all that?"

"Only vaguely," Christopher admitted.

"There's a plan in the undercroft," Hugo said, and he led us on, down wide, shallow steps this time, blue and soft like the passage, to a floor more palatial yet. My head was spinning by this time, but I sort of aimed my face where Hugo pointed and tried to look intelligent. "Ballroom, banquet room, music room, Grand Saloon," he said, and I saw vast spaces, enormous chandeliers, vistas of gold-rimmed sofas, and one room with about a hundred yards of table lined with flimsy gold chairs. "We don't use these more than two or three times a year," Hugo told us, "but they all have to be kept up, of course. There was going to be a grand ball here for Lady Felice's coming-of-age, but it had to be canceled when the Count died. Pity. But we'll be using them again in a couple of weeks to celebrate Count Robert's engagement. We had a spectacular ball here four years ago when the present Count was eighteen. Almost all the titles in Europe came. We used ten thousand candles and nearly two thousand bottles of champagne."

"Quite a party," Christopher remarked as we went past the main grand stairway. We craned and saw it led down into a huge hall with a streaky black marble floor.

Hugo pointed a thumb down the stairway. "The rooms down there are used by the Family most of the time—drawing rooms, dining rooms, library, and so on—but Staff are not allowed to use these stairs. Don't forget."

"Makes me want to slide down those banisters at once," Christopher murmured as Hugo took us to a much narrower flight of stairs instead, which came out into the hall behind the Family lift. He pointed to the various big black doors and told us which was which, but he said we couldn't look inside the rooms because Family might be using any one of them. We nodded, and our feet skidded in our new shoes on the black, streaky floor.

Then we thudded through a door covered with green cloth, and everywhere was suddenly gray stone and plain wood. Hugo pointed, "My father's pantry, Family china scullery, silver room, flower room, Staff toilets. We go down here to the undercroft."

He went galloping down a flight of steep stone steps. As we clattered down after him, I suddenly felt as if I were back at school. It had that smell, rather too warm and mixed with chalk and cooking, and like school, there was that feeling of lots of people about, many voices in the distance and large numbers of feet shuffling and hurrying. A girl laughed, making echoes, and—again like school—a bell rang somewhere.

The bell was ringing in the large stone lobby at the bottom of the stairs. There was a huge board there with row upon row of little round lights on it. One was flashing red more or less in the middle of it. A lady in a neat brown-and-yellow-striped dress and a yellow cap on her gray hair was looking up at the light rather anxiously.

"Oh, Hugo," she said gladly as we clattered off the stairs. "It's Count Robert."

Hugo strode across to the board. "Right," he said, and unhooked a sort of phone from the side, which seemed to stop the light flashing at once. I looked up at it as it went off. White letters under the light said *CR Bdm*. All the lights had similar incomprehensible labels. *Stl Rm*, I read. *Bkfst Rm*, *Dng Rm*, *Hskpr*, *C Bthrm*, *Stbls*. The only clear one was in the middle at the bottom. It said *Mr. Amos*.

Meanwhile, a voice was distantly snapping out of the phone thing. It sounded nervous and commanding. "Coming right away, my lord," Hugo said to it. He hung the phone up and turned to us. "I've got to go. I'll have to leave you here with Miss Semple. She's our Under-Housekeeper. Do you mind showing these Improvers round the undercroft?" he asked the lady.

"Not at all," she said. "You'd better go. He's been ringing for three minutes now." Hugo grinned at all of us and went racing up the stone steps again. We were left with Miss Semple, who smiled a mild, cheerful smile at us. "And your names are?"

"Conrad T—Grant," I said. I only remembered my alias just in time.

Christopher was just the same. He said,

"Christopher—er, er—Smith," and backed away from her a little.

"Conrad and Christopher," she said. "Two Cs." Then she made us *both* start backward by pouncing on us and straightening our neckcloths. "*That's* better!" she said. "I've just been putting your duty rosters up on our bulletin board. Come and look."

It was really more like school than ever. There was a long, long board, taking up all the wall beside the stairs. This was divided into sections by thick black lines, with black headings over each section: *Housemaids, Footmen, Parlor Staff, Stillroom, Laundry, Kitchen*, we read, and right at the end beside the stairs, we found *Improvers*. There were lists and timetables pinned under each heading, but it was like school again in the way there were other, less official notices scattered about the board. A big pink one said, "*Housemaids' Knees Up, 8:30 Thurs. All Welcome.*" Miss Semple tut-tutted and took that one down as we came to it. Another one read, in dark blue letters, "*Chef wants that hat returned NOW!!*" Miss Semple left that one up. She also left a yellow paper that said, "*Mrs. Baldock still wants to know who scattered those pins in the Conservatory.*"

When we came to the *Improvers* column, we saw

two large sheets of paper neatly ruled into seven and labeled with the days of the week. Times of the day, from six in the morning until midnight, were written on the left, and lines ruled for each hour. Almost every one of the boxes made like this was filled with neat gray spidery writing. "*6:00,*" I read on the left-hand sheet, "*Collect shoes to take to Blacking Rm for cleaning. 7:00, Join Footmen in readying Breakfast Rm. 8:00, On duty in Breakfast Rm . . .* " My eyes scudded on, with increasing dismay, to things like "*2:00, Training session in Laundry, 3:00, Training sessions in Stillroom and Kitchen annex 3 with 2nd Underchef.*" It was almost a relief to find a square labeled simply "*Mr. Amos*" from time to time. On down my eyes went, anxiously, to the last box, "*11:00–12:00.*" That said, "*On call in Upper Hall.*" Bad, I thought. I couldn't see one spare minute in which I might manage to summon a Walker, once I knew who was causing my Fate. And there didn't seem to be any boxes with meals marked in them either.

Christopher seemed to be trying to hide even worse dismay than I felt. "This is a *disaster!*" I heard him mutter as he scanned the closely filled right-hand sheet. He put a finger out to one of the only empty squares there was. "Er, someone seems to have forgotten to fill this square in."

"No mistake," Miss Semple said, in her high, cheerful voice. She was one of those nice, kind people who have no sense of humor at all. "You both have two hours off on Wednesday afternoons and two more on a Thursday morning. That's a legal requirement."

"Glad to hear it!" Christopher said faintly.

"And another hour to yourselves on a Sunday, so that you can write home," Miss Semple added. "Your full day off comes every six weeks and you can—" A bell began to ring on the board across the lobby. Miss Semple whirled around to look. "That's Mr. Amos!" She hurried over and unhooked the phone.

While she was busy saying, "Yes, Mr. Amos . . . No, Mr. Amos . . . ," I said to Christopher, "Why did you say this was a disaster?"

"Well, er," he said. "Grant, did you *know* we were going to be kept this busy when you applied for the job?"

"No," I said dolefully.

Christopher was going to say more, but Miss Semple hooked the phone back and hastened across the lobby again, saying confusingly, "You can take two free days together every three months if you prefer, but I shall have to show you the undercroft later. Hurry upstairs, boys. Mr. Amos wants a word with you before Tea is Served."

We ran up the stone stairs. As Christopher said late that night, if we had grasped one thing about Stallery by then, it was that you did what Mr. Amos said, and you did it fast. "Before he's said it, if possible," Christopher added.

Mr. Amos was waiting for us in the wood-and-stone passage upstairs. He was smoking a cigar. Billows of strong blue smoke surrounded us as he said, "Don't pant. Staff should never look hurried unless Family particularly tells them to hurry. That's your first lesson. Second— Straighten those neckcloths, both of you." He waited, looking irritated, while we fumbled at the white cloths and tried not to pant and not to cough in the smoke. "Second lesson," he said. "Remember at all times that what you really are is living pieces of furniture." He pointed the cigar at us three times, in time to the words. "Living. Pieces. Of furniture. Got that?" We nodded. "No, *no!*" he said. "You say, 'Yes, Mr. Amos—' "

"Yes, Mr. Amos," we chorused.

"Better," he said. "Say it smarter next time. And

like furniture, you stand against the walls and seem to be made of wood. When Family asks you for anything, you give it them or you do it, as gracefully and correctly as possible, but you do not speak unless Family makes a personal remark to you. What would you say if the Countess gives you a personal order?"

"Yes, your ladyship?" I suggested.

"No, *no!*" Mr. Amos said, billowing smoke at me. "Third lesson. The Countess and Lady Felice are to be addressed as 'my lady' and Count Robert as 'my lord.' Now bear these lessons firmly in mind. You are about to be shown to the Countess while we Serve Tea. You are there for this moment simply to observe and learn. Watch me, watch the footman on duty, and otherwise behave like two chairs against the wall."

His stone-colored eyes stared at us expectantly. After a moment we realized why and chorused again, "Yes, Mr. Amos."

"And chairs would be slightly more use," he said. "Now, repeat back to me—"

Luckily at that moment a bell shrilled downstairs in the lobby.

"Ah," said Mr. Amos. "The Countess has Rung

for Tea." He stubbed out his cigar on a piece of wall that was black and gray with having cigars stubbed on it and put the dead cigar into a pocket of his striped waistcoat. Then he stuck out both arms, rather like a penguin, to make his shirt cuffs show and shook his thick shoulders to settle his coat. "Follow me," he said, and pushed through the green cloth door into the hall.

We followed his solemn pear-shaped back out into the middle of the huge black-floored hall. There his voice rang around the space. "Wait here." So we waited while he went to one of the large doors on the other side of the hall and pushed the two halves of it gently open. "You rang, my lady?" His voice came to us, smooth and rich and full of respect.

Probably someone said something in the room beyond. Mr. Amos bowed and backed away into the hall, gently closing the doors. For a moment after that, I could hardly see or hear anything, because I knew I was now actually going to see the person causing my bad karma. I was going to *know* who they were and I was going to have to summon a Walker. My heart banged, and I could hardly breathe. My face must have looked odd, because I saw Christopher give me a surprised, searching look, but he had no time to say anything. At that moment the footman called Andrew backed out through the distant green door, carefully towing a high-tea trolley.

Later that day Christopher said this was when he began to feel he might be in church. Mr. Amos gestured to us to fall in on either side of Andrew, while he walked in front of the trolley himself and threw the double door wide open so that we could all parade into the room beyond in a solemn procession, with the trolley rattling among us. But it didn't go quite smoothly. Just as we got to the doorway, Andrew had to stop the trolley to let a young blond lady go through first.

She was very good-looking. Christopher and I agreed on that. We both stared, although we noticed that Andrew very carefully didn't look at her. But she did not seem to see me, or Christopher, or Andrew, though she nodded at Mr. Amos and said, "Oh, good. I'm in time for Tea." She went on into the room, where she sat bouncily on one of the several silk sofas, opposite the lady who was already there. "Mother, guess what—"

"Hush, Felice dear," the other lady said.

This was because the church service was still going on, and the other lady—the Countess—did not want it interrupted. She was one of those who had to have everything exactly so and done in the right order.

If you looked at her quickly, this Countess, you thought she was the same age as the good-looking one, Lady Felice. She was just as blond and just as slender, and her dark lilac dress made her face look pure and delicate, almost like a teenager's. But when she moved, you saw she had studied for years and years how to move gracefully, and when she spoke, her face took on expressions that were terribly *sweet*, in a way that showed she had been studying expressions for years, too. After that, you saw that the delicate look was careful, careful, expert makeup.

By this time two small jerks of Mr. Amos's chin had sent me and Christopher to stand with our backs against the wall on either side of the doorway. Andrew stopped the trolley and shut the doors—practically soundlessly—and Mr. Amos gently produced a set of little tables, which he placed out beside the ladies. Then back and forth he and Andrew went, back and forth from trolley to tables, setting a thin gold-rimmed plate and a fluted cup and saucer on three of the tables, then napkins and little forks and spoons. Then there was the teapot to place on its special mat on another table, a strainer in a bowl, a gold-edged jug of cream, and a boat-shaped thing full of sugar cubes. All just so.

Then there was a pause. The ladies sat. The teapot sat, too, steaming faintly.

Christopher, who was staring ahead looking so totally blank that he seemed to have no brain at all, said that at this point he was thinking the tea in the pot would soon be cold. Or stewed. So was I, a bit. But mostly I was feeling really let down. I stared and stared at the Countess, hoping I would suddenly *know* that she was the person causing my Fate. I even looked at Lady Felice and wondered, but I could tell she was just a normal, happy kind of person who was having to behave politely in front of the Countess. The Countess was a sort of hidden dragon. That was why I thought she might be the one. She was very like a teacher we had in my third year. Mrs. Polak *seemed* very sweet, but she could really give you grief, and I could see the Countess was the same. But I didn't get any *knowing* off her at all.

It has to be Count Robert, then, I thought.

"Amos," the Countess said in a lovely, melodious voice, "Amos, perhaps you could tell my son, the Count, that we are waiting to have tea."

"Certainly, my lady." Mr. Amos nodded at Andrew, and Andrew scudded out of the room.

We waited some more, at least five minutes to judge from the way my feet ached. Then Andrew slithered back between the doors and whispered to Mr. Amos.

Mr. Amos turned to the Countess. "I regret to tell you, my lady, that Count Robert left for Ludwich some twenty minutes ago."

"Ludwich!" exclaimed the Countess. I wondered why she didn't know. "What on earth does he need to go to Ludwich for? And did he give *any* indication of how long he proposed to be away?"

Mr. Amos's pear-shaped body bent in a bow. "I gather he intended a stay of about a week, my lady."

"That's what I was going to tell you, Mother," Lady Felice put in.

At this, something happened to the Countess's face, a hard sort of movement under the delicate features. She gave a tinkly little laugh. "Well!" she said. "At least the tea has had time to brew. Please pour, Amos."

Ouch! I thought. The Count's going to be in for it when he gets back!

This was the signal for the church service to go

on. Mr. Amos poured tea as if it were the water of life. It was steaming so healthily that Christopher said later that he was sure there was a keep-warm spell in the mat. Andrew offered cream. The Countess waved him away and got given lemon in transparent-thin slices by Mr. Amos instead. Then Andrew moved in with the sugar boat, and the Countess let him give her four lumps.

While the show moved on to Lady Felice, the Countess said, as if she were covering up an awkward pause, "I see we have two new page boys, Amos."

"Improvers, my lady," Mr. Amos said, "who will function as pages until they learn the work." His head jerked sharply at Christopher. "Christopher, be good enough to hand the sandwiches."

Christopher jumped. I could see his mind had been miles away, but he pulled himself together and heaved the sandwiches up off the trolley. There were scores of them, tiny, thin things with no crusts and thick, savory-smelling fillings, heaped up on a vast oval silver plate. Christopher sniffed at them yearningly as he hoisted the plate up, but he went and held the plate out to the Countess very gallantly, with a flourishing bow that matched the way he looked.

The Countess seemed startled, but she took six sand-wiches. Mr. Amos frowned as Christopher brought the plate to Lady Felice and went on one knee to hold it out to her.

Christopher had to go back and forth. It was amazing how much those two slim ladies ate. And all the while Mr. Amos stood back like a stuffed penguin and frowned. I could see he thought Christopher was too fancy.

"Ludwich!" the Countess complained after about her fifteenth sandwich. "Whatever does Robert *mean* by it? Without warning, too!"

She went on about it rather. Eventually Lady Felice dumped her eighteenth sandwich back on her plate in an irritated way and said, "Really, Mother, does it *matter*?"

She got a stare. The Countess had ice blue eyes, big ones, and the stare was glacial. "Of course it matters, dear. It's extreme discourtesy to *me*."

"But he was probably called away on business," Lady Felice said. "He was telling me that his bonds and shares—"

I could see this was quite a cunning thing to say, a bit like the way Anthea and I used to ask Uncle Alfred for money to stop him raging when we'd broken something. The Countess held up a small, gentle hand all over rings to stop Lady Felice. "Please, darling! I know nothing about finance. Amos, are there cakes?"

It was my turn to jump. Mr. Amos said, "Conrad, hand the cakes now, please."

They were at the bottom of the trolley on another huge silver plate. I almost staggered as I heaved it up. The plate was truly heavy and made heavier still by being piled so with all the tiniest and most delicious pastries you could imagine. Scents of cream, fruit, rosewater, almond, meringue, and chocolate hit my nose. I felt my stomach whir. It sounded so loud to me that I couldn't think of any elegant way to hand those cakes. I simply walked over to the Countess and held the plate out to her.

Mr. Amos frowned again. I could tell he thought I was too plain.

Luckily I didn't have to heave the plate about for very long. The Countess had just wanted to change the subject, I think. She only took three cakes. Lady Felice had one. How they could bear not to eat the lot, I shall never know.

After that we had the church service again, with everything being cleared back onto the trolley in the proper religious order. Mr. Amos and Andrew bowed. Both glared sideways at us until we realized we had to bow, too. Then we were allowed to push the trolley away into the hall.

"Tea ceremony over," Christopher muttered, under the clattering.

But it was not, not quite. In the middle of the hall Mr. Amos stopped and told us off. He made me at least feel quite awful. "In front of *Family!*" he kept saying. "One of you flounces like a pansy, and the other plods like a yokel!" Then he went on to the way we stood. "You do *not* gaze like half-wits; you do *not* stand to attention like common soldiers. You are in a proper household here. You behave *right*. Watch Andrew next time. He stands against a wall as if it were *natural*."

"Yes, Mr. Amos," we said miserably.

He allowed us to go away down the stone stairs in the end. And there the bewildering day went on and on. Miss Semple was waiting to show us the undercroft. Christopher tried to sidle off then, but she turned and shot him a mild but all-seeing look and shook her head. He came glumly to heel. I followed her resignedly anyway. It was clear to me that I was here for a week, until Count Robert came back, so I thought I might as well learn my way about.

The undercroft was vast. I had to be shown all over it again the next day because it was too big to take in that first time. All I remembered was a confusion of steams and scents from several kitchens and a laundry, and people in brown-and-gold uniform rushing about. There were cold stores and dry stores full of food, and a locked door leading to the cellars. There was at least one room dedicated entirely to crockery, where two girls seemed to be washing up all the time. I was very surprised when Miss Semple told us this was just crockery for Staff. The good china for the Family was upstairs in another pantry with another set of maids to wash it. Family and Staff were like two different worlds that only linked together at certain times and places.

Christopher became fascinated by this. "It's my amateur status, Grant," he told me. "It allows me to take a detached view of the tribal customs here. You must admit it's a strange setup when all these people chase about in the basement, just to look after two women."

He was so fascinated that he asked question after question at supper. Our part of the Staff had supper in the Upper Hall at seven, so that we would be ready to wait on the Family when they dined at eight. Their food was called Dinner and was very formal, but ours was fairly formal, too. A whole lot of Staff gathered round a big table at one end of a large sort of sitting room. There were chairs and magazines in the other end, and a smaller board with lights, in case anyone needed us while we were there, but no television. Andrew told me rather sadly that you couldn't get a signal up in Stallery, not for any money. Andrew was the nicest of the footmen by far.

Anyway, there were six footmen, and us, and a dismal old man with a snuffle (he was steward or accountant or something) and a whole lot of women. Miss Semple was there, of course, and she told me that the very smart elderly woman was the Countess's maid, and the almost as smart younger one was Lady Felice's. Those two weren't very nice. They only spoke to each other. But there were the Upper Stillroom Maid, the Head of Housemaids, the Head of Parlormaids, and several other Heads of Somethings. Apparently there should have been Hugo, too, but he had gone to Ludwich with Count Robert. All the other Staff ate in the Lower Hall, except Mr. Amos, who had his meals alone, Miss Semple said.

There was also Mrs. Baldock. She was Housekeeper, but I kept thinking of her as the Headmistress. She was the largest woman I had ever seen, a vast six-footer with iron gray hair and a huge bosom. The most noticeable thing about her was the purple flush up each side of her large face. Christopher said this didn't look healthy to him. "Possibly she drinks, Grant," he said, but this was later. At that supper she swept in after all the rest of us. Everyone stood up for her. Mrs. Baldock said a short grace, then looked down the table until she saw Christopher and me.

"I'll expect you two in the Housekeeper's Room promptly at nine-thirty tomorrow," she said.

This sounded so ominous to me that I kept my head down and said nothing for most of the meal. But Christopher was another matter. When supper came—and it was steak pie and marvelous, with massive amounts of potatoes in butter—it was brought in by four maids. Mrs. Baldock cut the pie, and the maids carried it around to us. Nobody started eating until Mrs. Baldock did.

"What is this?" Christopher said as the maid brought his slice.

"Steak pie, sir," the girl said. She was about

Christopher's age, and you could see she thought he was ever so handsome.

"No, I mean, the way there are Staff to wait on Staff," Christopher said. "When do *you* get to eat?"

"We have high tea at six-thirty, sir," the girl said, "but—"

"What a lot of meals!" Christopher said. "Doesn't that take another whole kitchen and a whole lot more Staff to wait on *you*?"

"Well, only sort of," the girl said. Her eyes went nervously to Mrs. Baldock. "Please, sir, we're not supposed to hold conversations while we're serving."

"Then I'll ask *you*," Christopher said to Andrew. "Do you see any reason why this serving business should ever stop? *We* have supper now, so as to wait on the Family, and these charming young ladies have theirs at six-thirty in order to wait on *us*. And when *they* are waited on, those people must have to eat at six, and before that some *other* people have to eat earlier still in order to wait on *them*. There must be some Staff who have supper at breakfast time in order to fit all this serving *in*."

Andrew laughed, but some of the other footmen were not amused. The one called Gregor growled, "Cheeky little beggar!" and the one called Philip said, "You think you're quite a card, don't you?" Behind them all four maids were trying not to giggle, and from the head of the table, Mrs. Baldock was staring. Well, everyone was staring. Most of the Head Maids were annoyed, and the two Lady's Maids were scandalized, but Mrs. Baldock stared with no expression at all. There was no way of knowing if she approved of Christopher or was about to sack him on the spot.

"Someone must be cooking all the time," Christopher said. "How do you manage with only three kitchens?"

Mrs. Baldock spoke. She said, "*And* a bakery. That will do, young man."

"Yes, ma'am," Christopher said. "Delicious pie, whichever kitchen it came from." He and Mrs. Baldock eyed each other down the length of the table. Everyone's heads turned from one to the other like people's at a tennis match. Christopher smiled sweetly. "Pure curiosity, ma'am," he said.

Mrs. Baldock just said, "Hmm," and turned her attention to her plate.

Christopher kept a wary eye on her, but he went on asking questions.

Seven

We had to jump up as soon as we had finished supper. We left the maids clearing plates and giggling at Christopher's back and hurried upstairs with the footmen to the dining room. This was a tall, gloomy room that matched the black-floored hall. Mr. Amos was waiting there to show us how to fold stiff white napkins into a fancy boat shape and then to instruct us in the right way to make two little silver islands of cutlery and wineglasses on the shiny black table. We had to put each knife, fork, and spoon exactly in its right place.

Christopher went rather pale while we were trying to get it right. "Indigestion, Grant," he told me in a sorrowful whisper. "Bolting pie and then running upstairs is not what I'm used to."

"That won't be the only thing that disagrees with you if Mr. Amos hears you," the surly footman—Gregor—said to him. "Hold your tongue. Put this cloth over that arm, both of you, and stand by that wall. Don't move, or I'll belt you one."

We spent the next hour doing just that. We were supposed to be attending to what Mr. Amos and the footmen did as they circled in and out around the two Ladies sitting each at their little island of glass and silver, but I think I dozed on my feet half the time. The rest of the time I stared at a big picture of a dead bird and some fruit on the opposite wall and wished I could be at home in the bookshop. The two Ladies bored me stiff. They talked the whole time about the clothes they were going to buy as soon as the time of mourning was over and where they would stay in Ludwich while they were shopping. And they seemed to go on eating forever.

When at last they were finished, we were allowed to go back to the undercroft, but we had to stay in the Upper Hall in case we were needed to bring things to the Ladies in the drawing room. Gregor watched us to make sure we didn't try to slip away. We sat side by side on a hard sofa as far away from

Gregor as we could get, trying not to listen to the two Lady's Maids, who were doing embroidery quite near to us and whispering gossipy things to each other.

"She's got a whole drawerful of keepsakes from him by now," said one.

The other one said, "If that gets found out, they'll *both* be in trouble."

"I wouldn't be in her shoes for any money," the first one said.

I yawned. I couldn't help it.

"Come, come, Grant," Christopher said. "On these occasions you have to keep going by taking an interest in *little* things, like those two maids do. We've been here a good seven hours by now. I know they seem the longest we've ever known, but you must have found *some* little thing to be amazed about *somewhere*."

I had, now he came to remind me. "Yes," I said. "How do the Countess and Lady Felice eat so much and stay so *thin*?"

"Good question," Christopher replied. "They fair put it away, don't they? The young one probably rushes about, but the old one is slightly stately. She ought by rights to be the size of Mrs. Baldock.

Perhaps the chef charms her food. But my guess is she takes slim spells. I dare you to go over and ask her Lady's Maid if I'm right."

I looked across at the two gossiping women. I laughed. "No. You do it."

Christopher didn't dare either, so we went on to talk about other things we had noticed. This was when Christopher told me his theory that Mrs. Baldock drank. But right at the end, just before Andrew came in and said we could go off to bed, Christopher astounded me by asking, "By the way, what or where is this Ludwich that the Countess is so peeved with the Count for vanishing to?"

I stared at him. How could he not know? "It's the capital city, of course! Down in the Sussex Plains, beside the Little Rhine. Everyone knows that!"

"Oh," said Christopher. "Ah. So the Count's gone on a spree, has he? The fact is, Grant, that one gets a little confused about geography, living with the Travelers. They never bother to say where we are or where we're going. So what part of the country are we in now?"

"The English Alps," I said. "Just above Stallchester." I was still astonished.

Christopher repeated, "The English Alps. Ah,"

looking grave and wise. "What other Alps are there, then—as a matter of interest?"

"French, Italian, Austrian," I said. "Those Alps sort of run together. The English Alps are divided off by Frisia." Christopher looked quite bewildered. He didn't seem to know any geography at all. "Frisia's the country on the English border," I explained. "The whole of Europe is quite flat between Ludwich and Mosskva, and the Alps make a sort of half-moon round the south of that. The English Alps are to the north of the plains."

Christopher nodded to himself. I thought I heard him murmur, "Series Seven—no British Isles here, of course."

"What?" I said. "What are you on about now?"

"Nothing," he said. "I'm half asleep."

I don't think he was, although I certainly was. When Andrew said we could go, I tottered into the lift, then out of it, and fell into the nightshirt and into bed and went to sleep on the spot. I dimly heard Christopher get up later in the night. I assumed he was visiting the toilet up at the end of the corridor, and I waited, mostly asleep, for him to come back. But he was away for so long that I went properly back to sleep and never heard him returning. All I knew was that he was in bed and asleep the next morning.

They woke us up at dawn.

We got used to this in the end, but that first morning was awful. We had to put on aprons and go around with a big basket collecting shoes to be cleaned, from the attics downward. Most doors had at least one set of shoes outside them. But Mr. Amos put out four pairs of small black shoes. The Countess put out a dozen pairs, all fancy. Lady Felice put out a stack of riding boots. We had to stagger down to the undercroft with the lot, where we were very relieved to discover that they employed someone else to clean them all. I could hardly clean my face that morning, let alone shoes.

Then we were allowed to have breakfast with a crowd of red-eyed, grumpy footmen. Andrew was off duty that morning, and Gregor was in charge, and he didn't like either of us and had it in for Christopher particularly. He sent us upstairs to the Family breakfast room before we'd really finished eating. He said it was important to have someone on duty there in case one of the Family came down early.

"I bet that was a lie!" Christopher said, and he

rather shocked me by helping himself to bread and marmalade from the vast sideboard. We found out that all the footmen did the same, when they finally loitered in.

And it was just as well they deigned to turn up. Lady Felice came in before seven, looking pale and pensive and wearing riding clothes. No one had expected her. Gregor had to shove the bread he was eating under the sideboard in a hurry, and his mouth was so full that one of the other footmen had to ask Lady Felice what she fancied for breakfast. She said, a bit sadly, that she only wanted rolls and coffee. She was going out riding, she said. And would Gregor go to the stables and ask them to get Iceberg saddled. Gregor couldn't speak still, or he would have sent Christopher. He had to go himself, scowling.

By the time the Countess stalked in, obviously seething for some reason, the sideboard had been lined with dishes under dome-shaped silver covers, most of them fetched from the food lift by Christopher or me, and she had a choice of anything from mixed grill to smoked kidneys and fish. She ate her way through most of them while she was interviewing the poor snuffly old accountant man.

His name was Mr. Smithers, and I think he had

only just started his own breakfast when she rang for him. He kept eyeing her plates sorrowfully. But he was a long time arriving, and Gregor sent Christopher to look for him, while the Countess drummed her long pearly nails angrily on the tablecloth.

Christopher marched smartly out of the room and marched smartly in again almost at once with Mr. Smithers, who behaved as if Christopher had dragged him there by his coat collar. Gregor looked daggers at Christopher. And honestly, that was one of a good many times that I didn't blame Gregor. Christopher was so pleased with himself. When he looked like that, I usually wanted to hit him as much as Gregor did.

Mr. Smithers was in trouble with the Countess. She had an awful way of opening her ice blue eyes wide, wide, and saying in a sweet, cold, cooing voice, "*Explain* yourself, Smithers. *Why* is this so?" Or sometimes she just said, "*Why?*" which was worse.

Poor Mr. Smithers snuffled and shifted and tried to explain. It was about some part of her money that was late coming in. We had to stand there and listen while he tried.

And it was odd. It was all quite ordinary stuff, like the income from the home farms and the inn she owned in Stallstead and her property in Ludwich. I kept thinking of Uncle Alfred telling me about Stallery's worldwide dealings and the huge markets that needed the possibilities pulled to work them, and I began to wonder if Uncle Alfred had got this right. He had told me about *millions* on the stock exchange, and here was the Countess asking about sixties and eighties and hundreds. I was really confused. But then I thought it had to be the Count who dealt in the big money. *Someone* had to. You only had to look at Stallery to see it cost a bomb to run the place.

But I didn't have much time to think. Mrs. Baldock rang for us the moment the Countess had polished off Mr. Smithers and her breakfast. Christopher and I had to pelt off to the Housekeeper's Room. By the time we got there, Mrs. Baldock was pacing about among her pretty floral chairs and little twiddly tables. The purple bits down the sides of her face were almost violet with impatience.

"I can only spare you five minutes," she said. "I have to be at my daily conference with the Countess after this. There's just time to outline the nature of your training to you now. We aim, you see, to ensure that whichever of you attains the post of valet to the Count is completely versed in all aspects of domestic science. You'll be learning, first and foremost, the correct care of clothing and the correct fashion for everything a gentleman does. Proper clothes for fishing are just as important as evening dress, you know, and there are six types of formal evening wear. . . . "

She went on about clothes for a good minute. I couldn't help thinking that the Count would have had to hire a lorry when he went to Ludwich if he really did take all the clothes Mrs. Baldock said he needed. I watched her feet tramping about on the floral carpet. She had huge ankles that draped over the sides of her buckled shoes.

"But just as important are laundering, house-cleaning, and bed making," she said. "And in order to learn to care for your gentleman in every way, you'll be having courses on flower arranging, hair-cutting, and cookery, too. Do either of you cook?"

While I was saying, "Yes, ma'am," I had the briefest glimpse of absolute horror on Christopher's face. Then he somehow managed a beguiling smile. "No," he said. "And I couldn't arrange flowers if my life depended on it. It's beginning to look as if Conrad's going to be the next valet, isn't it?"

"The Count will shortly marry," Mrs. Baldock pointed out. "The Countess is insisting on it. By the time *his* son is of an age to require a valet, even *you* should have learned what is necessary." She gave Christopher one of her long, expressionless looks.

"But why *cooking?*" he said despairingly.

"It is the custom," Mrs. Baldock said, "for the Count's son to be sent to university accompanied by both his tutor and his valet. They will take lodgings together, and the valet will create their meals."

"I'd far rather *create* a meal than *cook* one," Christopher told her frankly.

Mrs. Baldock actually grinned. She seemed to have taken to Christopher. "Get along with you!" she said. "I can see well enough that you can do anything you set your mind to, young man. Now go and report to the Upper Laundrymaid and tell her I sent you both."

We blundered our way through the stone warren of the undercroft and finally found the laundry. There the woman in charge looked at us doubtfully, then straightened our neckcloths, and then stood back to see if this had changed her opinion of us. She sighed. "I'll start you on ironing," she said pessimistically. "Things that don't matter too much.

Paula! Take these two to the pressing room, and show them what to do."

Paula materialized out of the steam and took us in tow, but unfortunately, she turned out to be no good at explaining things. She showed us to a bare stone room with various sizes of ironing tables in it. She gave Christopher a damp linen sheet and me a pile of wettish neckcloths. She told us how to turn the irons on. Then she left.

We looked at each other. Christopher said, "Penny for them, Grant."

"It's a bit like," I said, "that story where they had to turn straw into gold."

"It is!" Christopher agreed. "And no Rumpelstiltskin to help." He pushed his iron experimentally across the sheet. "This makes no difference—or possibly more wrinkles than before."

"You have to wait for the iron to get hot," I said. "I *think*."

Christopher lifted the iron and turned it this way and that in front of his face. "A touch of warmth now," he said. "How do these things work anyway? They don't plug in. Is there a salamander inside, or something?"

I laughed. Christopher's ignorance was truly

amazing. Fancy thinking a fire lizard could heat an iron! "They have a power unit inside—just like lights and cookers and tellies do."

"*Do* they? Oh!" said Christopher. "A little light came on at the end of this iron!"

"That *may* mean it's hot enough," I said. "Mine's got a light now. Let's try."

We got going. My first idea—that you could save time and effort by doing ten neckcloths at once—didn't seem to work. I cut the pile down to five, to two, and then to just one, which promptly turned yellowish and smelled. Christopher kept muttering, "I don't seem to be living up to Mrs. Baldock's high opinion of me—not at *all*!" until he startled me by crying out, "Great heavens! A *church window*! Look!"

I looked. He had a dark brown iron shape burned into the middle of his sheet.

"I wonder if it will do that again," he said.

He tried, and it did. I watched, fascinated, while Christopher printed a whole row of church windows right across the sheet. Then he went on to make a daisy shape in the lower half of it.

But at this point I was recalled to my own work by a cloud of black smoke and a very strong smell. I looked down to find that my iron had burned a neckcloth right in two and then gone on to burn its way into the ironing table beneath. I had a very deep black church window there. I found red cinders in it when I snatched the iron up.

"Oh, help!" I said.

"Panic ye not, Grant," Christopher said.

"I can't *help* it!" I said, trying to fan away rolls of brown smoke. "We're going to get into awful trouble."

"Only if things stay like this," Christopher said. He came across and looked at my disaster. "Grant," he said, "this is too deep for a church window. What you have here is probably a dugout canoe." He switched his own iron off and wagged it in my face. "I congratulate you," he said.

I nearly screamed at him. "It's not *funny*!"

"Yes, it is," he said. "Look."

I looked, and I gaped. The smoke had gone. The black boat shape was not there anymore. The ironing table was flat and complete, with its brown-blotched surface quite smooth, and on top of it lay a plain, white, badly ironed neckcloth. "How . . . ?" I said.

"No questions," Christopher said. "I shall just get

rid of my own artwork." He picked up a corner of his ruined sheet and shook it. And all the church windows simply disappeared. He turned to me, looking very serious. "Grant," he said, "you didn't see me do this. Promise me you didn't, or your dugout canoe comes back deeper and blacker and smokier than ever."

I looked from him to the restored ironing table. "If I promise," I said, "can I ask you how you did it?"

"No," he said. "Just promise."

"All right. I promise," I said. "It's obvious anyway. You're a magician."

"A magician," Christopher said, "is someone who sets out ritual candles round a pentangle and then mutters words of power. Did you see me do that?"

"No," I said. "You must be a very advanced kind."

Then I was half frightened, half pleased, because I thought I had made Christopher annoyed enough to tell me about himself. "*Piffle!* Pigheaded *piffle!*" he began. "Grant—"

To my great disappointment, Miss Semple hurried in and interrupted him. "You have to stop this now, boys," she said. "Make sure the irons are switched off. Mr. Avenloch has just brought in the produce for today, and Mr. Maxim wants you to start your cookery course by learning to pick out the best."

So off we hurried once more, to a chilly stone storeroom that opened off the yard, where Mr. Avenloch was standing watching a gang of lower gardeners carry in baskets of fruit and boxes of vegetables. One of the gang was the boy with the handmade boots. He grinned at us, and we grinned back, but I didn't envy him. Mr. Avenloch was one of those tall, thin, eagle-faced types. He looked a total tyrant.

"Wipe that smile off your face, Smedley," he said, "and get you gone back to that hoeing."

When the whole gang had gone scurrying out again, Mr. Maxim pranced forward. He was almost as full of himself as Christopher was. He was Second Underchef and he had been given the extra responsibility of teaching us, and this had made him really cocky. He rubbed his hands eagerly together and said to Christopher, "You are choosing for the table of the Countess herself. Pick me out—by sight only—all the best vegetables for her."

From the look on Christopher's face, I was fairly sure he had never seen a raw vegetable in his life before this. But he made a confident pounce toward a basket of gooseberries. "Here," he said, "are some splendid peas, really big ones. Oh no, they're hairy. It can't be good for peas to have bristles, can it?"

"Those," Mr. Maxim said, "are gooseberries for the Stillroom. Try again."

A little more cautiously, Christopher approached a small box of bright red chilies. "Now here are some fine, glossy carrots," he suggested. "They probably fade a bit when you cook them." He looked at Mr. Maxim. Mr. Maxim nearly dislodged his tall white hat by clutching at his head. "No?" Christopher asked. "What are they then? Pipless strawberries? Long, thin cherries?"

By this time I was leaning against the wall bent over with laughter. Mr. Maxim rounded on me. "This is no joke!" he shouted. "He's winding me up, isn't he?"

I could see he was furious. Cocky people hate being made fun of. I shook my head and managed to pull myself together. "No, he's not," I said. "He really doesn't know. He—you see—he's lived all his life as heir to a great estate—a bit like Stallery, really—but the family fell on hard times, and he had to get a job." I looked sideways at Christopher. He put on a modest look and did not try to deny what I said. Interesting.

Mr. Maxim was instantly sorry for Christopher. "My dear boy," he said, "I quite understand. Please go round with Conrad and let him identify the produce for you." He was wonderfully kind to Christopher after that and even *quite* kind to me when I mistook a pawpaw for a vegetable marrow.

"Thanks," Christopher murmured to me while we were arranging the fruit I had chosen in a great cut glass bowl. "I owe you one, Grant."

"No, you don't," I whispered back. "Dugout canoe."

But he did end up owing me one later that day. This was after we had stood against the wall in yet another eating room, each of us with a useless white cloth draped over one arm, watching the Countess and Lady Felice eat lunch. Part of the meal was actually the bowl of fruit we had arranged that morning. This gave me a good feeling, as if I had really *done* something at last. The Countess attacked the fruit heartily, but Lady Felice took one grape, and that was all.

"Darling," said the Countess, "you've hardly eaten anything. *Why?*"

It was the bad "*Why?*" with the stare. Lady Felice looked at her plate in order not to meet the stare and muttered that she wasn't hungry. This did not satisfy the Countess at all. She went on and on about it. Was Felice ill? Should she call a doctor? What were the symptoms? Or had breakfast disagreed with her? All in the sweet, high voice.

In the end Lady Felice said, "I just don't feel like food, Mother. All right?" Her face went pink, and she almost glared at the Countess.

And the Countess said, "There's no need to be coy, dear. If you're trying to lose weight, you're welcome to borrow my pills."

Christopher's eyes went sideways and met mine. She *does* take spell pills! his look said. Both of us nearly burst, trying not to laugh. Mr. Amos shot us a dirty look. So did Gregor. And by the time we had a grip on ourselves, Lady Felice had flung down her napkin and rushed out of the room, leaving the Countess looking annoyed and mystified.

"Amos," she said, "I shall *never* understand the young."

"Naturally not, my lady," Mr. Amos replied.

She smiled graciously, folded her napkin neatly, and walked elegantly to the door. "Tell Smithers to come to my boudoir with his revised accounts," she said as she left.

For some reason—I think it was watching her walk—I remembered Mrs. Potts saying that the Countess used to kick up her legs in a chorus line. I was staring after her, trying so hard to imagine her doing it—and I couldn't—that I jumped a mile when Mr. Amos shouted at me. He was really angry. He planted himself on the carpet face-to-face with us, and he told us off thoroughly for daring to laugh in front of the Ladies. He made me at least feel awful. It didn't seem to matter that he was the same height as I was and inches shorter than Christopher. He was like a prophet or a saint or something, hating us for being ungodly and thundering out of heaven at us.

"Now you will learn to be mannerly," he said in the end. "Both of you are to go out of this door and come in again as softly and politely as you can. Go on."

Even Christopher was quite cowed by then. We crept to the double door, crept out into the hall, and tiptoed apologetically in again. And of course that was not right. Mr. Amos made us do it over and over again, while Gregor kept shooting us mean smiles as he cleared the lunch away. We must have gone in and out fifty times, and Mr. Amos was just promising us that we would go on doing it until we got it right, when one of the other footmen came to say that Mr. Amos was wanted on the telephone.

"*What* a relief!" Christopher muttered.

"Gregor," said Mr. Amos, "set these two to cleaning the silver until we Serve Tea. If this is the call I was expecting, I shall be busy all afternoon, so you are to make sure they keep at it." And he hurried away on his small, shiny feet.

"I spoke too soon," Christopher said as Gregor came toward us.

"This way. Hurry up," Gregor said. He was positively gloating. Among his other drawbacks, Gregor was big. Hefty. He had the meaty sort of hands you could rather easily imagine giving you a wallop on the ear. We scuttled after him without a word, with our three sets of feet ringing, *clack-clack-clack*, around the hall. He led us through the green cloth door and along the wood-and-stone passage to a room right at the end, where there was a long table covered with newspapers. "Right," Gregor said. "Aprons behind the door. Roll your sleeves up. Here are the rags, and this is the polish. Get going." He whipped the newspaper away. "I shall be back to check," he said, "and I need to see my face in all this when I do."

He left us staring at two deep boxes of cutlery, silver teapots, silver coffeepots, several jugs, ladles, and two rows of the huge silver plates, all laid out on more newspaper. Rearing behind those were bowls, tureens, urns, and complicated twiddly candlesticks, most of them enormous.

"Straw into gold again, Grant," Christopher said, "and I think that would be easier."

"Most of it's quite shiny already," I said. "Look on the bright side."

"I *hate* bright sides," said Christopher.

But we knew Gregor would love to catch us slacking, and we got to work. I let Christopher rub on the pink, strong-smelling polish—because that was the easy part, and I was fairly sure that cleaning silver was another thing Christopher had never done before—while I took a pile of rags and rubbed and rubbed. After a while I got into the swing of it and began to read the newspapers under the silver and to think of other things. The cleaning room must have been next door to Mr. Amos's pantry. I could hear his voice as I worked, droning on in blasts and occasionally giving out a sort of booming bark, but I couldn't hear the words, just his voice. It got me down.

I mentioned this to Christopher. He sighed.

I made several other remarks to Christopher, and he did not answer any of them. I turned and looked at him. He was drooping over the table, panting a bit, and his face was almost the gray and white color of the newspaper on the table. He had turned his neckcloth back to front in order not to get polish on it, and I noticed that there was a gold chain with a ring threaded on it hanging out of his shirt. It kept tinking on the candlestick he was working on because he was all bowed over.

I remembered a boy called Hamish at my school who could never do Art because the paints gave him asthma. It looked as if something the same was wrong with Christopher. "What's the matter? Is the polish making you ill?"

Christopher put the candlestick down and held himself up with both hands on the table. "Not the polish," he said. "The silver. There's something about Series Seven that makes it worse than usual. I don't think I can go on, Grant."

Gregor, luckily, was lazy enough not to keep dropping in on us. But he was going to come in at some point. And Christopher was the one he disliked most. "All right," I said. "You keep a lookout by the door so that you can look busy when Gregor turns up, and I'll do it. There's no point making yourself ill."

"Really?" said Christopher.

"Truly," I said, and waited. Now he really did owe me one.

Christopher said, *"Thanks!"* gratefully, and backed away from the silver. He went a better color almost at once. I saw him glance down and notice the gold ring dangling out of his shirt. He looked quite horrified for an instant. He tucked the ring and its chain out of sight, double quick, and pulled his neckcloth around to hide it. "I owe you, Grant," he said as he went to the door. "What can I do for you?"

Success! I thought. I was so curious about Christopher by now that I very nearly blurted out that I wanted him to tell me all about himself. But I didn't. Christopher was the kind of person that you needed to go cautiously with. So I said, "I don't want anything at the *moment*. I'll let you know when I do."

"Fair enough," Christopher said. "What's this droning sound coming through the wall?"

"Mr. Amos phoning," I said, picking up the candlestick and starting to rub.

"What could a butler find to phone about all this time?" Christopher said. "The exact vintage of champagne? Or has he an old mother who insists on a daily report? Amos, dear, are you using those corn plasters I sent you? Or is it his wife? Hugo must have a mother, after all. I wonder where they keep her."

I grinned. I could tell Christopher was feeling all right again now.

"Talking of mothers," he said, "I don't care for the Countess at all, do you, Grant?"

"No," I said. "Mrs. Potts, who cleans the book-shop, says she used to be a chorus girl."

Christopher was absolutely delighted. "No? *Really?* Tell me every word Mrs. Potts said about her."

So I told him as I polished. From there I somehow went on to tell him about the bookshop, too, and about Mum and Uncle Alfred, and how Anthea had left. As I talked, it occurred to me that, instead of *me* finding out about Christopher, *he* was finding out about *me*. And I thought that was just typical of Christopher. Anyway, I didn't mind telling him, as long as he didn't get to know about my Evil Fate and what I had to do, and it did help the silver cleaning along wonderfully. By the time Gregor put his head around the door—and Christopher dashed to the table and pretended to buff up a jug—it was almost all done. Gregor was really annoyed.

"Tea is Served in ten minutes," he said, scowling. "Get washed. You two are pushing the tea trolley in today."

"Never an idle moment here, is there?" Christopher said.

Eight

There was never an idle moment. We were kept so hard at it that I never managed to read one word of my Peter Jenkins book. Most nights I fell into bed and went straight to sleep. But I did notice, that second night, while we were getting into the nightshirts, that there was no sign of the ring or the chain around Christopher's neck. Hidden by magic, I thought, and then fell fast asleep.

Then—you know how it is—after three more days I began to get into the rhythm of things and to know my way about. Everything started to feel much more leisurely. I had time that day to be maddened with curiosity about what Christopher was really doing at Stallery and about where he had come from. In fact I had time to be maddened by Christopher generally. He would keep calling me Grant in that superior way, and there were times when I wanted to hit him for it, or shout that it was only my alias, or—anyway, he really annoyed me. Then he would say something that doubled me up with laughter, and I discovered I liked him again. It was truly confusing.

There was a full moon that fifth night. Christopher said, "Grant, this darned moon is shining right in my eyes," and he pinned our curtains together so that the room was almost completely dark.

As I lay down and shut my eyes, I thought, Ah! He wants me to be asleep while he goes off like he did before. I was annoyed enough to do my best to stay awake.

I didn't manage it. I was sound asleep when I somehow realized that the door had just shut softly behind Christopher.

By then I was so maddened with curiosity that I more or less tore myself out of sleep. I stumbled out of bed. It was cold. Stallery didn't provide you with dressing gowns or slippers, so I was forced to climb quickly into my velvet breeches and drag the bedspread off my bed to make a sort of cloak. With the undone buckles of the breeches banging at my knees, I raced out into the corridor just as Christopher flushed the toilet and came out of the bathroom. I dodged back into our room again and waited to see where he would go.

And a right idiot I shall look if he just comes back to bed! I thought.

But Christopher went straight past our room and on in the direction of the lift. I tiptoed quietly after him, trying to tread on the parts of the chilly floorboards that didn't creak. But Christopher himself was making the floor creak so much that I almost need not have bothered. He strode on as if he thought he was the only person awake in the attics.

He marched straight past the lift and toward the clothing room. He stood there in front of the slatted doors for a moment, in moonlight blazing down on him from the big skylights, and I heard him mutter, "No, it *is* farther on, then." Then he swung half around and marched off down the corridor that led to the line painted on the wall and the women's rooms beyond.

I must admit I nearly didn't follow him. It would be a disaster to be sacked from Stallery before I had met Count Robert and settled my Evil Fate. But then I thought that there was no point in getting up half dressed in order to follow Christopher if I *didn't* follow him. So I went after him.

When I caught up with Christopher, he was in a wide bare space where moonlight shone bright and white through a row of windows. He was shivering in his nightshirt as he turned slowly around on the spot. "It *is* here," he was saying to himself, quite loudly. "I *know* it is! So why can't I *find* it, then?"

"What are you looking for?" I said.

He made a noise like "Eek!" and jumped around to face me. It was the nearest to undignified that I had ever seen Christopher be. "Oh," he said. "It's you. For a moment I thought you were the ghost of a hunchback. What are you doing here? I left a really strong sleep spell on you."

"I made myself wake up," I said.

"Bother you!" he said. "You must have a bigger talent for magic than I realized."

"But what are you *doing* here?" I said. "You'll get the sack. This is the women's part."

"No, it isn't," Christopher said. "The women's part is along there." He pointed. "There's a painted line there, too, that I suppose they're forbidden to go past as well. Go and look if you like. This part of the attics is empty, right from the front to the back, and there's something very odd about it. Can't you feel it?"

I was going to say, "Nonsense!" I was quite sure he was just trying to distract me from my curiosity. But when I had my breath all drawn in ready to say it, I let it out again without speaking. There *was* an oddness. It was not unlike the peculiar buzzing I used to feel in Uncle Alfred's workroom after Uncle Alfred had been doing magic, except that this strange vibration felt old and stale. And it did not feel as if it had been made by a person. It felt like a sort of earth tremor, only it was magical instead of natural.

"Yes, and it feels pretty creepy," I said.

"It goes right down through the building," Christopher said, "though it's strongest up here. I've been all over this beastly mansion by now, so I know."

I was distracted, even though I knew he meant me to be. "What, even into the women's part and Mr. Amos's pantry?" I said. "You can't have."

"I couldn't get into the wine cellar," Christopher said regretfully, "but I've been everywhere else.

Mr. Amos's pantry stinks of cigars and booze, and Mrs. Baldock's room is full of crinoline dolls. Mr. Amos's bedroom is even more spectacular than the Countess's is. He has a circular bed. In mauve silk."

I was even more distracted. I tried to see Mr. Amos rolling about in a round mauve bed. It was nearly as hard as seeing the Countess in a row of chorus girls. "You're joking," I said. "I've been with you all the time."

Christopher gave a chuckle that was half a shiver. He wrapped his arms around his nightshirt and said, "Ah, Grant, what an innocent you are! It's not difficult to make an image of yourself. I simply made an illusion of me standing by the wall while the Countess wolfs down her dinner. It's the one time I *know* Mr. Amos is busy waiting on her. Think about it, Grant. Have I looked at you or talked to you much during these last few dinnertimes?"

I realized that he hadn't. I was amazed. It was hard not to be even more distracted and pester Christopher to tell me how he did it, but I took a stern grip on myself. "Yes, but what have you been looking *for*? Tell me. You owe me."

"Grant," Christopher said, "you're a pest. You keep your nose to my trail like a bloodhound. All right. I'll tell you. But let's go back to our room first. I'm getting frostbite."

Back in our room, Christopher put on his smart linen jacket and wrapped himself in his bedclothes. "That's better," he said. "Why does it get so cold at night? Because this place is up in the mountains? How high *is* Stallery, Grant?"

"Three thousand feet, and you're trying to distract me again," I said.

Christopher sighed. "All right. I was just wondering where to start, really. I suppose I'd better begin by admitting that I don't come from this world of yours. I come from another one, a different universe entirely, that we call Series Twelve. This one, where *you* live, we call Series Seven. Do you have trouble believing that yours is not the only world in the world, Grant?"

"Not really," I said. "Uncle Alfred told me there might be other ones. He says it's all to do with possibilities."

"Right. Good," said Christopher. "One hurdle cleared. The next thing you should know is that I was born a nine-lifed enchanter—and that, believe me, Grant, is a *great* deal more than just being a magician—and although I only have a few lives left now, that doesn't make any difference to the kind of powers I have. And it means that, at home in my own world, I'm being trained to take over as what we call the Chrestomanci. The Chrestomanci is an enchanter appointed by the government to control the use of magic. Are you with me so far?"

"Yes," I said. "And what happens if you don't want the job?"

"Shrewd point," said Christopher. "I take off to Series Seven, I suppose." He laughed in a way that was not quite happy. "To be truthful," he said, "I was almost looking forward to being the Chrestomanci until I had a bad disagreement with my guardian, who happens to be the present Chrestomanci. He's a very serious and correct person, my guardian—one of those who *knows* he's always right, if you follow me, Grant."

"Then can't he train up someone else that he gets on with better?" I asked.

Across the dark room I could just see Christopher shaking his head. "No. As far as we know," he said, "there *is* no one else he can train up. Gabriel de Witt and I seem to be the only nine-lifed enchanters in all the known worlds. So we're stuck with each other. He disapproves of me, and I think he's boring. But the disagreement wasn't really about that. He's guardian to a lot of people my age—most of us live with him in Chrestomanci Castle—but one of us, an enchantress from Series Ten who likes to be called Millie, is a sort of special case. She only lives with us in the holidays because the people she came from insisted on her going to boarding school. Her latest school's in Switzerland—"

"Where's that?" I asked.

"You don't have it in Seven," Christopher said. "It's in the Alps, squashed in among France, Germany, and Italy—"

"I don't know of a Germany either," I said.

"The Teutonic States, then?" Christopher guessed.

"Oh, you mean the *Slavo*-Teutonic States!" I said. "I know about those. Mum says the Tesdi—my father's ancestors—came from there during the Conquest."

"You don't have to tell me history and geography are different here," Christopher said. "I *have* been educated. Do you want to hear the rest or not?"

"Go on," I said.

"Well," Christopher said, "Millie was really unhappy at this Swiss school. She said the girls and the teachers were horrible and she didn't *learn* anything and they were always punishing her just for being different, and she didn't want to go back last term. But of course our guardian sent her back because it was *right*. She cried. She's not one who usually cries, so I knew she was having a really horrible time. I tried to tell our guardian she was, but he wouldn't listen, and we had our first row. So then Millie got desperate, and she ran away from this school. Being an enchantress, she did it very cleverly, in a way that made the school and my guardian think she was hiding somewhere in Series Twelve. But I knew, right from the start, that she was in a different Series. I told my guardian, but he told me he wasn't going to listen to juvenile maunderings. That was our second row."

There was a short silence here. I could feel Christopher brooding. I knew it had been a very bad row. At length Christopher sighed and went on.

"Anyway, soon after that, I began to be sure that wherever Millie was hiding, she was in some kind of trouble. I even got worried enough to go to my guardian again. He more or less told me to shut up and go away." There was another short, brooding silence here. "That made our third row,"

Christopher said. "*He* said they were doing all they could to find Millie and I was to stop wasting his time, and *I* said, no, they weren't because he wouldn't *listen* to me. Honestly, Grant, if he hadn't been a nine-lifed enchanter, too, I'd have turned him into a *slug*, I was so angry!"

"So you came to look for her yourself," I said.

"That," said Christopher, "makes it sound much easier than it was. It's taken me *weeks* just to get this far. Finding out—secretly, of course—where Millie had gone was hard enough, and I now see that was the *simple* part. I got her pinned down in this part of Series Seven in a couple of days, and I worked out what *I* had to do to stop them coming after me in a matter of *hours*. My guardian thinks I'm hiding in Twelve B, but that's just cover for the way I cadged a lift from the Travelers. That's what started the delays. Travelers, you see, are some of the few people who are always moving from world to world—"

"You mean those two—three—five—caravans and that horse go to other worlds!" I said.

"All the time, Grant," Christopher said, "and there are tribes more of them and much better organized than they let you see. They go in a sort of spiral around the worlds—that was something I didn't know either, and I nearly went mad while they did. And they're more important than anyone thinks. You wouldn't believe the delays and disasters there were, while they coped with crises in Series One and so on, and I chewed my nails. It's been over a month before we even got into smelling distance of Series Seven. Then we had to get here. Luckily they always go to Stallery. There's something about Stallery that they need to keep contained, they tell me. The only good thing is that my guardian is probably as confused as I am about where I've been."

"You'll be in awful trouble with him, won't you?" I said.

"Grant, you are putting that too mildly," Christopher replied. "*Trouble* is not the word for what will happen if he catches up with me. You see . . . " Christopher paused, and this time he seemed to be seething with bottled-up misery, rather than brooding. "You see, Grant, when I was younger, I kept losing my lives. And my guardian, in his usual high-handed way, tried to stop me losing any more of them by taking one of my lives away and locking it in his safe under nine high-power charms that only he was allowed to break. As long as he had that life, I knew he could trace me wherever

I went. Anyway, I felt I had a right to my own life. So, before I left with the Travelers, I broke the charms, opened the safe, and took my life away with me. He's not going to forgive me for that, Grant."

That gold ring! I thought. I bet that's his life. This guardian of his sounded to be a total monster. "So what are you going to do," I asked, "when you find Millie?"

"I don't *know*! That's just the problem, Grant. I *can't* find her!" There were pounding noises across the room, where I could dimly see Christopher's fist rising and falling, beating at his knees. "I can *feel* her," he said. "She's *here*, I *know* she is! I felt her when we were coming here across the park, and I *keep* feeling her inside this house. When I get to that queer part beyond that line of paint, it almost feels as if I'm *treading* on her! But she's not *there*! I don't understand it, Grant, and it's driving me *mad*!"

He was pounding away at his knees in a frenzy by then. I was surprised because Christopher always seemed so cool. "Take it easy," I said. "Does she seem unhappy—as if she was a prisoner or something?"

"No, not really." Christopher calmed down, enough to stop beating his knees and think about this. "No, I don't think she's a prisoner—exactly. But she's not happy. It's—it's more as if she was stuck somehow, in a way she didn't expect to be—in a maze, or somewhere like that—and can't work out the turnings to find the exit. I think she panics quite often. My first idea was that she was working as a maid here and had signed a fifty-year contract or something, but I've seen all the girls who work here now, and none of them is Millie, not even in disguise."

"And the only place you *haven't* looked is the wine cellar?" I said.

"Yes, but I couldn't feel her at all when I stood outside the cellar door," Christopher said. "Though— come to think of it—that cellar door *is* right in the center of the strange bit of the house. . . . "

"We'd better get inside it, then," I said. "We could get round Mr. Maxim to take us in there for a wine tasting. And have you looked out-of-doors yet? There could be a maze in the gardens where she's stuck. Don't forget it's our free afternoon tomorrow. Let's go out and search the grounds then."

"Grant, you are a genius," Christopher said. "It *feels* like a maze, where she is—although she would have been inside it for months. There must be magic in it, or she would have starved to death by now."

"There *is* lots of magic in Stallery," I said.

"Everyone in Stallchester complains about it. We can't receive television because of it."

"Oh, I know there's lots of magic here all right," Christopher agreed. "It's all over the place, but I haven't a clue what most of it's doing. Some of it's to keep trespassers out, so that the *rest* of the magic won't be interrupted, but—"

I think I fell asleep at this point. I don't remember anything else Christopher said, and the next thing I knew, beastly Gregor was battering on our door, shouting that we were lazy lumps and to get out and get those shoes collected or he'd tell Mr. Amos.

"I hate Gregor," I said while we were going down in the lift with the shoe basket. "You couldn't do some magic to make him fall face first into the sandwiches at Tea, could you?"

Christopher was pale and tired and thoughtful that morning. "It's tempting," he said. But I could tell that his mind was on this Millie he was looking for. If it was me, I'd have been worrying more about that dreadful guardian of his, but I could see that Christopher was just angry, really, and hardly scared of his guardian at all.

Oh well, I thought, and got on with the day.

Nine

At breakfast, Lady Felice looked more cheerful than usual, even though she did nothing but scrunch her bread all over the table and make a mess that Gregor made me clear up before the Countess arrived.

It was spotting with rain that morning. Lady Felice looked at it and said she would do her riding later on, when the rain had stopped. Andrew had to run all the way to the stables to stop them getting her horse ready. I wished she had sent Gregor. Andrew came back red in the face and quite wet.

We were supposed to go to Mr. Maxim straight after the Countess had finished breakfast, but Mrs. Baldock sent for us first.

"Have you looked in the stables?" I asked Christopher on our way to the Housekeeper's Room.

"Not really," he said. "Just felt about there. I don't get on with horses. But you're right, Grant. We'd better investigate there, too, this afternoon."

It was about our afternoon off that Mrs. Baldock wanted to see us. "You'll have time to go up to Stallstead," she said, "and if you want to do that, I'll advance you some pay. But remember—you have to be back here at six o'clock promptly."

I was relieved. I was afraid she was going to tell us off for being up half the night. Christopher said, with great courtly politeness, "No, thank you, ma'am. We hoped to look round the gardens and perhaps take a tour of the stables, if that's all right."

"Oh, well, in that case," Mrs. Baldock said, and she smiled at Christopher. He was a real favorite with her by then. "There's no problem about the stables. Just ask one of the grooms. But the gardens and the park are another matter. Staff are not allowed to be seen there by the Family. In the gardens you must take care not to go where you can be seen from the windows, and if you see any member of the Family in the gardens or the park, you must get out of sight at once. If I get a complaint about that from the Family, there's nothing I can do but give you notice on the spot, and you wouldn't want that, would you?"

"No, indeed, ma'am," Christopher said, very seriously. "We'll be extremely careful." As we went back along the stone passage to find Mr. Maxim, he said, "You know, Grant, I was just getting really angry about the Family hogging all these acres of gardens, when I realized that I've never once seen a footman or a housemaid in the gardens at home. I think they must have the same rule there. Oh, and Grant, don't forget we're trying to persuade Mr. Maxim to take us into the wine cellar. That's urgent."

This turned out to be difficult. Mr. Maxim had us cooking eggs that day. "The simplest, quickest, and most nutritious form a light meal can take," he said, rubbing his hands together in his usual irritating way. "How many ways do you know of cooking an egg?"

"Poached, boiled," Christopher said, "er, omelets. What wine goes best with an egg, Mr. Maxim?"

"Later, later," Mr. Maxim said. "Conrad?"

"Scrambled," I said. "Fried. My sister sometimes used to do them in little pots in the oven. When she did, my uncle used to open a bottle of red wine—"

"Let's leave your family history out of this,"

Mr. Maxim retorted, "and come and look at the stove instead. I have a small pan of water boiling here and another full of melted butter. What is your next step? Christopher?"

He held a large bowl of eggs out to Christopher. Christopher thought hard for a moment. "Marinade!" he said. "That's the word! If I poured wine over these . . . "

"You could try boiling them in wine instead of water," I suggested, backing Christopher up. "Sort of poached de luxe?"

"Or we could put wine in the butter," Christopher said. "If I knew which wine—"

It was a wonder Mr. Maxim didn't throw all the eggs on the floor. I could see he wanted to. "Give me patience!" he all but screamed. "*Forget* wine! Learn the basics *first*! Christopher, how would you make me a plain boiled egg?"

"Um. I think I'd drop it in and let it boil for an hour or so," Christopher said. "But I do want to learn about wine, too," he added, looking hopeful.

Mr. Maxim said, with his teeth clenched together, "I . . . said . . . forget . . . wine. Wine is Mr. Amos's business, not yours. Conrad, what do you think of Christopher's suggestion?"

"He'd end up with a sort of poached bullet," I said. "Honestly, Mr. Maxim, we were hoping you'd let us do a little wine tasting today."

"Well, you can't," said Mr. Maxim. "Now boil me an egg."

The best thing about these lessons was that we were allowed to eat what we cooked. I suppose it was a good way to keep our minds on what we did. We ate boiled eggs—or I did. Christopher left his because he said his spoon bounced off it. We did omelets next. I think Christopher was hungry. He was very careful and attentive to his omelet. They were coming along beautifully, and I was really looking forward to eating mine, when there was a most peculiar feeling. It was as if the world jerked violently sideways.

Christopher cried out, "What was *that?*" His omelet flew out of his pan and fell on his feet. I only just saved mine—except that when I looked down at it, it was bacon and fried eggs. Christopher had a fried egg on each shoe and bacon caught on the buckles.

"What do you mean, *What was that?*" Mr. Maxim asked angrily. "You are a nightmare, boy, a cook's despair! I ask you to cook me the simplest meal there is, and you tip it on your shoes! Pick it up. Throw it away and try again."

Christopher's eyes met mine in a mystified stare. Instead of the big bowl of eggs waiting on the table to be cooked, there were rashers of bacon and four cups, each with an egg ready broken into it. But Mr. Maxim simply had not noticed.

"There's been a change, Mr. Maxim," I explained. "We were cooking omelets a moment ago. Someone's pulled the possibilities, I think."

Christopher's stare turned into an enlightened grin. "Really, Grant? A probability shift? I never knew they felt like *that*."

Mr. Maxim looked at us gloomily. "*My* memory is that I decided yesterday to teach you bacon and eggs," he said. "But I take your word for it. Staff are always telling me things have changed. I never notice." Then he went all suspicious and demanded, "You're not pulling my leg, are you?"

"No, I promise," I said. "The books in our shop used to change like this, too."

An idea struck Christopher. "If he really doesn't remember . . . " he murmured to me. And he said to Mr. Maxim, "I'd like to ask you about wine—"

"*Stop that!*" Mr. Maxim shrieked. "I tell you for

once and for all that there is *no* wine that goes with bacon and eggs! Now clean up your shoes."

"Hmm," said Christopher. He delicately slid a fried egg off each shoe into the waste bucket and shook the bacon off after them. "We obviously wanted a wine tasting in this probability as well. I think that means the cellar is important."

"What are you muttering about?" Mr. Maxim yelled.

"Nothing, nothing," Christopher said. "Just something we'd do on our afternoon off—I suppose *that* hasn't changed, has it, Grant?"

It hadn't. To our relief, as soon as the Countess had folded her napkin and left, Mr. Amos solemnly gave us leave to go. Because he was watching us, we walked soberly across the black floor of the hall, but once we were through the green door, we ran. We clattered down the stone steps and charged through the undercroft to the nearest outside door. It felt good just to run. The drizzle had stopped outside, and we galloped out into sun, laughing.

The stables, across the yard beyond the kitchens, were an enormous place like two barns joined together by a clock tower. I let Christopher talk to the groom on duty there. He could turn on the charm far better than I could. And he did. In next to no time we were walking on a soft passageway inside the big dim barn, gazing into spacious stalls lined with even softer stuff. The horses in the stalls put their faces over the doors and gazed back at us.

I found myself gripped with a sort of fierce wistfulness. If *only* I had not happened to be born and brought up in a bookshop, if *only* I had happened to be born a stableboy like the one who was showing us around, then I could have spent all day with these huge, beautiful horses. The smell of them went to my head, and the *look* of them turned my heart over. There was one really big horse, almost red-colored, who had a white streak down his bent and noble nose, that I liked particularly. He was called Teutron. All the horses had their names on a board outside their stalls.

The stableboy said Teutron had belonged to the old Count and would probably be sold soon. I wished I were rich enough to buy him. The new Count liked a different style of horse, the boy said, and showed us two smaller, darker horses that moved like cats, which he said were Count Robert's. They were called Dawn and Dusk. Christopher, whose nose was wrinkled in disgust and who was definitely not enjoying it here, said those were sissy names. Lady Felice had three horses, Iceberg, Pessimist, and Oracle. They were putting a saddle on Oracle, down at the end of the barn, ready for Lady Felice to ride. Lucky thing.

We watched them doing that, me with interest, Christopher yawning, until the boy happened to mention that the next barn was where they kept the cars.

"Ah," Christopher said, suddenly coming awake. "Lead me to the cars."

I took this to mean that Christopher had not found any trace of Millie in the horse barn. I followed him rather sadly into the barn next door, where the lovely hay and animal smell was replaced by fumes of motor fuel. A row of gleaming saloons there were being polished by six dapper mechanics.

"Better," Christopher said. "Penny for them, Grant. You look mournful."

I sighed. "I was thinking I made a mistake not getting reborn in this life as a stable hand. But perhaps they don't let you choose. Maybe whatever I did to get my bad karma meant I had to be born in the bookshop instead."

Christopher gave me one of his long, vague looks

as we edged along by the cars. "Why are you so sure that your soul has been recycled, Grant? There's no evidence of it that I can see."

"My Uncle Alfred knows," I said. "He said I was. I had a bad former life."

"Your Uncle Alfred's word is not law," Christopher said. "Oh, look. Here's a car with all its guts showing."

We leaned on the wall next to this car, and Christopher watched with ridiculous interest while a mechanic did things inside its open front. I yawned. "Can you tear yourself away, Grant?" Christopher said after an endless five minutes. "We must have a look at the gardens."

The man working on the car told us that the quickest way to the park was through the small door across the yard outside the car barn. Christopher sauntered off there beside me. I was just opening the small door when there was a terrific noise from a car—a really *bad* noise, like *pop-pop-pop BOOM*— and a small red sports car came bellowing into the yard through the big open gates. It stopped with a squeal, in a spray of stones and a gust of blue, smelly smoke. The two young men in it were laughing their heads off.

"That was quite horrible!" one of them said as the engine died with a final *pop*.

"At least it got us here," said the one who was driving.

Christopher, like lightning, pushed us both through the small door and then held it not quite shut, so that we could only see a slit of the yard with the red car in it. "Family, Grant," he said.

The two young men came vaulting out of the car, still laughing. The one who had been driving called out, "Lessing! I'm afraid we need you. This is a very sick car."

The mechanic we had been watching walked into view, saying, "What is it *this* time, my lord?"

The other young man swallowed a giggle and said, "A piece dropped off in the middle of Stallchester. Robert said it was only a piece of trim, but it obviously wasn't. I said if he was that sure, there was no point stopping and picking it up. A mistake."

"Yes, blame Hugo," said the driver. "He couldn't wait to get home, so we've had to push the darn thing up all the steepest Alps." Both young men laughed again.

I stared at them through the gap Christopher was

holding open. They were both in ordinary sort of clothes, and medium tall, and thin, with fairish hair. They might have been a pair of students, laughing and joking after a day out together. But the one with the fairer hair had to be Count Robert himself, and the other one, now I looked properly, was indeed Hugo. I just hadn't known him without his valet's clothes.

I looked at the Count then, expecting to *know* that he was the one causing my Evil Fate. But I had no feeling at all. The Count might have been any cheerful, healthy young man, like one of the students who came to Stallchester to ski. I put my hand into my waistcoat pocket and took hold of the port wine cork, hoping that would help me to *know*, but it made no difference at all. The Count was still nothing but a normal, good-looking young man. I couldn't understand it.

While I stared, Lessing was saying something about the pair of them only having to *look* at a car for it to go wrong and he'd better see what they'd done *now*. He shrugged humorously and went to fetch his tools.

When he was gone, the Count and Hugo turned to each other, not laughing anymore, and stood for a moment looking sober and rueful. "Ah, well, Hugo," the Count said. "Back to real life, I suppose." And they both followed Lessing into the car barn.

"Interesting," Christopher remarked, gently shutting the small door. "No sign of Millie here, Grant. We have to look elsewhere."

We followed a path around to the gardens at the back of the mansion. These were massive. We went through steep ferny parts, flat places with pools and water lilies, fountains and rose arches, and a huge stretch that was all gravel and trees carved into silly shapes, and came to the part directly behind the house. There the garden was like one of those jigsaws that are almost impossible to do, with flowers of all kinds stacked into acres of long beds and grass and paths between.

I hung back, rather. "We aren't supposed to be seen from the windows."

"I assure you," Christopher said, "that not a soul will see us, Grant. I'm not a nine-lifed enchanter for nothing, you know."

He strode on, and I followed much less boldly. We marched down an endlessly long path slap in the middle of the jigsaw, with frothy walls of flowers on both sides of us and our ears filled with the buzzing of bees. We were in full view from the rows of windows behind us, but nobody came after us with yells of anger, so I supposed it was all right.

"I can feel that strangeness here, too," Christopher said, "but not as strongly as at the top of the house."

As he said this, we came out into a wider bit, where the flowers bent outward to make a circle around a sundial. "Can you feel Millie here at all?" I asked him.

Christopher frowned. "Ye-es," he said, "and no." He went and leaned on the sundial. "She's here and *not* here," he said. "Grant, I don't understand this at *all*."

"You said a maze," I was beginning, when there came that sideways jerk that had changed the eggs that morning. Christopher was suddenly leaning against a statue of a chubby boy with wings. He sprang away with a squawk. "The Count," I said. "He's back. He must have done that."

"Nonsense," Christopher said. "Use your head, Grant. Someone was messing with the probabilities this morning, long before the Count got home. Come along, and let's look for a maze."

There didn't seem to be a maze. The nearest we

found to one was where the jigsaw puzzle petered out into a place where stone pillars stood in rows, hung with flowering creepers. Beyond that the gardens stopped. There was drop of about ten feet down into a ditch, and after the ditch, the parklands began, rolling away for miles ahead of us.

"A ha-ha," Christopher said.

"Nothing's funny," I said. I was too hot by then, and sick of searching for a girl who didn't seem to exist. I was beginning to think Christopher was imagining Millie was near.

"I mean that this drop into a ditch at the end of a garden is called a ha-ha," Christopher explained. "At least it is in my world."

"I don't think it is here," I said. The new gardener's boy, Smedley, was sitting in the ditch, a few yards along from us. He had his boots off, and he looked as hot and sulky as I felt. "Why not ask him?" I said.

"Good idea." Christopher bounded along the row of pillars and stuck his head through the creepers above where the boy was sitting. "I say! Smedley!"

The poor kid jumped a mile. His sweaty face went white, and he scrambled to his bare feet in a hurry. "Just coming, sir— Oh, it's *you*!" he said when he saw Christopher's face sticking out from the creepers above his head. "Don't call out at me in posh voices like that! Do you want to give me a heart attack?"

"This is my normal voice," Christopher said coldly. "What are you doing in that ditch anyway?"

"Skiving off, of course," said Smedley. "I'm supposed to be looking for that damn guard dog—the one you tamed when we was walking here. Brute disappeared this morning, and park security's doing his nut, thinking someone may have poisoned it. All us garden staff are out looking for it." He scowled. "I'm not risking getting bitten, thanks."

"Very sensible," Christopher said. "Tell me, does this garden have a maze?"

"No," said Smedley. "Oriental garden, rose garden, four flower gardens, water garden, shrubbery, topiary garden, fern garden, hedged garden, vegetable garden, fruit garden, six hothouses, one orangery, big conservatory, but no maze. Or it may have got caught in a trap, see."

"What—the maze? Or the whole garden?" Christopher asked.

"The dog, stupid!" Smedley said.

"We'll keep a look out for it for you," Christopher told him. "What do you call this ditch and wall at the end of this garden? Apart from a good place to lurk, that is."

"This? This is the ha-ha," Smedley said.

Christopher shot me a superior look. "There you are, Grant. Come along now." He jumped down into the ditch beside Smedley, who flinched away. "Fear me not," Christopher said. "Grant and I are merely going for a stroll in the park. We will not give you away."

I jumped down and went *squelch*. One of my buckled shoes came off. I took the other one off, too, and my striped stockings. Smedley seemed to me to have the right idea. The grass felt deliciously cool and wet as we climbed the bank and set off into the parklands.

"Your funeral if you tread on a bee!" Smedley shouted after me. Evidently Christopher's superior manner annoyed him as much as it annoyed me, because he added, "Poncy footmen!" when we were almost too far away to hear.

"Take no notice," Christopher said—as if I would have done. "Our friend Smedley has clearly been told that house staff are nothing but mincing lackeys and that gardeners do all the real work." We walked a little way. I curled my toes luxuriously into the grass and thought that Christopher *would* think this. He had no idea how irritating he could be. "Smedley may be right," Christopher added. "I've never minced so much in my life before." We walked some more, and Christopher began to frown. "The oddness is getting fainter," he said. "Can you feel?"

"Not really," I confessed. "I only properly felt it in the attics."

"Pity. Well, let's go as far as that clump of trees and see," Christopher said.

The clump of trees was more like a small bushy wood on top of a little hill. We pushed our way through, up the hill and down in a straight line. I had forgotten it had rained earlier. Willows wept on us, and bushes sprayed us. Christopher hardly seemed to notice. He pushed on, murmuring, "Fainter, fainter." I put my shoes back on my muddy feet, wishing we'd taken the time to put on ordinary clothes. We would both need to change into dry uniforms for this evening, or Mr. Amos would have our guts for garters. Count Robert would be there for Dinner, I supposed. Maybe the reason I hadn't *known* he was causing my Fate was because I hadn't been close enough to him. I could get to stand right beside him at Dinner. Then I'd surely *know*.

We were both so busy thinking of other things that we nearly missed seeing Lady Felice riding toward the wood on Oracle.

I said, "Oh-oh! Family!" and pulled Christopher back among the wet willows.

He said, "Thanks, Grant." Then we had to stand there, because Lady Felice was cantering straight toward the hill where we were. Water ran down our necks, along with itchy bits of willow, while we waited for her to swerve around the hill and ride out of sight.

Instead, she came careering straight toward the edge of the wood and pulled the horse to a stop there. Hugo came out of the bushes just below us, still in his everyday clothes, and stood there with his hair as wet as ours was, looking up at her. She stared down at Hugo. Everything went tense and still.

Hugo said, "The car nearly broke down. I thought I was *never* going to get back."

Lady Felice said, "I wish you or Robert had *warned* me. It felt like a hundred years!"

"For me, too," Hugo said. "Robert didn't want

any questions asked, you see. At least he didn't find Ludwich as dreary as I did. It was like being half *dead*."

Lady Felice cried out, "Oh, Hugo!" and jumped down off Oracle. Hugo sort of plunged forward to meet her, and the two of them flung their arms around each other as if it really had been a hundred years since they last met. Oracle wandered peacefully off and then stood, with the look of a horse that was used to this.

I stared at them and then stared at Christopher, who looked quite as uncomfortable as I felt. He made a very slight gesture and said, in his normal voice, "Spell of silence, Grant. They won't hear us. I guess we're looking at something here that mustn't get back to the Countess *or* Mr. Amos either."

Not altogether believing in the spell of silence, I was just nodding when there was another of those sideways jerks. It was quite strong, but nothing much seemed to change. It did not seem to affect Hugo and Lady Felice in the least, and we were still draped in trees—except that they were not willows now, but some other kind, just as drooping and just as wet. I noticed that my striped stockings were not in my hand anymore. When I looked down, I saw they were on my legs instead.

Christopher backed away out of sight of Hugo and his Lady, looking very excited. "That *definitely* came from the house!" he said. "Come on, Grant. Let's get back there quickly and find out what's doing it."

Ten

Christopher set off through the wet wood at a gallop. On the level grass beyond I had to work hard to keep up. He had such long legs. But he had to stop in the ditch in front of the ha-ha and wait for me to boost him up the wall.

"Found the dog?" Smedley called out from farther along.

"No," I panted, boosting hard.

Christopher held down his hands to help me scramble up and hauled me up as if I weighed nothing.

"What's the hurry, then?" Smedley said as my feet met the top of the wall and we both set off running again. "I thought the dog was after you!"

We were too breathless to answer. Christopher dropped to a jog-trot and kept on in a straight line toward the house, past yew hedges and tiny box hedges, and then between the banks of flowers. I had a feeling that some of this was new, but it all jogged past so fast that I was not really sure anything had changed until we came to the open circle where Christopher had leaned on the sundial. The chubby boy statue was now a stately stone young lady carrying an urn, which was spouting water.

I couldn't help laughing. "Lucky it didn't do that while you were leaning on it!"

"Save your breath," Christopher panted.

We jogged on, pounding on gravel, then clattering up stone steps, and more stone steps, until we were charging across a wide paved platform in front of the house itself. I tried to stop here. It was obviously a place where Staff were not allowed. But Christopher trotted on, into the house through an open glass door, across a parquet floor in a room that was lined with books. While Christopher was wrestling open the heavy door, I saw there was a ladder up to a balcony where there were more books, under a fancy ceiling, and I knew this was the library and we shouldn't be there.

The heavy door brought us out into the hall, with the main stairway ahead in the distance. Andrew was just crossing the black floor, carrying a tray. He said, *"Hey!"* as we dashed past him. I knew then that Christopher, in his hurry to discover what was making the changes, had clean forgotten to make us invisible—and forgotten that he had forgotten. Andrew stared after us as Christopher skidded around the banisters and led me charging up the forbidden stairway. I was just glad it was Andrew and not Gregor. Gregor would have reported us to Mr. Amos.

At the top, outside the ballroom, Christopher had to stop and bend over to get his breath. But as soon as he could stand up again, he stared around in a puzzled way and then pointed toward the lofty ceiling.

"I don't understand, Grant. I thought we'd be on top of it here. Up again."

So up we went again, to the floor where the Family bedrooms were. Here the next lot of stairs were not in a straight line from the lower lot. We had to tear along the palatial passage to get to them and around a corner. When we whirled around that corner, I thought for a moment we were in a riot. There were squeals and screams and girls in brown-

and-gold uniforms pelting everywhere. They all froze when they saw us. Then one of them said, "It's only the Improvers," and there were sighs of relief all around. I could see they were all the younger maids. None of them were much older than me or Christopher.

"It's line-tig," one of them explained breathlessly. "Want to play?"

"Love to," Christopher said, quite as breathlessly. "But we have to take a message." And he charged on to the next stairs and up those. "I suppose . . . have to have . . . fun . . . somewhere," he panted as we pounded upward.

"If I was them, I'd go and chase about in the nurseries where it's empty," I said.

"No . . . excuse for . . . being there," Christopher suggested.

He did not pause on the next floor with its smell of new carpets. He just shook his head, chased along to the next stairs, and clattered up them to the nursery floor. "Getting warmer," he gasped, and we trotted along to the creaking wooden stairs to the attics.

By this time I could feel the strangeness, too. It was buzzing actively. It did not surprise me in the least when, as soon as we panted into the attics,

Christopher plunged away past the lift toward the center of the house. I knew we were going to end up in that space beyond the line painted on the wall.

Christopher was galloping along, excitedly puffing out, "Warm, warmer, almost *hot*!" when we both more or less ran into Miss Semple coming away from the clothes stores.

"Steady *on*!" she said. "Don't you know the rule about not running?"

"Sorry!" we both said. Then, without having to think, I added, "We need new clothes. Christopher got mud on his breeches."

Christopher looked down at himself. He was covered in brick dust and moss as well as mud. "And Conrad's ruined his stockings," he said.

I looked at my striped legs and discovered that at least four of the stripes had converted into ladders, with my skin showing through. There were willow leaves stuck behind the buckles of my shoes.

"So I see," Miss Semple said, looking, too. "Come along, then." She marched us into the clothes room, where she made us change practically everything. It was such a waste of time. Miss Semple said we were a disgrace to Stallery. "And those stockings will have to come out of your wages," she told me. "Silk stockings are costly. Be more careful in future."

Christopher scowled and sighed and fretted. I whispered to him, "If we hadn't met her, she'd have gone down and caught those girls playing tig. Or she might have caught *us* going past the painted line."

"True," Christopher muttered. "But it's still maddening. The changes have *stopped* now, damn it!" He was right. I couldn't feel the strangeness buzzing at all now.

When we were clean and neat and crisp again, Miss Semple picked up the pile of towels she had been carrying and sailed away to the lift with them.

"Now, hurry," Christopher said, "before anything else interferes."

We tiptoed speedily and cautiously toward the center of the attics. In the distance, floors creaked and someone banged a door, but no one came near. I think we both gasped with nervous relief when we passed the line painted on the wall. Then we sprinted to the wide space with the row of windows.

"Here—it *is* here, the center of things!" Christopher said. He turned slowly around, looking up, looking down. "And I still don't understand it," he said.

There really did seem to be nothing but flaking

plaster ceiling above and wide old floorboards underfoot. In front of us, the rather dirty row of windows looked out over the distant blue mountains above Stallchester, and behind us was just wall, flaking like the ceiling. The dark passage on the other side that led to the women's side was identical to one we had come along.

I pointed to it. "What about Millie? Is she along there?"

Christopher shook his head impatiently. "No. Here. *Here* is the only place she feels anywhere near at the moment. It looks as if these changes are somehow connected to the way she's not here, but that's all I know."

"Under the floor, then?" I suggested. "We could take one of the floorboards up."

Christopher said, in an unconvinced way, "I suppose we could *try*," and we had, both of us, knelt down near the windows to look at the boards, when another sideways jolt happened. It was lucky we were kneeling. Up here the shift was savage. We were both thrown over by it. My head cracked against the wall under the windows. I swore.

Christopher reached out and hauled me up. "I see the reason for these painted lines now," he said, rather soberly. "If you'd been standing up, Grant, you'd have gone straight through the window. I shudder to think how far it is to the ground from here."

He was pale and upset. I was annoyed. I looked around while I was rubbing my head, and it was all exactly the same, wide floorboards, distant mountains through the windows, flaky plaster, and the feeling of something strange here as strong as ever. "What *does* it?" I said. "And *why*?"

Christopher shrugged. "So much for my clever ideas," he said. "If I have a fault, Grant, it's being too clever. Let's go down and check the nursery floor. Nothing seems to have changed at all this time."

Famous last words, my sister Anthea used to say. Christopher strode away down the passage, and there was a door blocking his way, a peeling red-brown door.

"Oh!" he said. "This is new!" He rattled at it until he found the way it opened.

It blew inward out of his hands. We both went backward.

Wind howled around us, crashing the door into the wall and flapping our neckcloths into our faces. We both knew at once we were somewhere different and rickety and very, very high up. We could feel the floor shaking under our feet. We clutched at each other and edged cautiously forward into the stormy daylight beyond the door.

There Christopher said, "Oooh!" and added airily, "Not afraid of heights, I hope, Grant?"

I could hardly hear him for the wind and the creaking of wood. "No," I said. "I like them." The door led out onto a small wooden balcony thing with a low, flimsy-looking rail around it. Almost at our feet, a square hole led into a crazy old wooden stairway down the side of what seemed to be a tall wooden tower. Our heads both bent to look through the hole. And we could see the stairway zigzagging giddily away, down and down, getting smaller and smaller, outside what was definitely the tallest and most unsafe-looking wooden building I had ever seen. It could have been a lighthouse—except that it had slants of roof sticking out every so often, like a pagoda. It swayed and creaked and thrummed in the wind. Far, far below, something seemed to be channeling the gale into a melancholy howling.

I tore my eyes from that tottering stairway and looked outward. Where the park should have been, the ground was all gray-green heathery moor, but beyond that—this was the creepy part to me—there were the hills around Stallery, the exact same craggy shapes that surrounded Stallchester. I could see Stall Crag over there, plain as plain.

After that I stood by the railing and looked upward. There was a very small slanting roof above us, made of warped wooden tiles, with a sort of spire on top that ended in a broken weathercock. It was all so old that it was groaning and fluttering in the wind. Behind and around us, the moor just went on. There was no sign of Stallery at all.

Christopher was white, nearly as white as the neckcloth that kept fluttering across his face. "Grant," he said, "I've got to go down. Millie feels quite near now."

"We'll both go," I said. I didn't want to be up at the top of this building when Christopher's weight brought the whole thing down, and besides, it was a challenge.

I don't think Christopher saw it as a challenge. It took him an obvious effort to unclench his hand from the doorjamb, and when he had, he turned around *very* quickly and clenched the same hand even harder on the rail beside the stairs. The whole balcony swayed. He kept making remarks—nervous, joky remarks—as he went carefully down out of sight, but the wind roared too hard for me to hear them.

As soon as Christopher was far enough down that I wouldn't kick his face, I scrambled onto the stairs, too. A mistake. Everywhere groaned, and the staircase, together with the balcony, swayed outward away from the building. I had to wait until Christopher was farther down and putting weight on a different part of it. Then I had to go slowly because he was. I could tell he was scared silly.

I was quite scared, too. I'd rather climb Stall Crag any day. It stays still. This place swayed every time one of us moved, and I kept wondering what lunatic had built the thing, and why. As far as I could tell, nobody lived in it. It was all cracked and weathered and twisted. There were windows without glass in the wooden walls. When Christopher was being particularly slow, I leaned over with the wind thundering around me and peered into the nearest window, but they were always just empty wooden rooms inside. There was a door on each balcony we came to, but when I looked down past my own legs—not a clever thing to do: I went quite giddy—I saw that Christopher was not trying to open any of the doors, so I left them alone, too. I just went on to the next flight, slanting the opposite way.

About halfway down, the sticking-out roofs were much wider. The stairs went out over the roofs there, to mad little spidery balconies hanging on the very edge, and then there would be another stair going down under that roof to the next one. When Christopher came to the first of these balconies, he just stopped. I had to hang on to the ladder and wait. I thought he must have found Millie, and that the howling sound I could still hear was being made by an injured girl in mortal agony. But Christopher went on in the end. And when I got to that balcony, I knew why he had stopped. You could see through the floor of it, down and down, and it was rocking. And the howling was still going on, below some-where.

I got off that balcony as quick as I could. So did Christopher after that. We had to climb over three more of the horrible things before we came to a longer, thicker stair, where there was actually a handrail. I caught up there. We were only one floor up by then.

"Nearly there," Christopher said. He looked ghastly.

"Millie?" I asked.

"I can't feel her at all now," he said. "I hope I don't understand."

As we clattered down the last few steps, the howling became a sort of squeaking. At the bottom, a great brown shape hurled itself at us, slavering. Christopher sat down, hard. I was so scared that I went up half the flight again without even noticing. "They left a wild beast on guard!" I said.

"No, they didn't," Christopher said. He was sitting on the bottom step with his arms around the creature, and the creature was licking his face. Both of them seemed to be enjoying it. "This is the guard dog that went missing today. Its name is"—he reached around the great tongue and found the name tag on the dog's collar—"Champ. I think it's short for Champion and not a description of its habits."

I went down the stairs again, and the dog seemed glad to see me, too. I suppose it had thought it was permanently lost. It put great paws on my shoulders and squeaked its joy. Its massive tail thumped dust out of the ground, which whirled in the wind, stingingly. "No, you've got it wrong," I told it. "We're lost, too. We are, aren't we?" I asked Christopher.

"For the moment," he said. "Yes. Stallery seems to

have been built on a probability fault, I *think*—a place where a lot of possible universes are close together and the walls between them are fairly weak. So when whoever—or *whatever*—keeps shifting to another line of possible events, it shifts the whole mansion across a *bit*, and that bit at the top of the house gets moved a *lot*. The top gets jerked somewhere else for a while. At least, I'm hoping it's just for a while. Now we know why those painted lines are *really* there."

"Do you think it's the Countess doing it?" I said. "Or the Count?"

"It may be no one," Christopher said. "It could just happen, like an earthquake."

I didn't believe that, but there was no point arguing until I met the person causing my Evil Fate and *knew*. Come to think of it, my Fate must have landed us here anyway. In order not to feel too bad about it, I said to Christopher, "You worked out what had happened on the way down?"

"In order not to think of dry rot and planks snapping," he said, "or the distance to the ground. And I realized that Millie must be stuck in one of the other probabilities, just beyond this one. Maybe she hasn't noticed which part of the mansion moves— Oh dear!"

We both understood the same thing at the same moment. In order to get ourselves back to the Stallery we knew, we had to be at the top of the tower when another sideways shift happened. We looked at each other. We got up, towing the dog, and backed away to where we could see the whole unpainted wooden height of the thing, moving and quivering in the wind, and the crazy stairway zigzagging up it. It looked worse from the ground even than from at the top.

"I don't think," Christopher admitted, "I can bring myself to climb that again."

"And we'd never get the dog up it anyway— Hang on!" I said. "The dog *can't* have been in the attics when it got here. It lives in the grounds."

"Oh, *what* a relief!" Christopher said. "Grant, you're a genius! Let's sit on the right line and wait, then."

So we did that. Christopher very carefully paced from side to side, and then back and outward, until he found the spot where the strangeness felt strongest. He decided that a lump of rock about forty feet from the tower was the place. We sat leaning against it—with the dog between us for warmth and the wind hurling our hair and neckcloths sideways—staring at the derelict front door of the tower and waiting. Gray clouds scudded overhead. An age passed.

"It's funny," Christopher said. "I have no desire at all to explore that building. Do you, Grant?"

I shuddered. The wind sort of moaned in the twisted timber, and I could hear doors opening and slamming shut somewhere inside. I *hoped* it was only the wind doing it. "No," I said.

Later on, Christopher said, "My stockings have turned into ladders held together by loops. If they take them out of our wages, how much do the things cost?"

"They're silk," I said. "You've probably worked all last week for nothing."

"Bother," he said.

"So have I," I said, "only I've ruined two pairs now. How long have we sat here?"

Christopher looked at his watch. It was nearly five-thirty. We were going to be late back on duty if another shift didn't happen soon. A whole set of doors slammed inside the tower, making us jump.

"I suppose I deserve this," I said.

"Why?" Christopher demanded.

"Because . . . " I sighed and supposed I might as

well confess. "This is all probably my fault. I have this bad karma, you see."

"*What* bad karma?" he said.

"There's something I didn't do in my last life," I said, "and now I'm not doing it in this life either—"

"You're talking perfect codswallop," Christopher said.

"Maybe it's something you don't have in your world," I said.

"Yes, we do. I was studying it, as it happens, just before I came away, and I assure you, my dear Grant—"

"If you're only in the middle of learning—" I started to say when we both realized that the wooden tower was now a dark stone building. Without any kind of warning, or blurring, or any sort of sideways jerk, it had become twice as wide, though no less derelict. It seemed to be built of long blocks of dark slate, sloping inward slightly, so that it tapered up to a square top, high, high above us. Its square stone doorway gaped in front of us, breathing out a dank and rather rotten smell. There were no stairs anymore.

"That's odd," said Christopher. "I didn't feel it change, did you? What do you say, Grant? Do we risk looking inside?"

"It looks more like a house than the wooden place," I said, "and we're stuck here if we don't do *something*."

"True," said Christopher. "Let's go."

We got up and lugged the dog over to the empty square doorway. The place smelled horrible inside, and it was absolutely empty in there. Light came in through enough small windows—just gaps between slabs of slate, really—to show us that the stairs were now indoors. They went zigzagging up one of the walls, and they were simply steps, with nothing to stop a person falling off the outside edge. They were made of slate like all the rest, but they were so old that they sort of drooped outward toward the empty middle of the place. And the trouble was, this building was as high as ever the wooden tower had been.

I told myself that it was no worse than Stall Crag. Christopher swallowed, rather. "One slip," he said, "one stumble, and we'll be dogmeat for Champ here. But I *think* I can keep us stuck to them by magic if we stay close together."

The dog refused to go inside at first. I knew it was the smell combined with the sight of those stairs, but Christopher explained cheerfully that poor Champ lived out-of-doors and was probably forbidden to go inside a house. It could have been true. Anyway, he towed the resisting beast to the bottom of the stairs. There Champ braced all four gigantic paws and would not budge. We tried climbing up a short way and calling beguilingly, but he simply went out into the middle of the dark, smelly floor and began to howl again.

Christopher said, "This is hopeless!" and he went down and tied his neckcloth into Champ's collar for a lead. He hauled. The neckcloth stretched. Champ stopped howling, but he shook all over and still refused to move.

"Do you think he knows something we don't?" I suggested. I was resting a hand on a step two stairs up, and it was slimy. It would be nice to have an excuse not to climb the things.

"He knows exactly what we know. He's a coward, that's all," Christopher said. "Champ, I refuse to put a compulsion spell on a mere dog. Come *on*. It's getting late. Supper, Champ. Supper!"

That did the trick. Champ came up the steps in a rush. I was barged into the slate wall, first by the dog and then by Christopher as Christopher was towed upward, and I had to scramble like a maniac to keep up with them. We took the first three zigzags at a mad run, but after that, when the hollow building was like a deep, smelly well around us, Champ seemed to realize he might need to save his breath, and he slowed down.

It was worse like that. I climbed sliding my back up the rough wall and hoped hard that Christopher's spell was a good strong one. Some of the steps higher up were broken and slanted outward more than ever. To take my mind off it, I asked, "Why did you say my bad Fate was codswallop—my karma?" My voice made a dead sort of booming around the place.

Christopher's voice made more dead echoes as he called downward, "I don't think you have any. You have a new, fresh feel to me. Either this is your very first life or your earlier ones were blameless."

I knew he was wrong. He was making me seem so childish. "How do you mean?" I boomed up at him.

And he echoed back, "Like Lady Felice. I don't think she's been around more than once at the most. Compare her with the Countess, Grant. *There's* an old soul if ever I met one!"

"You mean she has bad karma?" I boomed.

"Not particularly," he echoed down. "Not anything very bad from before, I think, though mind you she's laying up a bit this time round, if you ask me."

This made me sure he was just guessing. "You don't know really, do you?" I shouted back. "*Other* people can see my Fate! They *told* me!"

"Like who?" Christopher called down.

"Like my Uncle Alfred and the Mayor of Stallchester," I yelled upward. "So!"

By now it was getting hard to hear. The place was filling with echoes, and Champ, up ahead, was rasping out breaths as if Christopher's neckcloth were throttling him, but I am fairly sure Christopher said, "If you ask me, Grant, they were probably smelling their own armpits."

"Will you *stop* calling me Grant in that superior way!" I shouted at him.

I don't think he heard. Champ at that moment dived away sideways. I thought he was simply diving up the next zigzag, but it turned out to be the top of the stairs. Christopher, with his arm stretched out to hang on to the neckcloth, was jerked after Champ and out of sight. I thought for a moment that they had disappeared, but when I sidled up after them, I found a square slate passage leading through the top of the wall. There was light at the end of the passage, lighting up every slimy slab, and Champ was towing

Christopher along it at full gallop. I sprinted after them, expecting to come out on the roof.

But we all burst out onto big floorboards, in a place full of the warm smell of wood, where I saw that the light had been coming from a row of dusty windows looking out to the mountains above Stallchester. The ceiling was flaking plaster, and all around us was the feel, like an engine in the distance, of other people living and moving around here.

"Grant," Christopher whispered, "I believe we're back." He looked ghastly. It wasn't just that he was white and shaking and his stockings were laddered. He was covered with dark slime and cobwebs, too. And if the back of his waistcoat was anything to go by, mine was ruined. I could see my breeches were. And my stockings. Again.

"Let's go and check," I said.

We tiptoed back along the passage we seemed to have just come in by. It was wooden now. At the end of it we came to the streak of paint on the wall. Then we had only to peep around the corner to see we were certainly in Stallery. Andrew and Gregor were just coming out of the clothes store, adjusting crisp new neckcloths. People were hurrying and calling things and coming in and out of doors in the distance. We could tell that everyone was getting smartened up for supper and Dinner after that.

We dodged back into the part with the windows.

"We'd better let them go downstairs before we get more clothes," I said.

"I approve of the first part of your plan," Christopher said, "but you're forgetting Champ. We have to account for him, too. We must go down as we are. Then, if anyone sees us, we can say that we found him stuck in the drains. And if nobody does see us, we let him out of the nearest door for Smedley to find and *then* sneak up here for more clothes."

"Drains right up *here*?" I said.

"There have to be," he said firmly. "Where does our bathwater go—and so forth?"

I supposed it might work. It seemed to me a recipe for trouble. "Can't you magic our clothes?"

"Not for a whole evening," Christopher said. "It would be an illusion, and illusions wear thin after an hour or so."

I sighed. "Anyway, thanks for keeping us on those stairs."

Just for a second Christopher had such a blank, dumbfounded look that I knew he had forgotten to work any magic on those steps. I was glad I had not known while I was on them. "Think nothing of it, Grant," he said airily.

Then we hung about for a boring ten minutes. Champ did not help. He whined and drooled and made little rushes toward the passage. Either he knew he was not meant to be here or he could smell all the suppers cooking.

At length the bell went for maids' supper, making us all jump. Champ turned his jump into another surge down the passage. This time we followed him. There were still people about in the distance, and we could hear the lift working. That meant we had to go down the stairs, trying not to let Champ tow us down them too fast.

He took us in an eager rush down onto the matting of the nursery floor. Here he broke into a gallop whatever we said. Perhaps he thought the matting was grass and he was allowed to run on it. Anyway, he ran us straight past the top of the next stairs and dragged us on down the passage, to where the door was open on that long, empty nursery.

As we hurtled up to it, a young man in evening dress came out of the nursery. The dim light there showed his fair hair and the lost, rather drooping way he looked. But the look changed as he saw us. His head went back, and he went ramrod straight, with his face all firmed into haughty surprise.

"What the devil do you think you're doing?" he said.

It was quite obvious to all three of us that he was Count Robert.

Eleven

Christopher must have used some magic then. He and the dog both stopped as if they had run into a wall. I overran a little and stopped myself on a doorknob on the other side of the corridor. The Count turned himself so that his frosty look could hit me as well as Christopher.

I had no idea what to do, but Champ had no doubt. His tail thumped. He crawled forward, quivering with shame, to the full stretch of Christopher's neckcloth, and tried to get into licking distance of the Count's beautiful, shiny shoes. Christopher just stood and looked at the Count as if he were summing him up. This was where being an amateur was a big help. Christopher would not have minded being sacked on the spot. He had more or less found Millie now, and he could make himself invisible and come back to finish the job, but I still had my Evil Fate to think of. I stared at the Count, too, hoping and hoping to *know* he was the one causing my Fate, but all I could see was a young fellow in expensive evening dress who had every right to stare at us in outrage.

"Come on," Count Robert said. "Explain. Why are you dragging poor old Champ around up here?"

"It's more that *he* was dragging *us*," Christopher said. "From the look of him, I think he caught your scent, my lord."

"Yes, he did, didn't he?" Count Robert agreed, looking thoughtfully down at Champ, who wagged and groveled more than ever. "But that doesn't explain why he's here or why all of you are covered with black gunk." At this, Christopher drew breath, presumably to begin on the drains story. "No," said the Count. "Not you. I can see you'd just tell me something glib and untrue." Christopher looked hurt and indignant, and the Count turned to me. "*You* tell me."

It seemed to me that I'd nothing more to lose. I knew I was about to be sacked and sent home in disgrace. Wondering what Uncle Alfred would say, and then thinking dismally that I would be dead by next year anyway, so what did Uncle Alfred matter either, I said, "We went past the painted line in the attics. Champ was at the bottom of a wooden tower there, but we couldn't have got him back up it, so we waited until it changed into an empty slate building."

Christopher muttered, "Believe it or not, I was going to tell you that, too." The Count gave him a disbelieving sideways look. "Honestly," Christopher said. "I thought you'd probably guessed."

"More or less," said Count Robert. His frosty look tipped up at the edges and became a slight grin. "You were unlucky to get those two towers straight off. Hugo and I didn't run into them for years. Well, now what shall we do about it? I don't think any of you should be seen as you are. Amos is prowling round the next floor in a rage—"

"About us?" I said anxiously.

"No, no—about something I told him," the Count said. "But he'd certainly better not see you or Champ as you are. He'd fire you both on the spot if he knew where you'd been, so . . . " He considered for a second. "Give me the dog. Hugo and I can get him cleaned up in my rooms—luckily Champ is well known to be a friend of mine—and then I can take him down to the stables. You two go and get fresh clothes, or you'll be in real trouble."

We both said, with real gratitude, "Thank you, my lord."

Count Robert smiled. There was a sad sort of look to him, smiling. "No problem. Here, Champ!"

Christopher let go of the neckcloth. It was an ex-neckcloth really, more of a dirty string by this time. Champ immediately sprang to his hind legs and attempted to put both his paws on the shoulders of the Count's evening jacket. The Count caught the paws just in time, in a way that showed he had had a lot of practice, and said, "No, *down*, Champ! I love you, too, but there's a time and a place for everything." He put Champ down on all four feet and took firm hold of the ex-neckcloth. "Off you go," he said to us.

We scurried away to the attic stairs. I looked around as we went and saw Count Robert using one of his gleaming shoes to urge Champ into the Family lift. "Get on, stupid!" he was saying. "It's quite safe. Or do you *want* to meet Amos in a rage?"

Christopher was very excited as we sped back to

the clothes store. "My guess was right, Grant! You heard the Count, did you? There are lots more places beside those two frightful towers. Millie must be in one. Will you come with me to look for her tomorrow on our morning off?"

Well, of course I would. I could hardly wait to explore. Next time, I thought, I would take my camera with me, too, and collect some real evidence of other worlds, or dimensions, or whatever they were.

Before that, of course, we had to get into new clothes, hide the gunky ones in an empty room, and rush off to our supper. Then we had to stand by the dining room wall with those stupid cloths over our arms while Mr. Amos, Andrew, and two other footmen served the Family with their Dinner. Neither of us dared do a thing wrong. Mr. Amos was still in a rage. Whatever Count Robert had said to him, fury about it was bottled into Mr. Amos, so that he was like a huge pear-shaped balloon full of seething gas. Andrew and the other two tiptoed around him. Christopher and I tried our best to look like part of the wall.

The Countess was in a rage, too, but she wasn't doing nearly such a good job of bottling it as Mr. Amos was. I suppose she had no need to bother.

Nothing was right for her that evening. There was a thumbprint on her wineglass, she said, a speck of dirt on her fork, she said, and iron mold on her napkin. Then she found a smear of pink polish on the salt cellar. Each time one of us was sent whizzing away to fetch a new one of whatever was wrong, and then, while she waited for it, she turned to Count Robert, opened her eyes wide, and did her *"Why?"* at him. When I came back with a shiny new salt cellar, she was saying, "Really, darling, you *must* grow out of this habit of only pleasing yourself."

Count Robert stood up to it better than I would have done. He smiled and said, "But *you* asked me to arrange it, Mother."

"But not *now*, Robert. Not when we've got company coming to celebrate your engagement!" the Countess said. "Amos, this plate is dirty. See this speck on the edge here?"

Mr. Amos leaned over her shoulder and inspected the plate. "I believe that is part of the pattern, my lady." He shot Count Robert a mean look while he said it. "I'll have it replaced at once," he said, and snapped his fingers at Christopher.

By the time Christopher whizzed back with a fresh plate, Count Robert was really getting it in the neck. "And you haven't even considered where this hireling of yours will eat," the Countess said. "When I think of all the trouble I went to, to teach you that a gentleman should consider others, I quite despair of you, Robert! You behave like a greedy child. Greedy and selfish. Me, me, me! Your character is so weak. Why can't you learn to be strong, just for once? Why?"

Christopher rolled his eyes at me as he took up his place by the wall again. And it really was amazing the way the Countess went on at Count Robert, who after all *owned* Stallery, as if he were about six years old, just as if there were no footmen standing like wooden statues, or us listening to her, or Mr. Amos by the serving table looking meanly glad that the Count was in trouble. I was quite embarrassed. But I was also pretty curious to know what Count Robert had done to annoy the Countess and Mr. Amos so.

By this time the Countess was on about the way the weaknesses of Count Robert's character had shown up when he was a toddler and kept reminding him of bad things he had done when he was two and four and ten years old. The Count just sat there, bearing it. Lady Felice kept her head down over her plate. But the Countess noticed her, too.

"I'm glad to see that your silly little eating disorder is over, dear."

"It was nothing, Mother," Lady Felice said.

So then the Countess decided that the fish was overcooked and told Mr. Amos to send it back to the kitchen. Mr. Amos snapped his fingers at me to take it. "And be sure," he said, handing me the loaded tray, "to tell Chef exactly what her ladyship found wrong with it."

I missed the next bit, while I went away through the hall and the swing door, down the steps to the undercroft, and on to the kitchen, but Christopher said it was just more of the same. In the kitchen the Chef put his hands on his hips and stared at me humorously. All the footmen called him the Great Dictator, but I thought he was quite a nice man. "And what's supposed to be wrong with it?" he asked me.

"She says it's overcooked," I said. "She's in a really bad mood."

"One of *those* evenings, eh?" the Chef said. "Slimming spells disagreed with her, and she's saving herself for the roast, is she? All right, get back and tell her that yours truly grovels all over the carpet and you needn't mention that this fish was perfect."

Back I went, all the way to the dining room, where I managed to go in almost exactly as I was supposed to, slipping in sideways with nearly no noise. Mr. Amos was waiting there for me. Behind his bulky pear shape the room felt like a thunderstorm. "And what has Chef to say for himself?" he demanded, low and urgent.

"He grovels on the carpet and I'm not to say the fish was perfect," I said.

That was stupid of me. I think it was Christopher's influence that made me say it. Mr. Amos had the perfect opportunity to get rid of some of *his* bad temper on me. He gave me a glare from his stone-colored eyes that made my knees go weak. Luckily for me, Lady Felice chose that moment to jump up from her chair and fling her big white napkin onto the table. Two wineglasses went over.

"Mother!" she said, almost in a scream. "Will you *stop* going on at Robert as if he'd committed a crime! All he's done is hire the librarian you *asked* him to hire! So leave him *alone*, will you!"

The Countess turned to Lady Felice. Her eyes went wide, and her lips began shaping the "Wh—" of one of her dreadful *"Why?"*s.

"And if you say, 'Why, dear?,' *once* more," Lady Felice screamed, "I shall pick up this candlestick and *brain* you with it!" She gave out a sound like a laugh and a sob mixed, and rushed for the door. Mr. Amos and I both had to dodge. Lady Felice stormed past us and crashed out of the room like a warm, scented hurricane and slammed the door behind her.

In the rest of the room she left a feverish dead silence. Andrew and the other footmen sprang into action, silently and on tiptoe, mopping up spilled wine, taking away the fallen glasses, and whipping away all the knives, forks, and spoons still there at Lady Felice's place. The other two at the table simply sat there, while—just as if nothing had happened—Mr. Amos walked around to speak gently in the Countess's ear.

"Chef sends his profound apologies, my lady, and says it will not occur again. Allow me to bring on the next course, my lady."

The Countess, in a frozen way, nodded. Because the footmen were still busy wiping up wine, Mr. Amos beckoned Christopher and me over to the food lift and passed us tureens and sauceboats to carry over to the table. I was not sure where to put things, but Christopher whirled everything across and dumped them any old where and then bowed and patted the mats with both hands, as if he knew just what he was doing. Mr. Amos glowered at him over his shoulder as he picked up a massive platter piled with meat.

The Countess, still looking frozen, said to Count Robert, "Felice is so tiresome these days. I think it's high time she was married. I shall invite that nice Mr. Seuly to dinner with our other guests. I feel sure I can induce Felice to marry him."

Count Robert said, "Are you making some kind of a joke, Mother?"

"Not at all. I never joke, dear," said the Countess. "Mr. Seuly *is* Mayor of Stallchester, after all. He is wealthy, and widowed, and he has a very respectable position in life—and it's not important who Felice marries, the way it is for *you*, dear. *You* are engaged to a title, but—"

"*Give me patience!*" Count Robert suddenly shouted out. He leaped to his feet, whacked his napkin on the table and—like Lady Felice—made for the door with great strides just as Mr. Amos arrived with the platter of meat.

I never could work out how Mr. Amos missed Count Robert. The Count did not seem to see either

Mr. Amos or the meat. He just charged out through the door and banged it shut behind him. Mr. Amos somehow managed to raise the vast platter above both their heads and then to twirl himself away. The Countess sat, still frozen, watching Mr. Amos waltzing around with the great steaming dish.

When at last he stopped twirling, she said, "I don't understand, Amos. What is making my children so very tiresome lately?"

"I believe it is their extreme youth, my lady," Mr. Amos replied, laying the platter reverently down on the table. "They are mere adolescents, after all."

Christopher's eyes swiveled to mine in amazement. As he said to me afterward, you called people adolescents at his age and mine. "Lady Felice has come of age," he said, "even if they did have to cancel the party for it. And Count Robert must be in his twenties! Grant, do you think that the Countess is mad and Mr. Amos humors her?"

He said that much later, though. At that time we had to stand there while the Countess obstinately plowed through three more courses, half a bottle of wine, and dessert, and looked angrier with every mouthful. Mr. Amos's bottled rage grew so huge that even Christopher hardly dared move. The footmen all pretended they were invisible, and so did I.

And it did not stop there. The Countess laid down her napkin and went to the Grand Saloon, telling Mr. Amos that the Improvers could bring her coffee there. This meant that Christopher and I had to race upstairs after her with trays of comfits and chocolates, while Mr. Amos followed us with coffee, herding us like a rather heavy sheepdog.

The Grand Saloon was vast. It stretched from the front to the back of the house and was full of things to fall over, like golden footstools and small, shiny tables. The Countess sat in the middle of it, where Christopher and I had to keep dribbling coffee for her into a cup so small that it reminded me of the crucibles Uncle Alfred did his experiments in. I drizzled in coffee, and Christopher dripped in cream, while Mr. Amos stood by the distant door, rocking on his small, shiny feet and waiting for us to make a mistake so that he could vent some of his rage on us. We knew that the very least that could happen was that Mr. Amos would cancel our morning off, so we were very, very careful. We tiptoed and poured for what seemed a century, until the Countess said, "Amos, I wish to be alone now." By that time my arms were shaking and my calves ached with tiptoeing, but we hadn't made any mistakes, so Mr. Amos had to let us go.

"Whew!" I said when we were safely out of hearing. "What *has* Count Robert done to make them both so angry? Did you find out?"

"Well," Christopher said, scratching at his head so that his sleek hair separated into curls, "you probably know as much as I do, Grant. But while you were away with the fish, the Countess *did* say something about hiring penniless students to catalog the library here. Though why that should make anyone angry, I haven't a clue. After all, she's supposed to have *asked* Count Robert to hire someone. The Librarian at Chrestomanci Castle says you have to have a proper list of the books you've got or you can't find any of them. And I can't see why that should make Mr. Amos angry as well."

I felt suddenly full of an idea. "Could it be," I said, "that they have *secret* books in there? You know, books about pulling the possibilities or explaining how to work the changes at the top of the house?"

Christopher stood still in the passage outside our room. "Now that *is* a notion!" he said. "Grant, I think we ought to take a look at this library when we're free tomorrow morning."

Twelve

Naturally that next morning we went to look at the top of the mansion first. Christopher was seriously anxious about this girl Millie, and I was really excited about what we'd see there next. We went to the attics as soon as we were free.

On the way, I dodged into our room and got my camera. I wanted to have proof that we weren't imagining the strange towers. As it was a dull sort of day, with fog down in Stallchester valley and only Stall Crag sticking up out of it, I made sure the flash was working.

Christopher jumped at the sudden brightness. "Don't count your chickens, Grant," he said while we crept along to the streak of paint on the wall.

"You may not have anything to photograph."

This made me sure that my bad karma would cancel out any chance of the mansion changing. But we were in luck. Just as we passed the stripe of paint, there was the most almighty sideways wrench. Christopher and I were thrown against each other and sort of staggered around in a half circle, with me hanging on to Christopher's neckcloth for balance. And as soon as we were facing the other way, we realized that the passage we had just come through was now a tall pointed archway made of stone. Beyond it was somewhere so shadowy and stony that I was glad I'd remembered my camera flash.

"Looks like that tower we hauled the dog up again," Christopher said as we went through the archway.

It was nothing like the slate tower. The archway opened into a stone-floored gallery held up on one side by fancy stone pillars, each pillar a different shape. The roof was a basketwork of stone vaulting, and the other wall was blank stone. The vaulting and the carvings on the pillars must have been picked out in gold paint once, but a lot of the gold had flaked off, leaving the patterns hard to see. From the space beyond the pillars there came vast, soft, shuffling echoes. It felt huge out there, but not as if people were living in it. It was more like the time my school had gone around Stallchester Cathedral, when the guide had taken us up into the passages in the dome.

Christopher said, "Millie's here! Quite near!" and set off at a run to the other end of the gallery, where the gloomy light came from.

I raced after him with my camera bouncing on my chest. The gallery opened into a big curving stone staircase, leading down into the gray light. Christopher went plunging down the stairs, and I followed. And as soon as we came around the first curve, we realized we were on an enormous spiral— a *double* spiral, we realized after the next curve. There was another staircase opposite ours, sort of wrapped around the one we were on. When we leaned over the high stone side, we could see the two staircases spiraling down and down. When we looked up, we saw the inside of a tower overhead. It had fancy windows in it, but they were so dirty that it was no wonder the place was in such gloom.

Footsteps rang, like an echo of ours. We looked over at the other staircase, and there was a girl there, hurrying down to get to the same level as us.

"Christopher!" she shouted. "What are *you* doing here?"

It was hard to see what the girl was like because of the gloom and because the staircases were so big and so wide apart, but her voice sounded nice. She seemed to have a rounded face and straight brownish hair, but that was all I could see. I swung up my camera and photographed her as she dashed down opposite us, which made her stop and try to cover her eyes.

"Meet us at the bottom!" Christopher shouted at her. His voice boomed around in a hundred echoes. "I'll tell you then."

In fact he tried to tell her as we dashed on down and around, the two of us circling around Millie and Millie circling around us, while the space rang with our hurrying feet and the voices of the other two. They kept shouting at each other as they went, trying to explain what they were doing here, but I don't think either of them could hear properly because of the echoes. I could tell they were truly glad to see each other. I took several more photos as we went. It was such an amazing place.

I think Millie shouted something like "I'm so pleased you came! I've been having such a frustrating time! This house keeps changing, and I can't seem to get *out*!"

"Me, too!" Christopher bellowed back. "I had to take a job as a lackey. What do you get to eat?"

"There's always food downstairs," Millie yelled in reply, "but I don't know where it comes from."

"How did you get *in*?" Christopher roared. The echoes got worse and worse. Neither of us could hear what Millie shouted in answer to this. Christopher roared again, "You know the main changes happen at the top of the house, do you?" I think Millie yelled back that of *course* she did, she wasn't a fool, but she never seemed to *get* anywhere. And she seemed to try and describe her frustrations as we all hammered down several more spirals. Then Christopher began bellowing, across her description, that *one* of the places was bound to be the perfect place for the two of them to live in secret—but we shot down the last curve at this point, and there was ceiling over the staircase. The echoes quite suddenly cut off. And we found ourselves in a plain stone hallway. Christopher stopped shouting and turned to me. "Quick, Grant. Where's the other stairway?"

We both ran along the hall to the place we

thought the other spiral ought to come out, but there was only wall there. It had little windows in it that looked out on to woodland, so it was obviously wrong.

"We got turned around," Christopher panted, and he dashed back the other way so fast that I could barely keep up.

There was a door at the end of the hall that way. Christopher thundered through it and on into the middle of a largish room, where he stopped dead beside a pile of sofas and armchairs with a sheet draped on top of them. Beyond that, big windows showed a garden that was mostly weeds. Rain was falling on the weeds. There were more windows, showing more weeds, in the left-hand wall, a harp or something in one corner, and nothing but a big empty fireplace in the right-hand wall.

"Not here," Christopher said in a defeated way.

I only had time to take one photo of the harp thing before he was off again, back the way we had come, to the hall and the staircase again. "I think I saw a door," his voice said in the distance. "Ah, yes."

The door was behind the stairs. Christopher had opened it and rushed through before I caught up, but when I did, he was moving slowly and cautiously down the dark stone passage beyond. There was a door on each side and a door at the end. The door on the right was open, and we could see it was a sort of big cloakroom with a row of dusty boots on the floor, several grimy coats on pegs, and a cobwebby window that looked out onto wet woodland. Christopher made angry noises and barged me aside to open the door across the passage. The room there was a dining room, as neglected and dusty as the cloakroom, and its window looked on to the weedy garden.

Christopher expressed his feelings by slamming that door before I could take a photo. He plunged on to the door at the end of the passage.

There were kitchens beyond that, two quite cozy-looking places with rocking chairs and big scrubbed tables and some kind of a stove in the farther one. There was a scullery beyond that which opened into a rainy yard with red tumbledown sheds all around it. By this time even Christopher was having to admit that this house we were in was much, much smaller than the place with the double staircase.

"I don't *understand* it!" he said, standing miserably beside the table in the second kitchen. "I didn't *feel* any change. Did you?" He looked almost as if he might cry.

I wished he would keep his voice down. There were definite signs that someone had been in this kitchen recently. Warmth was coming from the stove, and there was a bag of knitting on one of the rocking chairs. I could see crumbs on the table around a magazine of some kind, as if someone had been reading while they had breakfast. "Maybe the change happened while you were shouting at Millie," I said, very quietly, to give Christopher a hint.

He looked around at the stove, the knitting, and the table. "This must be where Millie comes to eat," he said. "Grant, you stay here in case she turns up. I'm going back up the stairs to see if she's there any-where."

"Does Millie do much knitting?" I asked, but he had dashed off again by then, and he didn't hear me. I sighed and sat in the chair by the table. It was clear to me, if not to Christopher, that the two staircases split apart somehow on the last spiral. Millie must have ended up somewhere as different from this house as the wooden tower was from Stallery. And I didn't like this house. People lived here. They had left furniture, coats, and knitting about, and they might come back at any moment and accuse me of trespassing. I had no idea what I would say if they did. Ask if they'd seen Millie, perhaps?

In order not to feel too nervous, I pulled the magazine across and looked through it while I waited for Christopher. It was quite, quite strange, so strange that it fascinated me—so very strange, in fact, that I was not surprised to find it was dated 1399, February issue. It could not have been anything like that old. It smelled new. It was printed on thick, furry paper in weird washed-out blues and reds, in the kind of round, plain letters you get in books in infant school. *Gossip Weekly*, it was called. There were no photographs or advertisements in it at all, and it was full of quite long articles that had titles like "From Rags to Riches" or "Singer's Lost Honeymoon" or "Scandal in Bank of Asia." Each article was illustrated by a drawing. Blue and red drawings. I had never seen such bad drawings in my life. They were so bad that most of them looked like caricatures, though I could see that the artist had put in lots of red and blue shadings, trying to make the drawings look like real people. And here was the really queer thing—about half of them looked like people I knew. The lady at the top of "Rags to Riches" could almost have been Daisy Bolger, and one of the drawings for the bank scandal looked exactly like Uncle Alfred. But it *must* have been bad drawing. When I turned to the big picture beside an article called "Royal Occasion," the picture looked like our king, except the caption called him "Prince of Alpenholm." One of the courtiers bowing to him might almost have been Mr. Hugo.

Now come on, I thought. This is, actually and truly, a magazine from another world. For all I know, in this world someone just like Hugo really is a royal courtier. How amazing. And I started reading about the royal occasion. I had got most of the way down one washed-out blue column, without understanding what the occasion was, or why it happened, when I heard heavy, slow footsteps coming in through the scullery.

They were the footsteps of a person you definitely did not want finding you sitting in their house. They stamped. There was angry puffing with them, and bad-tempered grunting. I dropped the magazine and tried to slide quietly away into the farther kitchen. Unfortunately, my foot knocked the chair as I slid out of it, and it scraped on the floor, quite loudly. The person in the scullery put on speed and arrived in the doorway while I was still in the middle of the room. This is my Evil Fate at work again, I thought.

She was a heavily built woman with a blunt, mauve face. I could see at a glance she was the kind of woman who *knows* you're up to no good, even if you aren't, and calls the police. She had a rubber sheet over her head against the rain, and she was wearing big rubber boots and carrying a can of milk. And she was a witch. I knew this the moment she put the milk can down and said, "Who are you? What are you doing here?" I could feel the witch-craft buzzing off her as she spoke.

"A mistake," I said. "Just going."

I backed away toward the door as fast as I could. She came trudging toward me in her big boots with her hands hanging, ready to grab. "They always find me," she said. "They send spies, and they find me wherever I hide."

She was saying this to make me think she was mad and harmless. I knew she was because I could feel her casting a spell. It buzzed in my ears under her words until I could hardly think or see. So I did the only thing I could manage. I raised my camera and took her picture. She was nearer than I realized. The flash went off right in her face. She screamed, and her rubber sheet fell off as she put her hands up to hide her face. I heard her fall over the chair I had kicked as I pelted away through the other kitchen.

I ran like mad, through the corridor and out into the stone hall. I raced up those stone stairs, around and up, around and up, with the other set of stairs spinning dizzily past as I climbed, until my breath was almost gone, but I still hardly slowed up when I met Christopher coming down.

"*Run!*" I shrieked at him. "There's a *witch* in that kitchen! *Run!*"

He said, "We can do better than that, Grant," and seized hold of my elbow.

Before I could shake him off, we were somehow at the top at the stairs in a strong buzzing of magic. This buzzing was somehow wider and cleaner feeling than the buzzing the witch had made. As Christopher pulled me by my elbow along the gallery I remembered that he was supposed to be a nine-lifed enchanter, which made me feel a little safer, but I didn't really feel safe until we came out through the archway into the smell of warm wood and plaster in the attics of Stallery.

"*Phew . . . !*" I began.

Christopher said, "In our room first, Grant," and

turned me around. The archway had gone then, and we were able to scurry along the attic passages to our room, where we both sat heavily on our beds, me panting fit to burst and Christopher all limp, white and dejected. "Tell," he said, with his head hanging.

So I told him about the witch.

Christopher's head came up, and he said, "Hmm. I wonder if *she's* the reason Millie can't get out of there. Millie's an enchantress, you know. She *ought* to be able to leave. Instead, she seems to keep being shunted on to another probability. There was no sign of her on those stairs, and it could well be the witch doing it. We'd better go back and deal with the witch, then."

He got up. I got up, too, although my legs were weak and shaking, and followed him out beyond the stripe of paint again. Christopher groaned when we got there. There was no archway—nothing but the ordinary attics we had just come through. We sat on the floorboards for quite some time, waiting, but there was no change.

"You panicked me, Grant," Christopher said. "We should have gone down, not up. Oh, damn it! We were so close!"

"It was probably my bad karma," I said.

"Oh, don't talk nonsense!" he said. "Let's go and look for secret books in the library. I'm sick of sitting here. One of the maids is going to see us breaking the rules if we're not careful."

He was probably right. There seemed to be a lot of female noise coming from the other end of the attics suddenly, as if all the maids had arrived there at once. The empty space by the windows echoed to shrieks and giggles, and I could feel the floorboards creaking under me, the way they always did when everyone came up to bed. When we got up and went through our side of the attics, we found there was a fair amount of noise there, too. There were doors being slammed, running feet, and men laughing. A big deep man's voice was singing inside the nearest bathroom. It was so out of tune that I giggled.

Christopher raised his eyebrows at me. "Gregor?" he asked.

"Mr. Amos?" I said.

Christopher laughed then. It seemed to do him good. He was a lot more cheerful as we went down in the lift. He nodded at my camera, still hanging around my neck. "Are you intending to photograph the books, Grant?"

"No," I said. "I'd need a different lens. I just

forgot I'd got it. Why are we getting off at floor two? The library's on the ground floor."

"Ah. Admire my forethought and cunning, Grant," Christopher said. "That library has a sort of minstrel's gallery, and the door to it is on this floor. We can sneak in and make sure the Countess isn't in there consulting a cookery book or something."

"Ha, ha," I said. I was glad Christopher had cheered up, but there were times when his jokes really annoyed me.

But there *was* a woman in the library. When we softly opened the low wooden door and crept through onto a high balcony lined with shelves of books, we could see her through the carved wooden bars at the front of it. We both ducked down and knelt on the carpet, but she could have seen us through the bars, even so. She was sitting at the top of a long wooden stepladder, reaching for a book on a high shelf. The one good thing was that she wasn't the Countess, because she had dark hair, but that didn't alter the fact that she only needed to turn her head to see us there.

I grabbed for the door, ready to crawl out through it at once. "Never fear, Grant," Christopher said. I judged from the buzzing feeling I was getting that he had put a spell of invisibility around us on the spot. Then I gathered it was probably a spell of silence, too, because Christopher first sat down comfortably with his arms around his knees and then spoke in his normal voice. "We wait, Grant. Again. Honestly, Grant, I've never *done* so much waiting around as I have in this place."

"But she could be here for *ages*," I whispered. The stepladder was so close to the balcony that I couldn't help whispering. "I think she must be the penniless student who's supposed to catalog the books."

Christopher looked critically through the bars of the balcony. "She doesn't look penniless to me," he said.

I had to admit that she didn't. She was wearing a dark blue dress that was both flowing around her and clinging to her in an expensive way, and her feet, hooked on a rung of the ladder, were in soft red boots, really nice ones. Her dark hair fell to her shoulders in the same sort of costly hairstyle that Lady Felice had.

"She's a friend of the Family come to borrow a book," Christopher said.

While he was saying it, the lady took down a book and opened it. She looked at the title page, nodded, and made a note on the pad on her knee. Then she leafed through the book, shut it, looked at the binding, and shook her head. She slipped some kind of card into the front and turned to put the book carefully into a box that was fastened to the back of the ladder.

She was my sister, Anthea.

I stood up. I couldn't help it. I nearly called out. I would have done if Christopher had not grabbed me and pulled me down. "Someone else coming!" he said.

Thirteen

Christopher was right. The big main door of the library opened, and Count Robert came in. He shut the door behind him and stood smiling up at my sister. "Hallo, love," he said. "Are you on the job already? It was only a pretext, you know."

And my sister Anthea cried out, "Robert!" and came galloping down the ladder. She flung herself into Count Robert's arms, and the two of them began hugging and kissing each other frantically.

At this point Christopher got cramp in one leg. I think it was embarrassment, really. Or it could have been running up and down those stairs. But it was real cramp. He whipped himself into a ball and rolled about, clutching his left calf, with his face in a wide grin of agony. I was forced to park my camera on the lowest bookshelf and lean over him, pounding and kneading at his striped silk leg. I could feel the muscles under the stocking in a hard ball, and you know how much that hurts. It used to happen to me after skiing sometimes. I tried to make Christopher take hold of his own foot and pull his toes upward, but he didn't seem to understand that this was the way to cure cramp. He just rolled and clutched.

I kept glancing through the bars in case my sister or Count Robert had noticed us, but they didn't seem to. They were now leaning backward with their arms around each other's waists, laughing and saying, "Darling!" rather often.

"Ooh—ow! Ooh—ow!" Christopher went.

"Pull your *toes*!" I kept whispering.

"Ooh—*ow*!" he said.

"Then use some magic, you fool!" I said.

I heard the main door open again and looked. This time it was Hugo who came in. He stood and smiled at Anthea, too, all over his puggy face. "Good to see you, Anthea," he said, and then something that sounded like "Join the club." But Christopher's knee hit my chin just then, and I went back to kneading. When I next looked, the three of them had gone to the leather chairs by the window, where Count Robert and Anthea each sat on the arm of the same chair, while Hugo leaned on the back of it. Hugo was talking quickly and urgently, and Count Robert and Anthea looked up at him and nodded anxiously at what he said.

I wanted to know what Hugo was saying. I took hold of Christopher's ear, put my mouth to it, and more or less shouted, "Use some *magic*, I said!"

That seemed to get through. There was some frantic buzzing. Then Christopher abruptly straightened out and lay with his face in the carpet, panting. "Oh, horrible!" he gasped. "And deaf in one ear, too."

I looked down into the library again in time to see Count Robert kiss Anthea and get up. Hugo kissed her, too, a friendly kiss on one cheek, and they both turned to go. But the library door opened yet again. This time it was Mr. Amos who came in, looking anything but friendly. Christopher and I both froze.

"Has this young person got everything she requires?" Mr. Amos asked, with truly dreadful politeness.

"Well, not really," my sister said, cool as a cucumber.

"I was just explaining that I need a computer if I'm to do this job properly."

Hugo said, with an anxious look, "I told you, miss. Atmospheric conditions here in Stallery mean that your programming is liable to random changes."

Count Robert turned to Mr. Amos with his chin up, all lordly. "*Have* we a computer, Amos?"

It was a splendid cover-up from all three. Mr. Amos gave Count Robert a small bow and said, "I believe so, my lord. I will see to it personally." Then he went away, very slow and stately.

Count Robert and Hugo grinned at each other and then at Anthea. Hugo gave her a wink over his shoulder as he followed Count Robert out of the library.

"Phew!" said my sister. Then she swung around in a swirl of expensive skirt and came marching toward the balcony, looking really angry. "Come down out of there," she said, "whoever you are!"

I hardly needed to look at Christopher's face, squashed against the carpet, to know that he had forgotten all about his spells of invisibility and silence from the moment he got cramp. I stood up. "Hallo, Anthea," I said.

She caught hold of the stepladder and stared. She was really astonished. "*Conrad!*" she said. "What on *earth* are you doing here dressed like a lackey?"

"I *am* a lackey," I said.

"But that's ridiculous!" she said. "You ought to be at school."

"Uncle Alfred said I could go to Stall High as soon as I had expiated my Evil Fate," I explained.

"What evil fate? What are you *talking* about? Come down here this instant, and tell me properly," Anthea said. I had to smile. Anthea pointed over and over at the carpet in front of her as she gave her commands. It was so exactly what she used to do in the bookshop when she was annoyed with me that I felt almost happy as I climbed down the steep stair from the balcony. "And your friend," Anthea commanded, jabbing her finger toward another place on the carpet.

Christopher got up, quite meekly, and limped down the stair after me. Anthea looked from him to me.

"This is Christopher," I said. "He's a nine-lifed enchanter, and he's here on false pretenses like I am."

"Really?" Anthea said suspiciously. "Well, I felt someone doing magic, so I suppose that *could* be true. Now stand there, Conrad Tesdinic, and tell me all about this nonsense that Uncle Alfred's been putting into your head."

"I knew it was nonsense," Christopher said. "But I thought his name was Grant. Are you his sister? You look quite alike."

"Yes. Shut up, you!" Anthea said. "Conrad?"

Christopher, to my surprise, did what Anthea said. He stood there attentively, looking slightly amused, while I told her what Uncle Alfred had said about my bad karma and how it was going to kill me unless I dealt with the person who was causing it. Anthea sighed and looked at the ceiling. So I told her that Mayor Seuly and the rest of the Magicians' Circle had seen my Evil Fate clinging to me, too, and how they had given me the way to *know* the person responsible before Uncle Alfred sent me to Stallery. Anthea frowned heavily at this, and Christopher looked even more amused. But he seemed quite surprised when Anthea said, "Oh dear! I feel really guilty! I shouldn't have left you. And Mother? Didn't she even *try* to tell you Uncle Alfred was talking nonsense?"

"She's always busy writing," I said uncomfortably. "We never talked about my Fate. And it isn't nonsense, is it? Mayor Seuly thought it was true."

"Everyone knows he's a crook. He just wants his chance to make money the way Stallery does," my sister said. "I think he lied to you, Conrad, in order to find out how to pull the probabilities himself." She looked from me to Christopher. "Have you discovered yet who's doing it, and how?"

"No," we both said, and Christopher asked, "So it doesn't happen naturally, then?"

"Some of it does," Anthea said. "But someone is helping it along somehow. This is something Robert and I would really like to know about. It's one reason why I'm here. And what were you supposed to do, Conrad, when you found out who was doing it?"

"Summon a Walker," I said.

Christopher and Anthea both looked utterly puzzled.

"They gave me this wine cork," I said, fetching it out. I was feeling awful by then, stupid and taken in and, well, sort of pointless. If I didn't have a Fate, then what *was* I?

I felt worse when Christopher said, "I did try to tell him he hasn't any bad karma."

"But he might have an awful lot if he does what Mayor Seuly and Uncle Alfred seem to want!"

Anthea said. She gave me a worried, puzzled look. It made me feel worse than ever. "Conrad, for goodness' sake, what stopped Mother paying for you to go on at school?"

"She hasn't any money," I said. "Uncle Alfred owns the bookshop and—"

"But he *doesn't*!" Anthea exclaimed. "Oh, I should have written and *told* you! I admit that puzzled me, too, so I went and looked up Father's Will in the Record Office as soon as I got to Ludwich, and he'd left the entire shop to Mother."

"What? All of it?" I said.

"All of it," she said. "And to you and me after that. He left Uncle Alfred some money, but that's all. Come to think of it, I do remember Father saying to me when he was dying that he hoped Alfred would take his money and go, because he didn't trust him as far as he could throw him. . . . " She tailed off in an uncertain way. "Now why didn't I remember that before?"

She was looking vaguely at Christopher as she said this. He must have thought she was asking him because he said, "If he's a magician, this uncle, he could cast a selective forget spell quite easily. They're not difficult."

"He *must* have cast one," Anthea said, and went on decisively, "Conrad, I'm going to ring Mother up—I was going to anyway, and this makes it urgent—and see what she says."

There was a telephone in the corner of the library. Anthea marched across to it and dialed the number of our bookshop. I hurried after her and tried to listen in. Anthea turned the receiver so that I could distantly hear a bored woman's voice say, "Grant and Tesdinic. How can I help?"

Anthea mouthed at me, asking, "Who?" I said, "Daisy. New assistant after you left."

Anthea nodded. "Could I speak to Franconia Grant, please?" she said.

Daisy said, "Who?"

"The famous feminist writer," Anthea said. "I believe she married a Mr. Tesdinic, but we feminists don't mention that."

"Ooh!" Daisy went in the distance. "I get you. Just a minute and I'll see if she's free."

There were muffled footsteps running about and voices calling murkily. I heard Uncle Alfred, faint and far off, saying, "Not me— I don't have anything to do with those harpies!" Finally there was a clatter, and my mother's voice said, "Franconia Grant speaking."

From then on it was much easier to hear. Christopher was leaning over us, wanting to hear, too.

Anthea said cheerfully, "Hallo, Mother. This is Anthea."

My mother said, "Good heavens," which was not surprising. It *had* been four years. "I thought you'd left here for good," she added.

"I have, really," Anthea said. "But I thought you ought to know when your daughter gets married."

"I don't believe it," my mother said. "No daughter of mine would ever even think of enslaving herself to a male ethic—"

"Well, I am," Anthea said. "He's wonderful. I knew you'd disapprove, but I had to tell you. And how's Conrad?" There was a blank pause on the other end of the line. "My little brother," Anthea said. "Remember?"

"Oh," said my mother. "Oh yes. But he's not here now. He insisted on leaving school as soon as he was old enough, and he took a job right outside this district. I—"

"Did Uncle Alfred tell you that?" Anthea interrupted.

"No, of course not," my mother said. "You know

as well as I do that Alfred is a compulsive liar. *He* told me Conrad was staying on at school. I even signed the form, and then Conrad went off without a word, just like you did. I don't know what I've done to deserve two children like you." Then, while Anthea was trying to say that it was not true about me at least, my mother suddenly snapped, "Who is this wonderful man who has lured you into female bondage, Anthea?"

"If you mean marriage, Mother," Anthea said, "it's Count Robert of Stallery."

At this, my mother uttered something that sounded like "That impostor!," though it was more of a strange wailing yelp, and dropped the phone. We heard it clatter onto a hard surface. There was some kind of distant commotion then, until someone firmly put the phone back and cut us off.

As Anthea hung the whirring receiver back on its rest, I had the hardest job in the world not to burst into tears. Tears pushed and welled at my eyes, and I had to stand rigid and stare at the shelves of books in front of me. They bulged and swam. I felt utterly let down and betrayed. Everyone had lied to me. By now I didn't even know what the truth *was*.

Anthea put her arm around me, hard. Christopher

said, "I know how you feel, Grant. Something a bit like this happened to me, too, once."

Anthea asked him, "*Is* our mother under a spell, do you think?"

"She just doesn't care!" I managed to say.

"No, Grant, I think it's a bit more complicated than that," Christopher said. "Think of it as a mixture of lies and very small spells done by someone who knows her very well and who knows she'll go where she's pushed if she's pushed often enough and gently enough. It sounds as if much the same was done to you, Grant. What's this Walker you were supposed to summon? Why don't you try summoning it now and see what happens?"

The same dry-mouthed fear seized me that I had felt in the Magicians' Circle. I was horrified. "No, no!" I cried out. "I'm not supposed to do that until I *know*!"

"Know what?" my sister asked.

"The—the person who's—the one who I should have killed in my last life," I stammered.

I felt Anthea and Christopher look at each other across my head. "Fear spell," Christopher said. "And you *don't* know, do you, Grant? Then it's much safer to summon the thing now, before there's any real danger."

"Yes, do that. Do it at once, Conrad," Anthea said. "I want to know what he's making you do. And you," she said to Christopher, "if you really *are* an enchanter, you can stand guard on the door, in case that butler comes back with a computer."

Christopher's face was such a mixture of surprise and outrage that I nearly laughed. "*If* I am an enchanter!" he said. "*If!* I've a good mind to turn you into a hippopotamus and see how Count Robert likes you then!" But he went and stood with his shoulders against the door all the same, glowering at my sister. "Summon away, Grant," he said. "Do what the hippopotamus tells you."

Anthea still had her arm around me. "I won't let it hurt you," she said, just as if I were six years old again and she was putting plaster on my knee.

I leaned on her as I took the wine-blotched cork out of my waistcoat pocket. I still felt miserably ashamed of myself for believing all those lies, but the dry-mouthed fear seemed to have gone. And the cork was so ordinary. It had *Illary Wines 1893* stamped on it, and it smelled faintly sour. I began to feel silly. I even wondered if the Magicians' Circle had been playing a joke on me. But I pointed the cork at the end wall of the library and said, "I hereby summon a Walker. Come to me, and give me what I need. I think it's a hoax," I added to Anthea.

"No, it *isn't*," Anthea said, sounding sharp and stern. Her arm went tight around my shoulders.

There was a sudden feeling of vast open distances. It was a very odd feeling, because the library was still all around us, close and warm and filled with the quiet, mildewy scent of books, but the distances were there, too. I could smell them. They brought a sharp, icy smell like the winds over frozen plains. Then I realized I could *see* the distance, too. Beyond the books, farther off than the edge of any world, there was a huge curving horizon, faintly lit by an icy sunrise, and winds that I couldn't feel blew off it. I knew those were the winds of eternity. And real fear gripped me, nothing to do with any fear spell.

Then I realized that I could see the Walker coming. Across the huge horizon, lit from behind by the strange hidden sunlight, a dark figure came walking. He or she walked in an odd, hurried, careful way, bending a little over the small thing it carried in both hands, as if whatever it was might spill or break if it was jogged in any way. So it walked smoothly but quickly in little steps, and the winds blew its hair and its clothes out sideways—except that the hair and the clothes never moved at all. On it came, and on. And all the time I could see the shelves of books in front of me, in ordinary daylight, and yet I could see the distance and the Walker just as clearly.

Anthea's arm was clamped around me. I could feel her trembling. Christopher's shoulders thumped against the library door as he tried to back away, and I heard him mutter, "Gracious heavens!" We all knew there was nothing we could do to stop the Walker coming.

It came nearer and nearer with its strange pattering strides, and the winds blew its clothes and its hair and they still never moved, and it still bent over the small thing in its hands. When it was only yards away, and the room filled with gusts of arctic scent that we could smell but not feel, I could have sworn the Walker was taller than the library ceiling—and that was two stories high. But when it came right up to me, it was only a foot or so taller than Anthea. It was properly inside the room then, and I was numbed with the cold that I couldn't feel, only smell. It sort of bent over me. I saw a sweep of dark hair blown unmovingly away from a white face and long dark eyes. The eyes looked at me intently as it held out one hand to me. I had never seen any eyes so intent. I knew as I looked back that this was because the Walker was bound to get whatever it gave me exactly right. *Exactly* right. But I had to give it the cork first in exchange.

I put the cork into the hand it was holding out. That hand closed around the cork, and the other hand came out and passed me something else, something cold as ice and about twice as long and a good deal heavier. My face felt stiff and numb, but I managed to say, "Thanks," in a mumbling sort of way. The intent white face in front of me nodded in reply, once.

Then the Walker walked on past Anthea and me.

All our breaths, Christopher's, Anthea's, and mine, came out in a *Whoosh!* of pure relief. As soon as the Walker had gone past me, it had gone. The icy smell and the horizon of eternity had gone, too, and the library was once more an enclosed, warm room.

Christopher said, in a voice that was trying not to sound too awed, "Was it a man or a woman? I couldn't tell at all."

"I'm not sure that applies to a being like that," Anthea said. "What did it give you, Conrad?"

I looked at the thing in my hand. It felt quite warm now, or only cold the way metal always feels.

I looked at it and puzzled. It seemed to be a small corkscrew—very like the one I used to struggle with when the Magicians' Circle wanted a bottle of port opened—one of those with an open handle that you hook two fingers through, with little curls at either side for two more fingers. But there was a key sticking out from the top of the handle. If I held the thing one way up, it was a corkscrew, but if I turned it around, the corkscrew became the handle of the key.

I held the thing up to Anthea and twiddled it at Christopher. "Look. I'm supposed to *need* this. What do you think I *do* with it?"

Anthea leaned over me to look. "It *could* be the key to a wine cellar."

Christopher slapped the side of his velvet breeches. "That's *it*! The hippopotamus has got it in one! I *knew* it was important to get into that wine cellar! Come on, Grant. Let's go and do it before we have to go back on duty."

He rushed off to the gallery staircase. I followed him slowly, feeling upset and puzzled and let down. I had expected the Walker to give me something much more dangerous than a key or a corkscrew.

"Get a move on, Conrad," Anthea said. "That butler . . . "

So I hurried a bit, and lucky that I did. I had only just climbed into the gallery when the door below opened again. Mr. Amos came importantly in, followed by a line of footmen carrying a viewscreen, a tower, a keyboard, drums of flex, armloads of disks, a stack of power cells, a printer, boxes of paper, and a load of other accessories.

"I shall supervise the setting up of the equipment personally, miss," Mr. Amos said to Anthea.

Christopher dragged me through the door at the back of the balcony. "Good," he said when we were safely out in the corridor. "If he's busy in there, he can't possibly be in the wine cellar. Let's *go*, Grant!"

Fourteen

We galloped downstairs, and down again
to the undercroft. "Funny," I said to Christopher as
we tiptoed toward the stairs that led to the cellar. "I
didn't know any of those footmen with Mr. Amos.
Did you?"

"Hush," he said. "Utmost caution, Grant."

Actually there was no one about, and it was quite
safe. Christopher was just being dramatic because it
was all so easy. There were nice broad steps curving
down to the cellar and a light switch beside the door
at the bottom so that I could see to put the corkscrew
key into the keyhole. The keyhole looked far too big,
but the key went in, fitted exactly, and unlocked the
door when I turned it. The door swung open easily

and silently, and lights came on in the cellar as it opened.

"Lock it after you," Christopher said.

"No," I said. "We may need to get out quickly."

Christopher shrugged. I pushed the door shut, and we walked on into a set of low, cold rooms lined with wine racks and barrels. There were dusty bottles and shiny new bottles, rank on rank of them, little kegs labeled *Cognac* in foreign letters, bigger barrels labeled *herez* that Christopher said meant sherry, and whole walls of champagne.

"One could get awfully drunk here," Christopher remarked, surveying a dusty wall of bottles marked *Nuits d'été 1848*. "I have quite a mind to drown my sorrows, Grant. I *saw* Millie. I talked to her. Do you know how to open champagne?"

"Don't be a fool," I said. I pulled him away and led him on, and on, past thousands of bottles, until we came to another locked door in a wall at the end.

"Ah," said Christopher. "This may be it—whatever *it* is. Does your gadget work on this door, too?"

I tried the corkscrew key again, and it worked. This door creaked a bit as it opened, as if it were not used very much, and we saw why as soon as we were inside. Lights came on and showed another, newer-looking staircase that led to a trapdoor in the ceiling. Christopher looked up at the shiny new metal of the trapdoor very thoughtfully.

"I do believe," he said, "that we may be right under the butler's pantry here, Grant. In which case the important stuff is just round this corner."

The walls here were of quite new brick. It looked as if an extra room had been built, off at an angle to the main cellars. We edged around the corner to it. There we both stopped, quite bewildered. This room was lined—as closely as the wine cellars were lined with bottles—with lighted, flickering viewscreens. From floor to ceiling they were stacked in rows. Most were covered with green columns of figures that ran and jumped and changed all the time, but about a third of them, mostly on the end wall, were full of strange swirlings or colored jagged shapes. The jumping and flickering made me seasick. Worse than that was the peculiar buzzing of magic in the room, electric and alien and feeling like metal bars vibrating. I had to look at the floor for a while, until I got used to it. But Christopher walked up and down the room, watching the screens with interest.

"Do you understand this, Grant?" he asked.

"No," I said.

"I almost do," Christopher said, "but I'm going to need your help to be sure." He pointed to a screen of jumping numbers. "For instance, what does Coe-Smith mean?"

"Stock market," I said. "I think."

"Right!" Christopher said triumphantly. He pointed to another screen, where blue columns of numbers raced so fast that I couldn't read them. "What's Buda-Parich?"

"That's a city," I said, "over in the middle of the continent. It's where all the big banks are."

"And here's Ludwich," Christopher said, at another screen. "I know that one. More big banks and a stock exchange in Ludwich, am I right? But there can't be a city called Metal Futures, can there? This lot of screens must be stocks and shares, then. Yes, Chemics, Heavy Munitions, Carbon Products— it sort of makes sense. And . . . " He paused at a clump of screens where green and red lines zig-zagged, bent, and climbed. "These lot have to be graphs. But the really puzzling ones"—he went on, moving around to the end wall— "are *these*. They just seem to be patterns. What do you think this one is? The one that's all jagged moving shapes."

"Fractals?" I suggested.

"I wouldn't know a fractal if it jumped up and bit me," Christopher said. "Which it almost looks as if it could do. Oh, *look*. These must be the controls."

Under the possible fractals there was a sloping metal console. Rows of buttons took up the top half of it. The bottom part held a very used-looking keyboard. The lights from the screens painted winding colored patterns on Christopher's attentive face as he leaned both hands on the edge of the console and stared at the rows of buttons.

"Interesting," he said. "When controls are used a lot, you can see which the important ones are. This keyboard thingy is quite filthy with finger grease. Used every day, I should think. And this one on its own at the top has been used almost as much." His thin white finger pointed to a square button up on the right above all the others. The metal around this button was worn shiny and ribby, with a ring of grease around the shiny part. The label under it was all but worn away. As far as I could see, it said "shift."

"That must be—" I began, but Christopher turned to me, looking almost unholy in the colored lights.

"What do you think?" he said. "Dare we, Grant? Dare we?"

"No, we daren't," I said.

Christopher simply grinned and pressed the used square button firmly down.

We felt the shift like an earthquake down there. Our feet seemed to jerk sideways under us. All the screens blinked and began to flicker away madly in new configurations. Above the console, the strange patterns wove and writhed into quite different shapes and colors.

"*Now* you've done it!" I said. "Let's get out."

Christopher made a face, but he nodded and began to tiptoe away from the console. I had just turned to follow him, when a voice spoke. It was a woman's voice, very cultivated and rather deep. "Amos!" it said, and stopped both of us in our tracks. We stood, bent and on tiptoe, craning to look up at the round grid in the ceiling where the voice had come from. "Amos," it said. "Do pay attention. I don't think we can afford to make changes at the moment. We may have trouble this end. I told you about the ratty little fellow we caught sneaking around the office. Security locked him up, but he must have been some kind of magic user because he got away in the night. *Amos!* Are you listening?"

Christopher and I waited for no more. I clutched

his arm and he grabbed my shoulder and we bundled each other around the corner and out through the door. I could scarcely turn the corkscrew key in the lock for giggling. Christopher giggled, too. It was the silly way you behave when you feel you have almost been caught.

As we sped back past the ranks of wine, Christopher said in a giggling whimper, "That was never the Countess, was it?"

"No," I said. "Mrs. Amos?"

"A bit la-di-da for that," Christopher said.

We were still laughing when we came to the outer door and I locked that after us, and we didn't really get a grip on ourselves until we came to the lobby of the undercroft and I tried to fit the corkscrew key into my waistcoat pocket. It wouldn't go. It was more than twice as long as the wine cork, and it stuck out whatever I did.

Christopher said, "Here. Let me." He whipped a piece of string out of thin air, threaded it through the corkscrew handle, knotted the ends together, and hung the lot around my neck. "Under your shirt with it, Grant," he said.

While I was stuffing it out of sight under my cravat, Miss Semple came into the lobby, full speed ahead, striped skirts flying. "I've been looking all over for you two!" she said. "You're eating in the Middle Hall from now on, with the new Staff—" She stopped, went back a step, and put her hands up in horror. She was the sort of person who did that. "My goodness!" she said. "Go and get into clean uniforms at *once*! You've got two minutes. You'll be late for lunch, but it will serve you right."

We fled up the undercroft steps and dodged into the Staff toilets at the top. Christopher sagged against the nearest wall inside. "This has been quite the busiest morning of my life," he said. "*Damned* if I go all the way up to the attics again!"

This was my feeling, too. But when I looked over at the mirror, I saw why Miss Semple had been so horrified. We were both filthy. Christopher was covered in dust and carpet fluff. One of his stockings had come down, and his cravat looked like a gray string again. I had cobwebs all over me, and my hair stuck up. "Then work some magic," I said.

Christopher sighed and flapped one hand. "There." And we were once more smart flunkeys in crisp, clean shirts and neat cravats. "Drained," he said. "I'm exhausted, Grant. You've forced me to do permanent magic on us. At this rate, I shall be old before my time."

I could see he was all right, really, but he kept saying this sort of thing all the way back into the undercroft. I didn't mind. Neither of us wanted to talk about the Walker, or about the screens in the cellar and the voice from the ceiling. It was all too big to face just then.

We opened the door of the Middle Hall to find it almost entirely full of strangers, maids in yellow caps and footmen in waistcoats and striped stockings, who all seemed more than usually good-looking. Andrew, Gregor, and the other footmen we knew were sitting in a row down at the end of the long, low room, staring in a stunned way. One of the best-looking maids was standing on the table among the glasses and cutlery. As we came in, she held one hand up dramatically and said, "Oh when, oh when comes azure night and brings my love to me?"

And a fellow in a dark suit who was kneeling on the floor between the chairs said, "E'en before the twilight streaks the west with rose, I come, I come to thee!"

"Most rash," replied the young lady on the table.

"EH?" said Christopher.

Everyone jumped. Before I could believe it possible, every new maid and every strange footman was sitting demurely in a chair at the table, except for the man in the suit, who was standing up and pulling his coat sleeves down. And the girl—she really was *very* pretty—was still standing on the table.

"You *rats*!" she cried out. "You might have helped me down. Now I'm the one in trouble!"

"It's all right," I said. "We're only the Improvers."

Everyone relaxed. The man in the suit bowed to us. He was almost ridiculously tall and thin, with a sideways sort of hitch to his face. "Prendergast," he said. "Temporary underbutler. Temporary name, too," he added, hitching his face to the other side. "My stage name is Boris Vestov. Perhaps you have heard of me? No," he said sadly, seeing Christopher looking as blank as I felt. "I mostly play in the provinces anyway."

"We're all actors here, darlings," another good-looking maid explained.

"How? Why?" Christopher said. "I mean . . . "

"Because Mr. Amos is an extremely practical person," said the girl on the table. She knelt down and smiled at Christopher. She was blond and, face-to-face, quite stunning. Christopher looked as stunned as Andrew and the rest. Her name, I found out, was Fay Marley, and she was a rising star. I'd seen her last year on a friend's television, when I came to think about it.

I nudged Christopher. "It's true," I said. "She was in *Bodies* last year."

"So?" he said. "What has it got to do with Mr. Amos being practical?"

Fay Marley scrambled off the table and explained. They all explained. Nobody could have been friendlier than those actors. They laughed and joked and called us "darling," and they went on explaining while the ordinary maids came in with lunch. The ordinary maids were full of giggles and goggles. They kept whispering to me or to Christopher, "She's that young nurse in *Bodies*!" and "He's the one who jumps through the window in the chocolate ad!" and "He was the lost elf in *Chick-Chack*!" Mr. Prendergast/Vestov had more or less to push them out of the room.

Anyway, it seemed that practical Mr. Amos had, a long time ago, made an agreement with the Actors' Union that when Stallery needed more maids or footmen in a hurry, he would hire any actors who were not at that moment working.

"Being out of work is something actors are quite often," a glamorous footman said.

"But the Union makes strict conditions," a dark maid, who was quite as glamorous, told us. "If we get stage or film work while we're here, we're allowed to leave Stallery at once."

"And we take our meals together," a beautiful parlormaid said. "We're only allowed to work so many hours a day here. You'll be doing much longer hours than us, darlings."

"But," said Christopher, "what makes you think you can do the work at all?"

They all laughed. "There's not a soul among us," Mr. Prendergast told him, "who has not, at one time in his or her career, walked onto a stage and said, 'Dinner is served, madam,' or carried on a tray of colored water and wineglasses. We know the part quite well."

"And we've a day or so to rehearse in anyway," said another glamorous footman. He was Francis, and fair-haired like Fay. "I'm told that the guests don't arrive until the ladies get back from Ludwich."

They told us that they had all arrived by coach earlier that morning. "Along with that lovely wench who's checking the library," a pretty parlormaid added. "I'd give my eyeteeth for a complexion like that girl has."

We got told this bit more than once. This was because there were at least two more of those sideways changes during lunch. At each one, the conversation did a sort of jolt and went back a few stages. Christopher began to look just a little guilty. He rolled his eyes at me each time, hoping I would not say anything. By the end of lunch he was quite quiet and anxious.

Then the bell rang. Christopher and I had to go back on duty, along with Andrew, Gregor, and two of the actor footmen. And Mr. Amos was waiting at the top of the stairs, stubbing his cigar out in the usual place. I was sure he knew that we had been in his secret cellar. I almost ran away. Christopher went white. But it was the new footmen Mr. Amos wanted. He sent us on to the dining room ahead.

Whatever Mr. Amos said to the actors, it made them very nervous. They were awful. They got in one another's way all the time. Francis broke two plates, and Manfred fell over a chair. Andrew and Gregor were very scornful. And when the Countess came in, followed by Lady Felice and Count Robert, it was to the long clattering of knives pouring out of a drawer that Francis had pulled open too far. The Countess stopped and stared. She was all beautifully got up for her trip to Ludwich.

"I do beg pardon, my lady," Mr. Amos said. "The new Staff, you know."

"Is that what it was?" Count Robert said. "I thought it was a war."

The Countess gave him a disgusted look and stalked to her chair, while Francis, redder in the face than I thought a person could be, crawled about, scooping knives out of her path. Mr. Amos nodded me and Christopher off to help him. I was crawling about on the floor, and Manfred had just managed to slop soup over half the knives, when there came the most majestic clanging from somewhere, like someone tolling for a funeral in a cathedral.

"The front door," Mr. Amos said. "I beg you will excuse me, my ladies, my lord. Mr. Prendergast is not yet practiced in his duties." He seized Andrew's arm and whispered, "Put those two idiots against the wall until I get back." Then he fairly whirled out of the room.

Gregor gave me a sharp kick—typically—and made me serve the soup instead of Manfred. By the time I had given all three of them a bowlful, and the

Countess, spoon poised at her lips, was saying, "Now, Felice, dear, you and I are going to have a very serious talk about Mr. Seuly on the way to Ludwich," Mr. Amos came hurrying back. He looked almost flustered. As he shut the door in his soundless way, I could hear the voice of Mr. Prendergast outside it.

"I tell you I'm quite capable of opening a door, you pear-shaped freak!"

Everyone pretended not to hear.

Mr. Amos came and bent over Count Robert. "My lord," he said, "there is a King's Courier in the hall asking to speak with you."

The Countess's head snapped up. Her spoon clanged back into the soup. "What's this? Asking to speak to Robert? What nonsense!" She sprang up. Count Robert got up, too. "Sit down," she said to him. "There must be some mistake. *I'm* in charge here. *I'll* speak to this courier."

She pushed Count Robert aside and marched to the door. Manfred tried to make up for his mistakes by rushing to open it for her, but he slipped in the spilled soup and sat down with a thump. Christopher whisked the door open instead, and the Countess sailed out.

Count Robert simply shrugged, and while Francis

and Christopher were hauling Manfred up, he walked around the struggle and went to talk to Lady Felice. She was sitting with her head hanging, looking really miserable. I didn't hear most of what Count Robert said to her, but when Gregor shoved me over to wipe up the soup from the floor, the Count was saying, "Bear up. Remember she can't *force* you to marry anyone. You can say no at the altar, you know."

Lady Felice looked up at him ruefully. "I wouldn't bet on that," she said. "Mother's a genius at getting her own way."

"I'll fix something," Count Robert said.

The Countess came back then, very crisp and angry. *"Well!"* she said. "Such impertinence! I soon sent that man packing."

"What did he want, my lady?" Mr. Amos asked.

"There's a Royal Commissioner coming to the district," the Countess said. "They want me to entertain him as a guest at Stallery, of all things! I told the man it was out of the question and sent him away."

Mr. Amos went a little white around his pear-shaped jowls. "But, my lady," he said, "this must have been a request from the King himself."

"I know," the Countess said as Andrew pulled her

chair out for her and she sat down. "But the King has no right to interfere with *my* plans."

Mr. Amos gulped. "Forgive me, my lady," he said. "It is mandatory for peers of the realm to extend hospitality to envoys of the King when required. We would not wish to annoy His Majesty."

"Amos," said the Countess, "this person wishes to plant himself here, in my mansion, at the precise time when we have a house full of eminent guests. Lady Mary, the Count's fiancée, will be here with all her family and the people I have chosen to meet her. *All* the guest rooms will be full. The valets and lady's maids will be filling both upper floors. This Commissioner has a staff of ten *and* twenty security men. Where, pray, am I supposed to *put* them? In the stables? No. I told them to go to a hotel in Stallchester."

"My lady, I think that was most unwise," Mr. Amos said.

The Countess looked stonily at her soup and then across to the chops Andrew was fetching from the food lift. "I don't want this," she said. She slapped her napkin down and stood up again. "Come, Felice," she said. "We'll set off for Ludwich *now*. I'm not going to stay here and have my authority questioned all the time. Amos, tell them to bring the cars round to the door in five minutes."

She and Lady Felice hurried away in a brisk clacking of heels. Suddenly everyone else was rushing about as well. Andrew raced off with a message to the garage, Christopher was sent to fetch the two Lady's Maids, who were going to Ludwich, too, and the other footmen rushed away to bring down the luggage. Mr. Amos, looking thunderously upset, turned to Count Robert. "Will you wish to continue lunch now, my lord, or wait until the ladies have departed?"

Count Robert was leaning on the back of a chair, and I swear he was trying not to laugh. "I think you should go and lie down, Amos," he said. "Forget lunch. No one's hungry." Then, before Mr. Amos could send me off to the kitchens, he turned and beckoned me over to him. "You," he said, "go to the library and tell the young lady waiting there to meet me in the stable yard in ten minutes."

As I left, he was giving Mr. Amos a sweet, blank smile.

I found Anthea in the library sitting rather crossly in front of a computer screen. "They were quite right about the disturbances here," she said to me.

"Everything keeps hopping sideways, and when I get it back, it says something quite different."

When I gave her Count Robert's message, she jumped up, beaming. "Oh good! How do I find the stables in this barracks?"

"I'll take you there," I said.

We went the long way around, talking the whole way. I told her about the screens Christopher and I had found in the cellar. "And I think your computer went wrong when Christopher pressed the shift button," I said. "It felt magic to me."

"Very probably," she said. "So it's that pear-shaped butler messing up the world's finance, is it? Thanks. Robert will be very glad to know that."

"How did you meet Count Robert?" I asked.

My sister smiled. "At university, of course. And Hugo, too—though he was always popping off to visit Felice in her finishing school. I met Robert at a magic class on my first day, and we've been together ever since."

"But," I said, "the Countess says Count Robert has to marry a Lady Mary Something who's coming here soon."

Anthea smiled, happily and confidently. "We'll see about that. You'll find Robert's just as strong-minded as his awful mother. So am I."

I thought about this. "And what do *I* do, Anthea? I can't stay on here as an Improver, and Uncle Alfred won't let me go to school, because I didn't use the cork like he said—anyway, he'll know I know he's told me all those lies now. What do I *do*?"

"It's all right, Conrad," Anthea said. "Just hang on. Hang on and wait. Robert will make everything all right. I promise."

Then we got to the stable yard, where Count Robert was waiting in his red sports car. My sister rushed over to it, waving happily. I went away. She had an awful lot of faith in him. I didn't. I couldn't see someone like Count Robert ever sorting out this mess. Anthea's faith was just love, really.

Fifteen

The next couple of days were strange and hectic.

I hardly saw Anthea, except when she was dashing away from the Upper Hall after breakfast. She was out with Count Robert in his sports car almost all the time. I don't think she went into that library at all. And Count Robert didn't come in to meals, so I never set eyes on him either. Hugo, now, he was another matter. I seemed to run into him everywhere, wandering about, missing Lady Felice.

Because none of the Family were using the dining room, Mr. Amos used it to train the actor footmen in. He had me and Christopher and Andrew and Gregor in there all that first afternoon, sitting at the table, pretending to be Family, so that Manfred and the rest could pour us water into wineglasses and hand us plates of dried fruit and cold custard. To do those actors justice, they learned quickly. By the evening, Francis only dropped one spoon the last time he served me with custard, and Manfred was the only one still falling over things. But, none of us really fancied our supper.

Christopher summed up my feelings, too, when he poked his potato cheese with a fork and said, "You know, Grant, I find it hard not to see this as custard." The food turned into liver and cauliflower as he poked it. Christopher shot me a glum, guilty look. Since Mr. Amos had been giving the actors a hard time in the dining room all afternoon, we knew he had not been down to the cellar to push the shift button. So this change was Christopher's fault. I quite expected him to start persuading me to go to the cellar again with him that night. I was determined to say no. One time in that place was enough. The thought of its alien, technological magics made my flesh creep—and the thought of Mr. Amos discovering us there was even worse.

But all Christopher said was, "Things must be changing like this where Millie is, too. She could be lost for good if I don't get to her soon." And I half woke up in the night to hear him tiptoeing away to the forbidden part of the attics.

I don't know how long he stayed out there, but he was very hard to wake in the morning. "No luck?" I asked as we collected the shoes.

Christopher shook his head. "I don't understand it, Grant. There were no changes at all, and I sat there for hours."

Here the lift opened, and we found it crowded with actors acting a scene from *Possession*. This was the strange thing about actors. They loved acting so much that they did it all the time. They spoke in funny voices and imitated people if they didn't do scenes from plays. And the lift made a good place to act in, because Mr. Amos and Mrs. Baldock couldn't see them at it there. From then on, the lift was always liable to have a scene going on in it or some-one saying, "No, darling, the best way to see the part is like *this*," and then doing it. In between, Hugo rode broodingly up and down, looking as if he did not want to be disturbed. Christopher and I got used to taking the stairs instead.

The undercroft was crowded with the regular Staff, up early in hopes of catching one or other of the actors. The maids had all got it badly for the footmen. Francis was most popular, and Manfred next, because he looked dark and soulful, but even Mr. Prendergast got his share of giggles and fluttered eyelashes and shy requests for his autograph—and he was really odd-looking.

"It's something about greasepaint, Grant," Christopher said. "It acts like a love potion. What did I tell you?" he added as we ran into four of the regular footmen, Mr. Maxim, and the bootboy, who all wanted to know if we had seen Fay Marley that morning. "In the lift," Christopher told them, "pretending to be possessed by a devil or something."

Stallery echoed with rehearsals that day, not only actors acting, but with official ones. Mrs. Baldock and Miss Semple tore the maids away from the actor-footmen and the actor-maids out of the lift and drilled them all in their duties upstairs. Mr. Amos took Mr. Prendergast and all the footmen to the hall, where he trained them in how to receive the guests. Mr. Smithers was roped in to pretend to be a guest, and sometimes Christopher was, too. Christopher was good at grand entries. I was on the stairs, mostly, learning what to do with the dozens of empty suitcases Mr. Amos had found to be luggage for the pretend guests. Mr. Amos made me stack them in pairs in the lift and then take each one to the right bedroom. This always took ages. If Hugo was not in the lift, then it was two of the actresses, looking exhausted.

"If I have to make one more bed or lay out one more breakfast tray, I shall *drop*, darling!"

"Why does Miss Semple *insist* on *counting* everything? Does she think I'm a *thief*, darling?"

And when I arrived in the right bedroom with my empty luggage, Mrs. Baldock usually grabbed me and trained me in all the other things I might have to bring to people's bedrooms. I was made to carry in trays, newspapers, drinks, and towels. Mrs. Baldock seemed to think she had as much right to me as Mr. Amos did. I several times caught myself thinking that this must be my Evil Fate at work—in fact I *kept* thinking it and then realizing all over again that Uncle Alfred had probably invented it. It gave me a strange, hectic feeling at the back of my mind all day. On top of that, I kept waiting for Mr. Amos to discover that Christopher had pressed that shift button.

Luckily, Mr. Amos was too busy in the hall just then. I came back to my station on the main stairs to find a full-scale rehearsal just starting.

"Right, *go*!" Mr. Amos shouted. He was standing

in the middle of the hall like the director of a film.

The great doorbell solemnly clanged. At this signal, footmen in velvet breeches and striped waistcoats and stockings came rushing from behind the stairs and formed up in two slanting rows on either side of the front door.

"Like a flipping *ballet*," Mr. Prendergast said, gloomily standing beside me with his arms folded and too much wrist showing beyond the sleeves of his smart dark coat.

Mr. Amos paced solemnly toward the front door. He took hold of the handles. He stopped. He called over his shoulder, "Prendergast! Where are you *this* time?"

"Coming, coming," Mr. Prendergast called back, walking slowly and importantly down the stairs.

"Hurry it up, can't you?" Mr. Amos boomed up at him. "Do you think you're the King, or something?"

Mr. Prendergast stopped. "Ah, no indeed," he said. "It's these stairs, you see. No actor can ever resist a fine flight of stairs. You feel you have to make an entrance."

Mr. Amos, for a second, seemed about to burst. "Just . . . hurry . . . up," he said, slowly, quietly, and carefully.

Mr. Prendergast went on down the stairs, in a sort of royal loiter, and crossed the hall to stand behind Mr. Amos's left shoulder.

"My *right* shoulder, you fool!" Mr. Amos practically snarled.

Mr. Prendergast took two measured steps sideways.

"*Now!*" said Mr. Amos, and threw open the two halves of the door. Francis jumped forward and grabbed one half and Gregor took the other and they each dragged their half wide open. Mr. Amos bowed. Mr. Prendergast did a much better bow. And Mr. Smithers edged apologetically indoors. Christopher followed him, airily strolling, looking every inch an important guest. . . .

But here one of the sideways changes happened, and the show broke down. Everyone was suddenly in a different position, milling around, with Mr. Amos in the midst of the chaos almost screaming with rage. "No, no, *no*! Francis, why are you over there? Andrew, it is *not* your job to fetch luggage in. *You* take Mr. Smithers's coat."

Mr. Amos really did not seem to see that there had been a change. It began to dawn on me that he might be as insensitive to the shifts as Mr. Maxim was. It was an odd thing, because Mr. Amos must have been some sort of a magician, and I would have thought he ought to have known when his own magic machinery was working, but I could see that he didn't. That was a relief! Christopher was looking at Mr. Amos consideringly, as if he was thinking the same things as me. Beside him, Mr. Smithers stared around anxiously for the right footman to hand his imaginary coat to.

"Start again," Mr. Amos said. "And *try* this time."

"I try, I try!" Mr. Prendergast said, arriving beside me again. "I am exercising every thew and sinew to persuade that man to give me the sack, but *will* he?"

"Why?" I said.

"The union must have been right when they told me that a reasonable-looking underbutler was very hard to find at short notice," Mr. Prendergast said dolefully.

"No, I meant why do you want to be sacked?" I said.

Mr. Prendergast grabbed each of his elbows in the opposite hand and hitched his face mournfully sideways. "I don't like the man," he said. "I don't like this house. It strikes me as haunted."

"You mean the changes," I said.

"No," said Mr. Prendergast. "I mean haunted. As in ghosts."

And the strange thing was that by lunchtime everyone was saying that Stallery was haunted. Several agitated people told me that that someone— or something—had thrown a whole shelf of books on the library floor. I tried to find Anthea to ask her, but she was out with Count Robert. By teatime all the maids were saying that things in the bedrooms kept being moved. Some of them had heard strange hammerings and knockings there, too. By the end of the day Mr. Prendergast was not the only actor who was talking about leaving.

"It's just the changes," Christopher said as we climbed the stairs that night; the lift was full of a courtroom drama just then, with Mr. Prendergast as the judge and a very glamorous dark girl called Polly Varden being accused of murdering Manfred. "Actors are some of the most superstitious people there are."

"I'm glad Mr. Amos doesn't seem to notice the changes," I said.

"It is lucky," Christopher agreed. Here he began looking very anxious and raced ahead to the attics.

He didn't go into our room at all. I think he spent all night out in the forbidden part of the attics. I woke up to find him already dressed and bending over me urgently. "Grant," he said, "there were no changes last night either. I think that fat swindler turns his machines off before he goes to bed. I'm going to have to look for Millie by day. Be an absolute cracker and cover up for me, will you?"

"How do you mean?" I asked sleepily.

"By saying I'm ill. Pretend I'm up here covered in green and yellow spots. Please, Grant." Christopher had been learning from the actors. He went down on one knee and raised his hands to me as if he were praying. "Pretty please, Grant! There's a *witch* out there—remember?"

I woke up enough to start thinking. "It won't work," I said. "Miss Semple is bound to come up and check on you, and when you're not there, I'll be in trouble, too."

Christopher went, "*Oooh!*" desperately.

"No, wait," I said. "The way to work it is for you to *show* Mrs. Baldock that you're really not well. Can't you work some magic to make yourself look ill? Give yourself bubonic plague or something? Then stagger into her room looking like death."

Christopher stood up. "Oh," he said. "Thanks, Grant. I wasn't thinking, was I? It's easy, really. All I have to do is to get hold of some silver, and Series

Seven will do the rest. But you'll have to be the one who brings meals and medicines to my sickbed. Will you do that, Grant?"

"All right," I said.

So, when we took the boots and shoes down, we took them by way of the big main staircase. There was no one about to see us at that hour. This made it all the more puzzling when we found a big red rubber ball, which must have come from the nurseries, bouncing slowly down the stairs in front of us.

"I wonder if there *is* a ghost after all," Christopher murmured.

We were too busy with our plan to get hold of something silver to bother much about it. When the ball rolled away across the black marble floor of the hall, we simply dumped our baskets of footgear outside the breakfast room and sneaked in through the door. Christopher went on a rapid search of the sideboard in there. In no time he selected a very small silver spoon from one of the big cruet sets and stuffed it into his waistcoat pocket. "This'll do," he said.

The effect was almost instant. His face went bluish white, and by the time he was back at the door, his legs were staggering. "Perfect," he said. "Come on."

We dodged out into the hall again, where, as far as I could see, the red rubber ball had vanished. But I didn't have any opportunity to look for it because Christopher was now—honestly and completely— too weak to carry his basket. He panted and he wavered and I had to carry one handle of it for him.

"Don't look so concerned, Grant," he told me irritably. "It's only a sort of magical allergy."

Actually, I was staring anxiously after the vanished rubber ball with shudders creeping up my back, but I didn't like to say so. I helped Christopher to the undercroft, and to dump the baskets in the bootroom, and then to the Middle Hall for breakfast. By the time everyone else arrived there, he was looking like death warmed up.

All the actors exclaimed. Fay Marley took Christopher along to Mrs. Baldock herself, and Mrs. Baldock believed he was at death's door like everyone else did. Christopher reappeared in the Middle Hall doorway, blue pale and staggering between Fay on one side and Mrs. Baldock on the other.

"I must have Grant!" he gasped. "*Grant* can take me upstairs!"

I knew he meant that we had to put the silver spoon back before Mr. Amos noticed it was missing.

I jumped up at once and draped Christopher's arm artistically across my shoulders. Christopher collapsed against me, so that I staggered, too.

To my surprise, everyone protested. "You're not his servant!" several actors said. Most of the others added, "Let Fay help you take him!" and Gregor said, "I could probably carry him." Mrs. Baldock said anxiously, "Are you sure you're strong enough, Conrad? He's a big lad. Let someone else try."

"Grant!" Christopher insisted expiringly. "*Grant!*"

"Not to worry," I said. "I can get him as far as the lift, and we can go up in that."

They let us go, rather doubtfully. I heaved Christopher along to the lift, which was about as far as I could manage. Christopher was looking so unwell by then that I was quite alarmed. I took the spoon out of his waistcoat pocket and put it in mine, before I opened the lift, in case anyone was listening for me to do that. Hugo was in the lift, sitting on the floor with his arms around his knees, staring at nothing. So I shut the lift again. When I turned to Christopher, there was color back in his face and he was standing on his own— it was as quick as that.

"Keep tottering," I said, and we pretended to stagger to the lobby.

We met Anthea there, dashing past us from the stairs. "What's wrong with him?" she wanted to know.

"Muscular dysfunctional debilitation," Christopher said. "MDD, you know. I've had it from the cradle."

"You look pretty healthy to me," Anthea said, but she was, luckily, in too much of a hurry to ask any more.

We tottered artificially on, up into the hall and across it to the breakfast room, where Christopher took a swift look around to make sure that nobody was there. "You put it back, Grant," he said. "I have to get going." And he went dashing away up the main stairs.

I was a bit annoyed, but I sighed and slipped into the breakfast room.

As soon as I was inside, I was quite positive there was a ghost in there. The room had a heavy *occupied* feeling, and the air seemed thicker than it ought to be. It smelled of damp and dust instead of the usual coffee and bread smell. I stood for a moment wondering which was worse, facing a ghost or being accused of stealing the silver. Facing Mr. Amos, I thought. Definitely worse. But my back shuddered all over when I finally made myself scuttle over to the sideboard. As quick as I could, I laid the shiny little spoon back where I thought it came from.

There was a thudding sound behind me.

I whirled around to see the big bowl of fruit in the middle of the table in the act of tipping over. The thud had been the orange that tipped out first. It was followed by apples, pears, nectarines, and more oranges, which went rolling across the table and off its edges, while the bowl stood on its edge to shake out a floppy bunch of grapes.

"Don't *do* that!" I shouted.

The bowl thumped back to its right position. Nothing else happened. I stood there for what must have been five minutes, feeling as if my hair was trying to pull itself up by its roots. Then I made myself scramble to pick up the fruit and put it back.

"I'm only doing this because of what Mr. Amos will say," I said as I crawled after apples. "I'm not helping you. Go and annoy Mr. Amos, not me. *He's* the one that needs a fright." I crammed the last handful of apples in anyhow, on top of the grapes, and then I ran. I don't remember anything on my way to the Middle Hall. I was too scared.

The next thing I remember is being *in* the Hall

and being greeted merrily by the actors. "Come and sit down," they called. "We saved your breakfast. Do you want my sausage?"

Polly Varden said, "I'm glad you're not ill, too. We enjoy having you here, Conrad."

"But you're too humble with Christopher, you know," Fay Marley said. "Why did it have to be *you* who hauled him to the attics?"

I couldn't answer that. All I could think of to say was, "Well, Christopher's—er—special."

"No, he's not, no more than you are," Francis said.

"Darling, he just *thinks* of himself as a star," Fay said. "Don't get taken in by the posing."

And Mr. Prendergast explained, "A person may have the *quality*, but he still has to earn his right to be a star, see. What has young Christopher done that makes him so special?"

"It's—more the way he was born," I said.

They didn't like that either. Mr. Prendergast said he didn't hold with aristocracy, and the rest said, in different ways, that it was *work* that made you a star. Polly made me really embarrassed by saying, "But you don't put on airs, Conrad. We *like* you."

I was quite glad when it was time to go and stand against the wall while Count Robert bolted his breakfast—he seemed to be in as much of a hurry as Anthea. The ghost was still in there. I think it was the ghost that made Manfred drop a steaming squashy haddock on his feet—but it could have been Manfred on his own, of course.

Sixteen

That morning Mr. Amos had us all up on the ballroom floor, first in the great Banqueting Hall, learning how to lay it out for a formal dinner, and after that in the Grand Saloon, where he made half of us pretend to serve coffee and drinks to the other half. It did not go well. There was change after change, sideways jerk after sideways jerk, and each change caused someone to make a mistake. There was a golden footstool that turned up in so many places that even Mr. Amos noticed. I suppose it was hard to miss after Manfred had booted it across the room six times. Mr. Amos thought it was me playing practical jokes.

"No, no, you wrong the lad," Mr. Prendergast

said, stepping up between me and Mr. Amos. "There is a ghost in this place. You need an exorcist, not a lecture. You need a divine with bell, book, and candle. As I have played the part of a bishop many times, I would be happy to stand in the role of cleric and see what I could do."

Mr. Amos gave him an even nastier look than he had been giving me. "There has never," he said, "been a ghost at Stallery, and there never will be." But he gave up lecturing me.

Despite what Mr. Prendergast said, the maids told me that they thought the ghost had been busy in the bedrooms all morning, making loud thumps on the walls and rolling soap about. Mrs. Baldock had had to go and lie down. The maids were scared stiff. And they may have been right, and it *may* have been the ghost. The trouble was, it was so difficult to tell, with all the changes. The sideways jerks seemed to be happening twice as often that day.

The maids crowded around and told me all about it when I went to the kitchens at lunchtime to fetch a tray of food for Christopher. I had to push my way through them. I knew that if I didn't take the food to Christopher quickly, then Fay or Polly would tell me I was being too humble and take the tray up herself. And either she would find Christopher looking perfectly healthy, or he would not be there at all.

Mr. Maxim handed me the tray with a wonderful domed silver cover on it and whispered, "You'll never guess! Mr. Avenloch has gone missing! The garden staff don't know what to do!"

"You mean, like the dog, Champ?" I asked.

"*Just* like that," Mr. Maxim said. "A real mystery!" He was loving it, I could see.

I rushed off to the lift with the tray before any of the actors could start acting in there. And it was just as well I took it. Christopher was not in our room. There was no sign of him anywhere in the attics. I wondered what to do for a while. Then it occurred to me that the silver dome would make Christopher ill anyway, and so would the silver cutlery Mr. Maxim had given him, so I might as well eat the lunch myself. I sat on my bed and ate it all, peacefully.

I was finishing with the trifle when there was a really big sideways jerk. I sat there feeling a little sick, wondering if the trifle had changed into something else on the way down. As long as it wasn't sardines! I was thinking, when I heard footsteps clattering on bare boards in the distance.

Christopher's back! was my first, rather guilty thought. I laid the tray on my bed and hurried out to explain that I had eaten his lunch, but he could pretend to get well and go down and eat mine. By the time I reached the bathroom on the corner, I could clearly hear that there were two separate sets of footsteps, one heavy and one lighter. He's found Millie! I thought. Now we're going to have problems!

I shot anxiously through into the forbidden middle of the attics.

Mr. Avenloch, the head gardener, was there, along with the new gardener's boy, Smedley. They were clattering around, both of them looking tired, sweaty, and bewildered. "*Now* where have we got to?" Mr. Avenloch was saying, in an angry sort of moan. "This is different *again!*"

Smedley saw me. He shook Mr. Avenloch's earthy tweed sleeve. "Sir, sir, here's Conrad! We must be back in Stallery!" His face was bright red, and he was almost crying in his relief. "This *is* Stallery, isn't it?" he implored me.

"Yes, of course it is," I said. "Why? Where have you been?" I had a fair idea, of course.

"Half the morning outside a ruined castle," Mr. Avenloch said disgustedly. "With a lake to it, all weeds. Ought to have been drained and replanted years ago, but I suppose there was no one there to do it. Can you show us the way down from here, boy? I was only ever in the undercroft before now."

"Certainly," I said, in my best flunkey manner. "This way." I took them along toward the lift, collecting the tray on the way. They thumped along after me in their great crusty boots.

"It wasn't only a castle," Smedley said. "It was never the same castle anyway. It kept turning different. Then it was a huge place made of glass—"

"All cracked and dirty," said Mr. Avenloch. "Such neglect I never saw."

"And after that there were three palaces with white marble everywhere," Smedley chattered on. I knew how he felt. He had been having the sort of experience you just have to talk about. "And then there was this great enormous brick mansion, and when we went inside, it kept changing all the time. Stairs in all directions. Old furniture, ballrooms—"

"Didn't you see any people at all?" I asked, hoping to get news of Christopher.

"Only the one," Mr. Avenloch said repressively, "and she in the distance all the time." I could see he thought Smedley was talking too much.

I thought nervously of the witch. "What, like an old woman in rubber boots?" I asked.

"She seemed like a young girl to me," Mr. Avenloch replied, "and ran like a hare when we called out to her."

"That was what brought us up here," Smedley explained. "She ran away upstairs in the mansion— well, it was more like a cathedral by then—and we chased up after her, wanting to know what was happening and how to get out of there. . . . "

We were at the lift by then. Its door slid aside to show Mr. Prendergast pretending to be Mr. Amos. I hadn't realized that Mr. Prendergast was such a good actor. He was tall and thin, and Mr. Amos was short and wide, but he had Mr. Amos's way of holding his head back and slowly waving one hand so exactly that I almost saw him as pear-shaped. Mr. Avenloch and Smedley both gaped at him.

"Lunch is served," Mr. Prendergast said. "I require you to be furniture against the wall. Furniture with legs of flesh." Then he did a Mr. Amos stare at Mr. Avenloch and Smedley. "And what are you doing with a rake and a wheelbarrow, Conrad, may I ask?"

"It's a long story," I said. Hugo was in the lift, too,

behind Mr. Prendergast, grinning all over his face. "Can we come down in the lift with you?" I asked.

"Feel free," Hugo said. "He came up looking for you anyway."

Mr. Prendergast waved the two gardeners into the lift, like Mr. Amos ushering the Countess. "Enter. It is not your place to wait upon your fellow Improver, Conrad," he said to me, and I really felt for a moment as if it were Mr. Amos telling me off. "Enter, and place the rake in that corner and the wheelbarrow by the wall here. Hold your tray two inches higher. We will now descend." He pressed the lift button with a Mr. Amos flourish. "I will now," he said, "make use of our descent to instruct you upon the correct way to place chairs for a banquet. All chair legs must be exactly in line. Having placed them at the table, you must then crawl along behind them, measuring the distance of chair from chair, with a tape measure carried in the waistcoat pocket for the purpose."

He went on like this all the way down to the undercroft. Smedley could not help giggling—and kept getting a Mr. Amos glare, followed by "Know your place, wheelbarrow"—and even Mr. Avenloch began to grin after a while. Hugo was laughing as much as I was.

When we got to the undercroft, Mr. Prendergast announced, "Mr. Hugo will now repair to the Upper Hall, while I march Conrad off to his fate in the Middle Hall. You two implements—"

"Please, sir," Smedley interrupted imploringly, "have we missed our lunch, sir?"

"Take this tray," Mr. Prendergast said, removing it from me and dumping it on Smedley, "and proceed with your mentor to the kitchens, where you will find they have been anxiously awaiting your return. Off with you now." He pretended to look at his watch. "You have exactly two minutes before they feed your lunch to the dogs."

Smedley went racing off. Mr. Avenloch paused to say, "That was as good as a play. But don't let Mr. Amos catch you at it. You'd be in for it then."

"It's probably the one thing he wouldn't forgive me for," Mr. Prendergast agreed cheerfully. "Which is why I am rehearsing the part. Come, Conrad. Your lunch awaits."

I had to have another lunch. They really did not like me running after Christopher. And I really could not explain. I was half asleep for the rest of the afternoon, until around suppertime, when I was suddenly ravenous and wide-awake. And, I don't know why, I was quite convinced that Christopher was back. I sneaked off early to the kitchens and asked them to give me Christopher's tray now. I did not want Mr. Prendergast butting in again.

It was so early that the regular maids were all gathering there for their high tea. They told me that the ghost had been bouncing that red rubber ball up and down the corridors all afternoon. They weren't frightened by then, they said, just annoyed by it. Besides, who wanted to leave, one of them added, when there was a chance of getting to know Francis? Or Manfred, said another. A third one said, "Yes, if you want gravy poured down your neck!" and they all shrieked with laughter.

The men's end of the attics seemed very quiet after this. I went along to our room and got the door open—which is not easy when you're carrying a tray—and Christopher seemed to be there. At least he was in bed and asleep when I went in, but when I turned around from putting the tray on the chest of drawers, there was no one there. The bed was flat and empty.

"Oh, come *on*!" I said. "Don't be stupid. It's only me. What happened? Didn't you find Millie, then?"

A girl's voice answered, "Oh dear. What's gone wrong? You're not Christopher."

I spun about, looking for where the voice came from. Christopher's bed was still flat and unused, but there was a dip in the edge of my bed, the sort of dent a person makes sitting on the very edge. She was obviously very nervous. I said, "It's all right. I'm Conrad. I work here at Stallery with Christopher. You're Millie, aren't you? He said you were an enchantress."

She became visible rather slowly, first as a sort of wobble in the air, then as a blur that gently hardened into the shape of a girl. I think she was ready to whip herself invisible again and run away if I seemed to be hostile. She was just a girl, nothing like as glamorous as Fay or Polly, and a bit younger than Christopher. She had straight brown hair and a round face and a very direct way of looking at a person. I thought she seemed nice. "Not that *good* an enchantress," she said ruefully. "You're that boy who was with Christopher on those stairs, aren't you? I made a real mistake getting into all those mansions. There never seemed to be a way to get *outside* them."

"It may have been the witch keeping you in," I said.

"Oh, it *was*," she said. "I didn't realize at first. She was sort of kind, and she had food cooked whatever kitchen I got to, and she kept hinting that she knew all about the way the buildings changed. She said she'd show me the way out when things were ready. Then she suddenly disappeared, and as soon as she was gone, I realized that it was that knitting of hers—she was sort of knitting me in, trying to take me over, I think. I had to spend a day undoing her knitting before I could get anywhere."

"How did you get here?" I asked.

"Christopher shouted across those double stairs to go to the top and then find the room with his tie on the doorknob," Millie said. "I was so tired by then that I did."

"Then he's still out there?" I said.

Millie shrugged. "I suppose so. He'll be back in the end. He's good at that kind of thing—having nine lives and so on."

She seemed a bit cool about it. I began to wonder if the witch had grabbed Christopher instead, because he was stronger, and that this was how Millie got out. "Oh well," I said. "He's not here, and you are. He's supposed to be ill, and I'm supposed to bring his meals. Would you like this supper now I've brought it?"

Millie brightened up wonderfully. "Yes, *please*! I don't know when I've *ever* been so hungry!"

So I passed her the tray. She arranged it on the bedside table, which she pulled in front of the bed, and began to eat heartily. The food changed from egg and chips to cottage pie while she ate, but she hardly seemed to notice. "I had nothing to buy food with, you see," she explained. "And the witch only did breakfast. The last breakfast was days ago."

"Did you run away from school without any money, then?" I asked.

"Pretty well," Millie said. "Money from Series Twelve wouldn't work in Series Seven, so I only took what was in my pocket. I was going to be a parlor-maid and earn some money. Except when I got inside those mansions, there was nobody there to be a maid *for*. But . . . " She looked at me very earnestly. I could tell she was wanting me to believe the next bit particularly. "But I *had* to run away from that school. It really was an awful place—awful girls, awful teachers—and the lessons were all things like dancing and deportment and embroidery and how to make conversation with an ambassador, and so on. I told

Gabriel de Witt that I was miserable and not learning a *thing*, but he just thought I was being silly."

"And you told Christopher," I said.

"In the end," Millie said. "Only as a last resort— Gabriel never listens to him either. And Christopher was just as overbearing as I knew he would be. *You* know, 'My dear Millie, set your mind at rest, and *I* will fix it,' and this time he was worse. He decided we were going to go and live together on an island in Series Five. And when I said I wasn't sure I wanted to go and live all alone with Christopher— Well, would *you* want to, Conrad?"

"No," I said, very definitely. "He's far too fond of his own way. And the way he makes superior jokes all the time—I want to hit him!"

"Oh, doesn't he just!" Millie said.

After that, all the while Millie was eating the pudding—which started as jam roly-poly and then became chocolate meringue—we both tore Christopher's character to shreds. It was wonderful fun. Millie, from having known Christopher for years, found two faults in him where I only knew one. His clothes, she told me, he fussed about his clothes being perfect *all* the time. He'd been like that for three years now. He drove everyone in

Chrestomanci Castle mad by insisting on silk shirts and exactly the right kind of pajamas. "And he could get them right anyway by magic," Millie told me, "if he wasn't too lazy to learn how. He *is* lazy, you know. He hates having to learn facts. He knows he can get by just *pretending* to know—bluffing, you know. But the thing that *really* annoys me is the way he never bothers to learn a person's *name*. If a person isn't important to him, he *always* forgets their name."

When Millie said this, I realized that Christopher had never once forgotten *my* name—even if it was an alias. It suddenly seemed to me to be rather mean, talking about Christopher's faults when he wasn't here to defend himself.

"Yes," I said. "But I've never known him do anything really nasty. I think he's all right underneath. And he makes me laugh."

"Oh, me, too," Millie agreed. "I *do* like him. But you can't deny that he's *maddening* a lot of the time— Who's that?"

It was Mr. Prendergast again. We could hear him outside in the corridor, doing his Mr. Amos act. "Grant," he called out. "Conrad, stop lurking in sickrooms and descend to the undercroft immediately. Supper is being served!"

He was nearer than we realized. The next moment he flung the door open and stood looming in the doorway. Millie made a sort of movement, as if she was thinking of turning invisible, but then realized that it was too late, and stood up instead. Mr. Prendergast hitched his face sideways at her, and his eyebrows traveled up and down his forehead like two sliding mice. He looked at me, and then at the tray.

"What is this?" he said. "Is Christopher really a girl?"

"No, no," I said. "This is Millie."

"She's not another wheelbarrow," Mr. Prendergast said. "Is she?" And when Millie simply looked completely confused, he narrowed his eyes at her and said, "So where are you from, young lady?" For a moment he looked so utterly serious that he made goose bumps come up on my arms.

Millie probably felt the same. "Er, from Series Twelve, really," she admitted.

"Then I think I don't want to know," Mr. Prendergast said. He hitched his face the other way, and I remembered, with great relief, that he was simply a very good actor. "I think," he said to me, "that she'd better be a feather duster."

"What *are* you talking about?" Millie said, exasperated and frightened, but almost laughing, too. This was the effect Mr. Prendergast seemed to have on people.

"We can't have Conrad embarrassed," he said to her, "and he would be if you went on sharing his room like this. So I think you'd better come downstairs and get turned into another new housemaid. Luckily there are so many just now that one more will hardly be noticed. Come along to the lift, both of you. No, let *her* carry the tray, Conrad. It makes her look the part more."

Hardly able to believe it, we followed Mr. Prendergast to the lift. Hugo was in it. He stared at Millie with gloomy surprise.

"New feather duster," Mr. Prendergast told him airily. "She's the child star of *Baby Bunting*—you won't know it yet, it's on trial in the provinces, but it'll be a hit, I assure you."

Millie went bright red and gazed hard at her tray, biting her lip. I think she was trying not to laugh.

Mr. Prendergast said nothing more until the lift was nearly at the undercroft. Then he said suddenly. "By the way, where *is* Christopher?"

"Around," I said.

Millie added, "He went to the bathroom."

"Ah," said Mr. Prendergast. "Indeed. That accounts for it, then."

Rather to my surprise, he didn't ask any more. He just stalked with us to the Middle Hall, where he took Fay aside and murmured a few words to her. It was like magic, really. Fay and Polly and two other girls instantly took charge and hurried Millie off to the maids' cloakroom. When they came back, Millie was wearing a brown-and-gold-striped dress just like the other girls, and a proper maid's cap. She sat and chatted to them and the other actors while the rest of us had supper.

Fay and Polly must have found somewhere for Millie to sleep that night. When I saw her at break-fast the next morning, she had her hair up on top of her head, under her cap, and Fay or someone had done things to her face with clever makeup, so that Millie looked rather different and quite a bit older. I think she was enjoying herself. She had a surprised, happy look whenever I saw her.

I kept out of Millie's way on the whole. I dreaded the moment when Miss Semple spotted Millie. Miss Semple's mild, serious, distracted eyes didn't miss much, and I was sure she would realize that Millie was not a real maid before long. Then the fat would be in the fire, and Mr. Prendergast would probably get the sack. I was fairly sure he had made Millie into a feather duster in order to get sacked.

But Miss Semple—nor Mrs. Baldock—did not notice Millie all day. Some of the reason was the ghost. It distracted people by playing pranks, dragging the sheets off all the newly made beds on the nursery floor, smashing tooth glasses, and bouncing that red rubber ball down flights of stairs. It had done something new every time Mrs. Baldock took me over to train me upstairs. But some of the distraction was due to the changes Christopher had started by pressing that button in the cellar. Everything kept moving about, so that when you put something down and then turned around to pick it up again, it wasn't where you'd left it. Most people who noticed—and it was hard not to notice before long—thought this was the ghost's doing, too. They just sighed. Even when all the sheets and towels got shifted to quite different cupboards on different floors, they said it was the ghost again and sighed.

But no one could blame the ghost when, late in the afternoon, all our uniforms suddenly changed color. Instead of gold and brown stripes, we were suddenly wearing bright apple green and cream.

Miss Semple was really distressed by that change. "Oh Conrad!" she said, "what *is* going on? These are the colors we had in my mother's day. My mother changed them because they were thought to be unlucky. Green *is*, you know. Things had gone wrong then until Stallery had barely enough money to buy the new colors. Oh, I do hope we aren't in for any more bad luck!" she said, and went rushing off past me in her usual way.

We were all still rushing about exclaiming, when the Countess and Lady Felice came back unexpectedly.

Seventeen

The Countess and Lady Felice were not expected until the next morning, just before all the guests arrived. But they had finished their shopping early, it seemed, and now there they were, in three cars drawing up outside the great front entrance.

Their arrival caused a general stampede. I had just arrived in the kitchens for my cookery lesson, but Mr. Maxim sent me away again, because he had to help get together a proper dinner for the ladies in a hurry. He told me to go and help in the hall instead. Hugo shot out of the lift as I went by and raced to the garage to find out where Count Robert had gone with Anthea, and to get him back if he could. In the black-floored hall, there was the main stampede, for what Mr. Prendergast called "the dress rehearsal for the real show tomorrow." Footmen raced down from the attics and up from the undercroft, and the marvel was that we all arrived there just as Mr. Amos—with Mr. Prendergast haunting his right shoulder like a skinny black scarecrow—threw open the huge front doors and Francis and Andrew pulled them wide.

The Countess sailed inside with a new fur wrap trailing from her shoulders. As she handed the wrap off to Manfred, she gazed around at us all with gracious satisfaction, but she seemed, for a second, a little puzzled to see us all in our green-and-cream stripes. "Amos . . . " she began.

Mr. Amos said, "Yes, my lady?"

"I forgot what I was going to say," said the Countess. Evidently she was as insensitive to the changes as Mr. Amos was. "Has all been well?"

"Naturally, my lady," said Mr. Amos. He turned and *looked* at the red rubber ball that came trundling out of the library as he spoke. Then he looked at me. I picked it up—and it felt just as if I was wrenching the ball out of someone's resisting hand. I shuddered and shoved it into the library and shut the door on it.

"Then where is Count Robert?" the Countess demanded.

"Mr. Hugo is currently searching for him, my lady," Mr. Amos replied.

"Oh," the Countess said ominously. She marched away to the stairs, saying, "See to the luggage, will you, Amos."

It needed all of us to see to it. The three cars were stuffed with boxes, carrier bags, and parcels. I could not believe that two ladies could have bought so much in such a short time—though I suppose there were four ladies at it, really. The two Lady's Maids came in with armfuls of parcels and made a great pother about things being handled *gently* and being carried *right way up*. You could see they had been enjoying themselves. But Lady Felice, who hurried through while we were all handing parcels and carrier bags along like a bucket chain, did not look happy. She kept her head down, but I could see she had been crying.

She still looked that way when I was waiting on the Family at Dinner that night. This was such a magnificent meal that you would never have guessed that the Great Dictator and Mr. Maxim had been taken by surprise like the rest of us and had—so Mr. Maxim told me—made it up as they went along, wrestling also with the way chickens became salmon and cream became parsley as the food was fetched to the kitchens. The changes were quite bad that evening.

"You know I never notice," Mr. Maxim told me, "but Chef *does*, and he sorrowed, Conrad."

It struck me as a pity that neither Lady Felice nor Count Robert seemed to feel much like eating. Count Robert, who arrived back from some inn outside Stallstead, had certainly had supper with my sister before Hugo found him. He pushed food about on his plate, while the Countess told him that he should have been in the hall to meet her and how discourteous he was not to be there. He didn't even point out that she had come home a day early. But he stopped even pretending to eat when she went on to describe all the things he was expected to do and say when Lady Mary Ogworth arrived tomorrow.

So much for Anthea's chances! I thought, standing against the wall on my own. Christopher was still missing, and I was beginning to worry about him. With all these changes happening, he could be in castles and towers and mansions moving farther and farther away from Stallery all the time, and if the witch had not caught him yet, she *would* catch him if he was stuck out there again when Mr. Amos turned his machines off for the night. But there seemed nothing I could do. . . .

"As for Felice," I heard the Countess say, "the very *least* I insist on is that she be polite to Mr. Seuly."

At this, Lady Felice threw her fork down with a clatter.

Count Robert leaned forward. "Mother," he said, "does this mean that you've made some kind of arrangement for this Mr. Seuly to marry Felice?"

"Of course, dear," said the Countess. "We called on him on our way to Ludwich, and we had a long talk. He has made a very handsome offer for Felice, financially speaking."

"As if I was a *horse*!" Lady Felice said violently.

The Countess ignored this. "As I *keep* telling Felice," she said, "Mr. Seuly is even richer than Lady Mary Ogworth."

"Then," said Count Robert, "why don't you marry him yourself?"

This caused an astonished silence. Mr. Amos stared, the Countess stared, Gregor's mouth came open, and even Lady Felice raised her face and looked at her brother as if she could not believe her ears. At length, the Countess said, in a fading, reproachful whisper, "Robert! *What* a thing to say!"

"*You* said it first. To Felice," Count Robert pointed out. And before the Countess could pull her wits together, he went on, "Tell me, Mother, why are you so very set on your children marrying for money?"

"*Why?*" gasped the Countess, with her eyes very wide and blue. "*Why?* But, Robert, I only want the best for you both. I want to see you properly settled—with plenty of money, naturally—so that if anything happens, you'll both be all right."

"What do you mean, 'if anything happens'?" Count Robert demanded. "What do you imagine *might* happen?"

The Countess looked to one side and then to the other and seemed not to know how to answer this. "Well, dear," she said finally, "all sorts of things might happen. We might lose all our money—or—or . . . This is a very uncertain world, Robert, and you *know* Mother knows best." She was so much in earnest, saying this, that big tears trembled on the ends of her eyelashes. "You've hurt me very much," she said.

"My heart bleeds," Count Robert answered.

"At all events," the Countess said, in a sort of imploring shriek, "you have to *promise* me, darlings, both of you, to behave properly to our guests!"

"You can count on us to behave," Count Robert said, "but neither of us is going to promise more than that. Is that clear?"

"I *knew* I could count on you!" the Countess announced. She smiled lovingly from Count Robert to Lady Felice.

They both looked confused. I didn't blame them. It was really hard to tell what anyone had promised by then. I looked at Mr. Amos to see what he thought. He was scowling, but that might have been because he could see a speck of dust on the glass he was holding to the light. I wished Christopher were there. He would have known what was going on underneath this talk.

But Christopher was not there that night, and he did not turn up in the morning either. I had to make two journeys to collect all the boots and shoes. I was annoyed. After that I was working almost too hard to remember Christopher. But not quite. People are wrong when they say things like "I didn't have time to think." If you're really worried, or really miserable, those feelings come welling up around the edges of the other things you're doing, so that you are in the feelings even when you're working hard at something else. I was thinking—and feeling—a lot all the time the guests were arriving. Thinking about Christopher, worrying about Anthea, and feeling for myself, stuck here without even an Evil Fate to account for what I was doing.

The guests began arriving from early afternoon onward. Very stately people rolled up to the front doors in big cars and came in past the lines of footmen, wearing such expensive clothes that it seemed like a fashion parade in the hall. Then Mr. Prendergast would give out calls of "Lady Clifton's luggage to the lilac room!" or "The Duke of Almond's cases to the yellow suite!" and I would be rushing after Andrew and Gregor, or Francis and Manfred, with a heavy leather suitcase in each hand. When no guests were arriving, Mr. Amos had us measuring the spaces between the chairs at the banquet table to make sure they were evenly spaced. He really did that! And I'd thought Mr. Prendergast had been joking! Then the bells would clang, and it would be back to the black marble hall to carry more luggage.

And all the time I was more miserable and

wishing Christopher would get back. Millie was quite as worried about him by then, too. I kept meeting her racing past with trays or piles of cloths. Each time, she said, "Is Christopher back yet?" and I said, "No." Then, as things got more and more frantic, Millie simply said, "Is Christopher?" and I shook my head. By the middle of the afternoon, Millie was just giving me a look as we shot past each other, and I hardly had time even to shake my head.

This was when Lady Mary Ogworth arrived. She came with her mother—who reminded me more than a little of the Countess, to tell the truth. Both of them were wearing floaty sort of summer coats, but the mother looked like just another guest in hers. Lady Mary was beautiful. Up till then I'd never expected to see anyone who was better-looking than Fay Marley, but believe me, Lady Mary was. She had a mass of feathery white-fair curls, which made her small face look tiny and her big dark blue eyes look enormous. She walked like a willow tree in a breeze, with her coat sort of drifting around her, and her figure was perfect. Most of the footmen around me gasped when they saw her, and Gregor actually gave out a little moan. That was how beautiful Lady Mary was.

Count Robert was in the hall to meet her. He had been hanging about beside Mr. Prendergast on the stairs, fidgeting and shuffling and pulling down his cuffs, exactly like a bridegroom waiting by the altar for the bride. As soon as he saw Lady Mary, he rushed down the stairs and across the hall, where he took Lady Mary's hand and actually kissed it.

"Welcome," he said, in a choky sort of way. "Welcome to Stallery, Mary." Lady Mary kept her head shyly bent and whispered something in reply. Then Count Robert said, "Let me show you to your rooms," and he took her, still holding her hand, across the hall and away up the stairs. He was smiling at her all the way.

Gregor had to poke me in the back to remind me to pick up my share of her luggage. I was staring after them, feeling horrible. Anthea doesn't have a *chance*! I thought. She's deluding herself. Count Robert has simply been fooling about with her.

As soon as I'd dumped the suitcases, I sneaked to the library to find my sister, but she wasn't there. The ghost was. A book sailed at my head as soon as my face was around the door. But there was no sign of Anthea. I dodged the book and shut the door. Then I went to look for Anthea in the undercroft, but she was nowhere there either. And the under-croft was in an uproar because Lady Mary never stopped ringing her bell.

"Honestly, darling," Polly said, flying past, "you'd think we'd put her in a pigsty! *Nothing's* right for that woman!"

"The water, the sheets, the chairs, the mattress," Fay panted, flying past the other way. "This time it was the towels. Last time it was the soap. We've all been up there at least six times. Millie's up there now."

Miss Semple rushed down the stairs to the lobby, saying, "Mr. Hugo's fixed her shower—he thinks. But . . ."

Then the bell labeled *Ldy Ste* rang again, and they all cried out, "Oh, what is it *now*?"

Miss Semple got to the phone first and made soothing Yes madams into it. She turned away in despair. "*Oh,* I do declare! There's a spider in her water carafe now! Fay—no, you're finding her more shoe trees, aren't you?" Her mild, all-seeing eye fell on me. "Conrad. Fetch a clean carafe and glasses and take them up to the lady suite on one of the best gilt trays, please. Hurry."

If I had been Christopher, I thought, I would have

found an amusing way to say that my arms had come out of their sockets from carrying luggage. As I was just me, I sighed and went to the glass pantry beside the green cloth door. While I loaded a tray with glittering clean glassware and took it up in the lift, I decided that it must be the changes that were upsetting Lady Mary. They were going on remorselessly now. Before I got to the second floor, the lift stopped being brown inside and became pale yellow. It was enough to upset anyone who wasn't used to it.

The lift stopped and the door slid back. Millie, still looking very smart and grown up in her maid's uniform, was waiting outside to go back down. She gave me another of her expressive looks.

"No," I said. "Still no sign of Christopher."

"I didn't mean that this time," Millie said. "Are you taking that trayful to Lady Mary?"

"Yes," I said. "Fay and them have had enough."

"Then I don't want to prejudice you," Millie said, "but I think I ought to warn you. She's a witch."

"Really?" I said as I got out of the lift. "Then . . ."

Millie turned sideways to go past me. I could see she was angry then, pink and panting. "Then nothing!" she said. "Just watch yourself. And, Conrad, forget all the mean things I said about

Christopher—I was being unreasonable. Christopher *never* misuses magic the way that—that—*she* does!"

The lift shut then and carried Millie away downward. I went along the blue moss carpet and around the corner to the best guest suite, thinking about Christopher. He could be very irritating, but he was all right, really. And now I considered, he had set off to rescue Millie like a knight errant rescuing a damsel in distress. That impressed me. I wondered why I hadn't thought of Christopher that way before. I wished he would come *back*.

I knocked at the big gold-rimmed double door, but no one told me to come in. After a moment I knocked again, balanced the tray carefully on one hand, and went in.

Lady Mary was sitting sprawled in a chair that must have come from another room. Everything in the huge frilly room was pink, but the chair was navy blue, with the wrong pattern on it. Fay or Polly or someone must have lugged it in here from somewhere else. Lady Mary was clutching its arms with fingers bent up like claws and scowling at the fireplace. Like that, she looked almost as old as the Countess and not very beautiful at all. There was a half-open door beyond her. I could hear someone sobbing on the other side of it—her lady's maid probably.

"Oh, shut up, Stevens, and get on with that ironing!" Lady Mary snarled as I came in. Then she saw me. Her big blue eyes went narrow, unpleasantly. "I didn't say you could come in," she said.

I said, very smoothly, like Mr. Prendergast imitating Mr. Amos. "The fresh carafe and glasses you rang for, my lady."

She unclawed a hand and waved it. "Put them down over there." She waited for me to cross the room and put the tray on a small table, and then snapped, "Now stand there and answer my questions."

I was glad Millie had warned me. The hand waving must have been a spell. I found myself standing to attention beside the table, and the door to the corridor seemed a mile off. Lady Mary waved her hand again. This time I felt as if there was a tight band around my head, so tight that it somehow gave me pins and needles down both arms. I couldn't loosen it however hard I tried. "Why are you doing that?" I said.

"Because I want to know what I'm taking on here," she said, "and you're going to tell me. What do you think of Count Robert?"

"He seems nice enough—but I really hardly know him," I said. By this time I was panting and sweating. The pressure around my head seemed to be worse every second. "Please take this off," I said.

"No. Is Count Robert a magic user?" Lady Mary said.

"I've no idea—I don't think so," I said. *"Please!"*

"But *someone* here is," she said. "Someone's using magic to change things all the time. Why?"

"To make money," I found myself saying.

"Who?" Lady Mary asked.

I thought of Christopher pressing that shift button. I thought of Mr. Amos. I thought my head was going to burst. And at the same time I knew I wasn't going to tell this horrible woman anything else. "I don't—I don't know anything about magic," I said.

"Nonsense," Lady Mary said. "You're stuffed with talent. For the last time, *who?*"

"Nobody taught me magic," I gabbled desperately. My head was going to crack like an egg any moment, I thought. "I *can't* tell you because I don't *know!*"

Lady Mary screwed her mouth up angrily and muttered, "Why don't any of them know? It's ridiculous!" She looked at me again and said, "What do you think of the Countess?"

"Oh, she's awful," I said. It was a relief to be able to tell her *something*.

Lady Mary smiled—it was more of a gloating grin really. "They all say that," she remarked. "So it must be true. I'll have to get rid of her first thing then. *Now* tell me . . . "

A change came just as she said this. I never thought I'd be glad of a change. The tightness around my head snapped—*ping!*—like a rubber band that had been stretched too much. I staggered for a moment, pins and needles all over, eyes all blurry, but I could just see that the carafe and glasses on the tray had turned into a teapot, an elegant cup and saucer, and a plate of sugary biscuits.

I took a look at Lady Mary. She was behaving as if the rubber band had snapped itself in her face, blinking her big eyes and gasping. "Enjoy your tea, my lady," I said. Then I turned and ran.

I went down in the lift feeling awful. The pins and needles went away, slowly, but they left me feeling very miserable indeed. Lady Mary was obviously going to take over Stallery the moment she was married to Count Robert—or maybe even sooner. She would give me the sack at once, because I knew what she was like. I had no idea what I would do then. It was no good asking Anthea—she was as badly off as I was. And Christopher was not here to ask.

That was the good thing about Christopher. He never seemed to think anything was hopeless. If something went wrong, he made one of his annoying jokes and thought of something to do about it. I really needed that at the moment. I stopped the lift and sent it upward instead, just in case the changes had brought Christopher back. But our room was empty. I looked at Christopher's tie dangling from the doorknob and felt so lost that I began to wonder if Uncle Alfred was right after all about my Evil Fate. Everything went wrong for me all the time.

Eighteen

Middle Hall was crowded that evening.
Mr. Smithers and quite a few Upper Maids were
sent to eat with the actors, because Upper Hall was
filled with valets and lady's maids who had come
with the guests. They had to help the guests get
dressed, of course, so they had supper later. Mrs.
Baldock was holding a special cocktail party for
them in her Housekeeper's Room before that.
Polly, Fay, Millie, and another girl had to bolt their
food in order to race off and wait on Mrs. Baldock
and her guests. The rest of us hardly had time to
finish before bells began pealing and Miss Semple
came rushing in.

"Quick, quick, all of you! That's Mr. Amos

ringing. The company will be down in five minutes. Mr. Prendergast, you're in the Grand Saloon in charge of drinks—"

"Oh, am I?" Mr. Prendergast said, unfolding to his feet. "Menial tasks, nuts, and pink gin, is it?"

"—with Francis, Gregor, and Conrad," Miss Semple rushed on. "All other menservants to the Banqueting Hall to make ready there. Maids to the ballroom floor crockery store and service hatches. Hurry!"

The undercroft thundered with our feet as we all raced away.

The part in the Grand Saloon is a bit of a blur to me. I was too anxious and upset to notice much, except that Mr. Prendergast plonked a heavy silver tray in my hands, which made my arms ache. The guests were mostly a roar of loud voices to me, fine silk dresses and expensive evening suits. I remember the Countess graciously greeting them all, in floating blue, with a twinkly thing in her hair, and I remember Count Robert coming and snatching up a glass from my tray, looking as if he really needed that drink—and then I noticed that the glass he had taken was orange juice. I wondered whether to call out to him that he had made a mistake, but he was off by then, saying hallo to people, chatting to them and working his way over to the door as if he expected Lady Mary to come in any minute.

Lady Mary didn't arrive until right near the end. She was in white, straight white, like a pillar of snow. She went to Count Robert almost at once and talked to him with her head bent and a shy smile. I could hardly believe she had spent the afternoon complaining and casting spells and making her maid cry.

"That," Mr. Prendergast said, looming up beside me, "is a classic example of a glamour spell. I thought you might like to know."

"Oh," I said. I wanted to ask Mr. Prendergast how he knew, but he said, "Your tray's slanting," and surged away to fetch Gregor a fresh soda siphon.

Lady Felice arrived, wearing white, too, and looking horribly nervous. She went nearly as white as her dress when Mr. Amos flung the door open and boomed, "The Mayor of Stallchester, Mr. Igor Seuly."

Mr. Seuly looked really out of place. He was just as well dressed as everyone else, but he seemed smaller somehow, a little sunken inside his good clothes. He walked in trying to swagger, but he looked as if he was crawling, really. When the

Countess rustled graciously up to him, he took hold of her hand with a grab, as if she was rescuing him from drowning. Then he caught sight of me and my tray and came and took the largest glass as if that was a rescue, too.

"Have you found out how they pull the possibilities yet?" he asked me in a whisper.

"Not quite," I said. "I, er, we—"

"Thought not," Mr. Seuly said. He seemed relieved. "Not to worry now," he said. "When I'm spliced to Felice, I'll be part of the setup, and I'll be able to handle it for you. Don't you do anything until then. Understand?"

"But Uncle Alfred said—" I began.

"I'll fix your uncle," Mr. Seuly answered. Then he turned around and marched away into the crowd.

Shortly after that, Mr. Amos unfolded the double doors at the end of the room and said, in his grandest manner, "My lords, ladies and gentlemen, Dinner is served."

Everyone streamed slowly away into the Banqueting Hall, and it got quite peaceful. While Francis, Gregor, and I were clearing up spilled nuts and piling glasses on trays to give to Polly and the other maids at the door, Mr. Prendergast stretched himself out with a sigh along the most comfortable sofa.

"An hour of peace at least," he said, and lit a long black cigar. "Pass that ashtray, Conrad. No, make that nearly three hours of peace. I'm told they're having ten courses."

The double doors opened again. "Prendergast," Mr. Amos said. "You're on front hall duty. Get on down there."

"But surely," Mr. Prendergast said, sitting up protestingly, "everyone's arrived who's going to arrive."

"You never can tell," Mr. Amos said. "Events like this often attract poor relations. Stallery prides itself on being prepared."

Mr. Prendergast sighed—it was more of a groan, really—and stood up. "And what do I do in the unlikely event that penniless Cousin Martha or drunken Uncle Jim turn up and start hammering at the front door? Deny them?"

"You use your discretion," Mr. Amos growled. "If you have any. Put them in the library, of course, man, and then inform me. And *you*—Gregor, Francis, Conrad—in the Banqueting Hall as soon as you've finished here. Service is slower than I would like. We need you."

So, for the next two and a half hours, I was hard

at it, fetching dishes for other footmen to hand over elegant shoulders and carrying bottles for Mr. Amos to pour. Manfred had done quite well and only dropped one plate, but Mr. Amos would not let Manfred or me do any of the actual waiting at table. He said he was taking no chances. But we were allowed to go around with cheese boards, near the end. By this time the chinking of cutlery and the roar of voices had died down to a mellow rumble mixed with the occasional sharp *tink*. Mr. Amos sent Andrew back to the Grand Saloon to make coffee. And after I had carried around special wine for the speech and the toasts, he sent me to the Saloon, too.

Mrs. Baldock and Miss Semple were there, arranging piles of chocolates enticingly on silver plates. Mrs. Baldock seemed a little unsteady. I thought I heard her hiccup once or twice. And I remembered Christopher saying the first night we were here that he thought Mrs. Baldock drank— although she *had* just given a party, I suppose. I reached out to sneak a chocolate, thinking of Christopher. There had been no changes for hours now. Mr. Amos must have switched off his equipment, so Christopher was stuck for yet another night. Here Miss Semple slapped my reaching hand

and brought me back to reality. She sent me hustling up and down the huge room, planting the piles of chocolates artistically on little tables. So I was able to snitch a chocolate anyway, before Andrew called me over to help him rattle out squads of tiny coffee cups and ranks of equally tiny glasses.

I was thinking of Christopher, so I said what Christopher might have said. "Are we having a dolls' tea party?"

"Liqueurs are served in small glasses," Andrew explained kindly, and showed me a table full of round bottles, tall bottles, triangular bottles, flat bottles, red, blue, gold, and brown bottles, and one big green one. He thought I didn't know about liqueurs. If he had been Christopher, he would have *known* I was joking. "The big round glasses are for brandy," Andrew instructed me. "Don't go making a mistake."

Before I could think of a Christopher-type joke about this, the Countess came sailing in through the distant doors, saying over her shoulder to a stout man with a beard, "Ah, but this is Stallery, Your Grace. We never have *new* brandy!" Other guests came slowly crowding after her.

Mrs. Baldock and Miss Semple vanished. Andrew and I went into furniture mode. The rest of the guests gradually filtered out across the room and settled into chairs and sofas. Mr. Seuly had a lot of trouble over this. He kept trying to sit in a chair next to Lady Felice, but Lady Felice always stood up just before he got to her and, with a sad, absentminded stare, walked away to another chair in another part of the room. Count Robert somehow got buried in the crowd. He was never anywhere near Lady Mary, who was sitting on a golden sofa beside her mother, looking lovelier than ever.

Then Mr. Amos arrived. He closed the double doors on a violent crashing—Manfred was dropping plates again, I think, as the rest of the footmen cleared away the feast—and beckoned me and Andrew over to the table with the coffee cups. I was kept very busy taking around tiny clattery cups. The main thing I remember about this part is when I had to take coffee to Lady Mary and her mother. As I got to their sofa, the mother put out her hand to take one of the chocolates on the table beside them. Lady Mary snapped at her, in a little grating voice, "Mother! Those are bad for you!"

The mother took her hand back at once, looking so sad that I was sorry for her. I handed Lady Mary a cup of coffee, and managed to make it rattle and clatter so much that Lady Mary put out both hands to it and turned to give me a dirty look. Behind her, I saw the mother's hand shoot out to the chocolates. I think she took about five. When I handed the mother her coffee, she gave me a look that said, Please don't give me away!

I was just giving her a blank, furniture look in reply that said, Give away *what*, my lady? when the door to the service area behind us opened and Hugo and Anthea came quietly into the Saloon. They were wearing evening dress, just like the guests. Hugo looked good in his, and far more natural than Mr. Seuly. My sister was in red, and she looked stunning.

Nobody seemed to notice them at first except me. They walked slowly side by side out into the middle of the room, both looking very determined. Hugo was so determined that he looked almost like a bulldog. Then Anthea made a small magical gesture, and the Countess looked up and saw them. She sprang up and swept toward them in a swirl of silky blue.

"*What* is the meaning of this?" she said in a fast, angry whisper. "I will *not* have my guests disturbed in this way!"

At this, Lady Mary looked up, looked at Anthea, and looked venomous. Beside my sister's black hair and glowing skin, Lady Mary hardly seemed to be there. She was like a faded picture, and she knew it.

Across by the little cups and glasses, Mr. Amos looked up, too. He stared. Then he glared. If looks could have killed, Hugo would have dropped dead then, followed by Anthea.

But Lady Felice was now standing up, slowly and nervously. She was so obvious in her white dress that most of the guests turned around to see what she was doing. They looked at her, and then they looked at Hugo and Anthea. The talk died away. Then Count Robert stood up and walked forward from the other end of the Saloon. Everyone stared at him, too. One lady got out a pair of glasses on a stick in order to stare better.

"I apologize for the disturbance," Count Robert said, "but we have a couple of announcements to make."

The Countess whirled around to him and began to make her *Why, dear?* face. She was sweetly bursting with rage. By the look of him, so was Mr. Amos, only not sweetly. But before either of them could speak, the main door at the far end of the Saloon opened and Mr. Prendergast stood and loomed there.

"The Honorable Mrs. Franconia Tesdinic," he announced, in his ringing actor's voice.

Then he backed out of the room, and my mother came in.

My mother looked even more unkempt than usual. Her hair was piled on her head in a big, untidy lump, rather like a bird's nest. She had found from some cupboard, where it must have hung for twenty years or more, a long yellow woolen dress. It had turned khaki with age. I could see the moth holes in it even from where I was. She had added to the dress a spangled bag she must have bought from a toy shop. And she sailed into that huge room as if she were dressed as finely as the Countess.

I have never been so embarrassed in my life. I wanted to get into a hole and pull it in after me. I looked at Anthea, sure that she must be feeling at least as bad as I was. But my sister was gazing at our mother almost admiringly. With an affectionate grin growing on her face, she said to Hugo, "My mother is a naughty woman. I know that dress. She saves it to embarrass people in."

My mother sailed on like a queen, through the room, until she came face-to-face with the Countess. "Good evening, Dorothea," she said. "You seem to have grown very fine since you married for money. What became of your ambition to go on the stage?" She turned to the lady with the glasses on a stick and explained, "We were at school together, you know, Dorothea and I."

"So we were," the Countess said icily. "What became of your ambition to write, Fanny? I don't seem to have read any books by you."

"That's because your reading skills were always so low," my mother retorted.

"What are you doing here?" the Countess demanded. "How did you get in?"

"The usual way," my mother said. "By tram. The lodge keeper remembered me perfectly well, and that nice new butler let me into the house. He said he had had instructions about poor relations."

"But why are you here?" the Countess said. "You swore at my wedding never to set foot in Stallery again."

"When you married that actor, you mean?" said my mother. "You must realize that only the most pressing reason would bring me here. I came—"

She was interrupted by Mr. Amos. His face was a strange color, and he seemed to be shaking as he arrived beside my mother. He put a hand on her moth-eaten arm. "Madam," he said, "I believe you may be a little overwrought. Would you allow me to take you to our housekeeper?"

My mother gave him a short, contemptuous look. "Be quiet, Amos," she said. "This has nothing to do with you. I am here purely to prevent my daughter from marrying this Dorothea's son."

"*What?*" said the Countess.

From the other end of the room, Lady Mary said, "WHAT?" even louder and sprang to her feet. "There must be some mistake, my good woman," Lady Mary said. "Robert is going to marry *me*."

Count Robert gave a cough. "No mistake," he said. "Or only slightly. Before the three of you settle my fate between you, I'd better say that I've already settled it myself." He went over to Anthea and pulled her hand over his arm. "This is one of the announcements I was about to make," he said. "Anthea and I were married two weeks ago in Ludwich."

There were gasps and whispers all over the room. My mother and the Countess stared at each other in almost identical outrage. Count Robert smiled happily at them and then at all the staring guests, as if his announcement was the most joyful thing in the world.

"And Hugo married my sister, Felice, this morning in Stallstead," he added.

"*What?*" thundered Mr. Amos.

"But she can't, dear," the Countess said. "I didn't give my consent."

"She's of age. She didn't need your consent," Count Robert said.

"Now look here, young lord," Mr. Seuly said, getting up and advancing on Count Robert. "I had an understanding—"

Mr. Amos cut him off by suddenly bellowing, "*I forbid this!* I forbid *everything*!"

Everyone stared at him. His face was purple, his eyes popped, and he seemed to be gobbling with rage.

"*I* give the orders here, and *I* forbid it!" he shouted.

"He's mad," some duchess said from beside me. "He's only the butler."

Mr. Amos heard her. "No, I am *not*!" he boomed. "I am Count Amos Tesdinic of Stallery, and I will *not* have my son marry the daughter of an impostor!"

Everyone's faces turned to the Countess then, my mother's very sardonically. The Countess turned and stretched her arms out reproachfully to Mr. Amos. "Oh, Amos!" she said tragically. "How *could* you?

Why did you have to give us all away like this?"

"Too bad, isn't it?" Hugo said, with his arm around Lady Felice.

Mr. Amos turned on him, so angry that his face was purple. *"You . . . !"* he shouted.

Goodness knows what might have happened then. Mr. Amos threw a blaze of magic at Hugo and Lady Felice. Hugo flung one hand up and seemed to send the magic back. Lady Mary joined in, with a sizzle that shot straight at Anthea. My mother whirled around and sent buzzing lumps of sorcery at Lady Mary. Lady Mary screamed and hit back, which made my mother's bird's nest of hair tumble down into hanks on her shoulders. By then Mr. Seuly, Anthea, Count Robert, and some of the guests were throwing magics, too. The room buzzed with it all, like a disturbed wasps' nest, and there were screams and cries mixed in with it. Several chairs fell over as most of the guests tried to retreat toward the Banqueting Hall.

Mr. Prendergast threw open the door again. His voice thundered over the rest of the noise.

"My lords, ladies and gentlemen, your attention, please! Pray silence for the Royal Commissioner Extraordinary!"

Nineteen

The magics and the shouting stopped. Everyone stared. Mr. Prendergast stood aside from the doorway and announced each person as he or she came in. There was quite a crowd of them. The first two were large solemn men in dark suits, who went at once to stand on either side of Mr. Amos.

"Sir Simon Caldwell and Captain William Forsythe," Mr. Prendergast boomed, "personal wizards to His Majesty the King."

Mr. Amos looked from Sir Simon to Captain Forsythe in an astonished, hunted way and then looked a little happier when two smartly dressed ladies came to stand on either side of Count Robert.

"The Princess Wilhelmina and Madame

Anastasia Dupont, Sorceresses Royal," Mr. Prendergast announced. Count Robert went very pale, hearing this.

Quite a lot of the guests went pale, too, as the next group was announced. Mr. Prendergast intoned, "Mrs. Havelok-Harting, the Prosecutor Royal; Mr. Martin Baines, Solicitor to His Majesty; Lord Constant of Goodwell and Lady Pierce-Willoughby, King's High Justices. . . . " I forget the rest, but they were *all* legal people, and Mrs. Havelok-Harting in particular was an absolute horror, gray, severe, and pitiless. They all stared keenly at everyone in the Saloon as they spread out to make room for the next group of people.

"The Chief Commissioner of Police, Sir Michael Weatherby, Inspectors Hanbury, Cardross, and Goring," Mr. Prendergast boomed. This lot was in police uniform.

It dawned on me around then that *these* were all the people the Countess had told the courier to send to a hotel in Stallchester. I felt a trifle dizzy at the Countess's nerve. I tried to imagine them all crowded into the Stallchester Arms or the Royal Stag— probably both, considering how many of them there were—and I simply could not see it. The Countess obviously knew what she had done. She had both hands to her face. When the woman Inspector Goring came and stood stonily beside her, the Countess looked as if she might faint. The other two Inspectors went to stand by Hugo, who looked grim, and Mr. Seuly, who went a sort of yellow, and the Chief Commissioner marched through the Saloon and went to stand by the doors to the Banqueting Hall. Some of the guests who had been edging toward those doors went rather hastily to sit down again.

"The household wizards to the Royal Commissioner," Mr. Prendergast announced, and another group of sober-looking men and women filed in. They brought with them a cold, clean buzz of magic that reminded me somehow of the Walker.

"And," Mr. Prendergast proclaimed, "by special request of His Majesty the King, the Royal Commissioner Extraordinary, Monsignor Gabriel de Witt."

Oh no! I thought. Gabriel de Witt was every bit as terrifying as Christopher had led me to believe. He made Mrs. Havelok-Harting look ordinary. He was very tall, and dressed in foreign-looking narrow trousers and black frock coat, which made him seem about eight feet high. He had white hair and a gray, triangular face, out of which stared the most piercing eyes I had ever seen. He brought such strong age-old magic with him that he made my whole body buzz and my stomach feel as if it were plunging down to the center of the earth. I must warn Millie! I thought. But I didn't dare move.

After all this, I was not surprised when Mr. Prendergast swept his large right hand toward his own chest and added, "And also myself, the King's Special Investigator." Of course Mr. Prendergast was a detective, I thought. It made perfect sense.

Gabriel de Witt stepped slowly forward. "I must explain," he said. He had an old, dry voice, like a corpse speaking. "I came to Series Seven initially in search of two of my young wards, who seemed to have got themselves lost in this world. Naturally I went to the King first and asked his permission to continue my search in this country. But the King had problems of his own. It seemed that somebody in this country kept changing the probabilities for this world. There had been so many shifts, in fact, that *all* Series Seven was in danger of flowing into Series Six on one side and Series Eight on the other. The King's wizards were very concerned."

Mr. Amos, looking very startled, shook his head and made denying gestures. "It couldn't possibly have that effect!" he said.

"Oh yes, it could," Gabriel de Witt said. "I assure you that this is true. I noticed it from the moment I stepped into this world. There are beginning to be serious climate changes and even more serious disruptions to geography—mountains subsiding, seas moving about, continents cracking apart—as this Series tries to conform to the Series on either side. Altogether these changes constitute such a serious misuse of magic that when the King asked me for my help, I had no hesitation in agreeing. I and my staff started to investigate immediately. As a first result of our inquiries, a woman calling herself Lady Amos was arrested yesterday and her offices in Ludwich closed down."

"No!" Mr. Amos cried out.

"Yes," said Gabriel de Witt. "I fancy she is your wife. And"—he looked at Hugo—"your mother, I believe. We now have enough evidence to make further arrests here in Stallery. Mrs. Havelok-Harting, if you would be so good as to read out the charges."

The gray, pitiless lady stepped forward. She rattled open an official paper and cleared her throat with a rather similar rattle. "Robert Winstanley Henry Brown; Dorothea Clarissa Peony Brown, née Partridge; Hugo Vanderlin Cornelius Tesdinic; and Amos Rudolph Percival Vanderlin Tesdinic," she read, "you are all four hereby charged with treasonous imposture, the working of magic to the peril of the realm, fraud, conspiracy to defraud, and high treason. You are under arrest—"

"Not high treason!" Mr. Amos said. He had gone a queer pale mauve.

Count Robert—or plain Robert Brown, as I suppose he really was—had turned the same sort of color Christopher went when he touched silver. "I deny treason!" he said chokingly. "I told Amos I wasn't going along with his pretense anymore. I told him as soon as I got back from marrying Anthea."

My sister, who was clearly trying not to cry, opened her mouth to speak, but Mrs. Havelok-Harting simply turned implacably to one of the legal people. "Make a note," she said. "Tesdinic the elder and the male Brown enter pleas of not guilty as charged."

"And *I* am *innocent!*" the Countess said sobbingly. If she was not crying, she was doing a good job of pretending to. "I never did any of this!"

"No more did I," Mr. Amos said. "This is all some kind of trumped-up . . . "

He stopped and backed away as the red rubber ball came sailing through the Saloon. When it reached Mr. Amos, it began bouncing up and down vehemently in front of him.

"Mistake," Mr. Amos finished, eyeing the ball queasily.

"One moment." Gabriel de Witt held up his hand and strode toward the bouncing ball. "What is this?"

"It's a ghost, Monsignor," said one of the royal wizards beside Mr. Amos.

The other wizard added, hushed and shocked, "It says it's been murdered, sir."

Gabriel de Witt caught the ball and held it in both hands. There was dead silence in the Saloon as he stood there inspecting it, his face growing grimmer every second. "Yes," he said. "Indeed. A female ghost. It says the evidence for the murder will be found in the library. Sir Simon, would you be so good as to accompany this unfortunate ghost to the library and bring the evidence back here to me?"

He passed the wizard the ball. Sir Simon nodded and carried it away past Mr. Prendergast and out through the door.

"This has nothing to do with me," Mr. Amos declared. "You must understand, all of you!" He spread his arms pleadingly. The trouble was that everyone was so shocked and frightened by the presence of a murdered ghost that nobody really took Mr. Amos seriously. My thought was that Mr. Amos looked like a short pear-shaped penguin as he went on passionately. "You *must* understand! I only acted for the sake of Stallery. When my father, Count Humphrey, died, Stallery was bankrupt. The gardens were a wilderness, the roof was falling in, and I had to mortgage everything to pay what Staff we had—and they were a second-rate, slipshod lot anyway. It nearly broke my heart. I *love* Stallery. I wanted to have it as it *should* be, well run, restored, beautiful, full of properly respectful servants. I knew that would take millions, I knew it would take all my time and energy, I knew it would take magic—specially applied magic, magic I invented *myself*, I'll have you know, and secretly installed in the cellars! And in order to make my money, I had to have control of those cellars. The only person who has control of the cellars is the butler, so naturally I had to become the butler. You must see I had to be the butler! I paid a young actor to take my place—Rudolph

Brown and I looked much alike in those days——"

"Yes, and you turned your own brother—my husband—out," my mother said, suddenly and bitterly. "So he wouldn't get in your way. Hubert never got over it."

Mr. Amos stared at her as if he had forgotten she was there. "Hubert was quite happy running a bookshop," he said.

"No, he wasn't," my mother retorted. "The bookshop was *my* idea."

"You are ignoring two things, Count Amos," Gabriel de Witt put in. "First, that your elevation of your actor friend meant you were deceiving the King, which is treason, and second, that your attempt to restore Stallery was bound to come to nothing."

"Nothing?" said Mr. Amos. He held up a hand and flourished it around the Grand Saloon, the guests, the chandeliers, the beautifully painted ceiling, the golden chairs and sofas. "You call this nothing."

"Nothing," Gabriel de Witt repeated. "You must have seen that all the other buildings constructed over this probability fault are, without exception, empty ruins. This probability fault is like a sink. It would have pulled Stallery into the same ruined state in the end, however much magic you used, however much money you poured into it. I imagine this place costs more to run every year. . . . Ah, here is Sir Simon again."

He turned away from Mr. Amos's look of horrified disbelief as Sir Simon came striding among the lawyers and wizards. Of course, on this floor, he could go in through the balcony to the library and be there and back in minutes. Sir Simon came up to Gabriel de Witt, holding the rubber ball in one hand. With the other hand he was dangling my camera.

"Here we are, Monsignor," he said. "The victim claims that the murderer killed her by trapping her soul in this camera."

For a moment I could not breathe. I swear my heart stopped beating. Then, all of a sudden, my heart thundered into life again, hammering in my ears until everything went gray and blotchy and I thought I was going to pass out. I remembered then, I had parked that camera on a bookshelf when Christopher got cramp. I remembered the flashlight going off in the face of that witch as she started to put a spell on me. And I remembered that peculiar magazine, illustrated with bad drawings. Not photographs, *drawings*. The witch came from a world where nobody dared take a photo, because that trapped the person's soul inside the camera. I was a murderer. And I thought, I really do have an Evil Fate, after all.

I only dimly heard Gabriel de Witt saying, "I must ask every person here to wait, either in this room or in the Banqueting Hall with the servants. I or my staff or the police must question each of you under a truth spell."

Quite a number of the guests protested. I thought, I must get out of here! I looked around and realized I was quite near the service door. I had been pushed back toward it when all the people had come in with Gabriel de Witt. While Gabriel de Witt was saying, "Yes, it may indeed take all night, but this is a case of murder, madam," I began backing, very slowly and gently, toward that door. I backed while more guests protested. As I reached the door, Gabriel de Witt was saying, "I apologize, but justice must be done, sir." I went on backing until the door had swung open, just a small bit, behind me. Then, quite thankful that Mr. Amos had made me practice going in and out of rooms so much, I took hold of the door and slid myself around it. I let it close itself on top of my fingers so that it would not thump and then stood for a moment, hoping that no one had noticed me.

"Gabriel de Witt's in there, isn't he?" somebody whispered.

I shot sideways and saw Millie pressed against the wall beside the door. She looked almost as terrified as I was.

"And the house is full of policemen," she said. "Help me get away, Conrad!"

I nodded and tiptoed toward the service stairs. I told myself Millie would be much more frightened if I said why I needed to get away even more urgently than she did. I just whispered to her as she followed me, "Where are they mostly, these policemen?"

"Collecting all the maids and the kitchen staff and taking them to the Banqueting Hall to be questioned," she whispered back. "I kept having to hide."

"Good," I said. "Then we can probably get out through the undercroft. Can you make us both invisible?"

"Yes, but a lot of them are wizards," Millie whispered. "They'd *see* us."

"Do it all the same," I said.

"All right," she said.

We tiptoed on. I couldn't tell if we were invisible

or not. I think we must have been, though, because we passed the lift before we got to the stairs and a policeman came out of it, pushing Mrs. Baldock and Miss Semple in front of him, and none of them saw us. Both housekeepers were crying, Mrs. Baldock in big, heaving sobs and Miss Semple noisy and streaming. "You don't *understand*!" Miss Semple wept. "We've both worked here most of our *lives*! If they turn us off over this, where do we *go*? What do we *do*?"

"Nothing to do with me," the policeman said.

Millie and I dodged around them and fled down the stairs to the ground floor. I pushed the green cloth door open a fraction there. There was a lot of noise in the entrance hall, where more policemen seemed to be marshaling gardeners, stablemen, and chauffeurs up the main stairs. Most of them were protesting that only Family were allowed to go up this way. I let the door shut itself, and we scudded away, down to the undercroft.

I had never seen the undercroft so deserted. It was dim, empty, and echoing. I could almost believe that the probability fault had already swallowed all the life down here. I led Millie as fast as I could toward the door between the kitchens and the cellars where the gardeners usually brought their vegetables and fruit.

This bit was not empty. Light was shining up the cellar steps from the open door at the bottom. There were sounds of people busy in the cellars. Millie and I both jumped violently when a strong, wizardly voice shouted upward, "Go and tell him that shift key is completely stuck at *on*! If I turn the power on, we'll have changes all over the place again. Go on. Hurry!"

I nearly laughed. Christopher stuck that key down! I thought. But somebody began coming up the steps at a run. Millie seized my wrist, and we sprinted past the top of the stairs and into the produce lobby, before the person could get to the top of the cellar steps and see us. I opened the door, and we tiptoed out. Really out, outside into the gardens.

I was very dismayed to find that it was pitch-dark out there, but I said, "Now, run!"

Actually we went at more of a lumbering trot, with our arms out in case we hit something, trying to follow the pale lines that were probably paths. I think that misled us a bit. We may have been following things that were accidentally pale. At any rate, after lumbering for what seemed half an hour, we found ourselves bursting out beyond some midnight black bushes into the wide-open spaces of the park, not the garden as I had expected. It seemed much, much lighter out there.

"Oh, good, we can *see*!" Millie said.

And be seen! I thought. But we had to get outside the grounds somehow. I began to run, quite hard, toward where I thought the main gate was, taking a straight line over the driveway and across the mown turf of the parkland. I felt I couldn't get away from Stallery fast enough.

There was a deep *woof!* somewhere near us, followed by the pounding of mighty paws. I had forgotten Champ. I said a bad word and slowed down. So did Millie.

"Is that a guard dog?" she asked. She sounded even more nervous than I felt.

"Yes, but don't worry," I said, trying to sound thoroughly confident. "He knows me." And I called out, "Champ! Hey, Champ!"

We could trace Champ by the paws and the enormous panting at first. Then his huge dark shape appeared out of the gloom at a gallop. Millie and I both panicked and clutched at each other. But Champ simply swerved toward us, showing us he knew we were there, and went hurtling on, uttering another deep *woof.*

A second later there was the most terrible noise in the distance. Champ burst out barking, a deep, chesty baying, like thunder. Another dog joined in, this one high and ear-piercing, and yapped and yapped and yapped, making even more noise than Champ. A horse started whinnying, over and over, madly. Mixed in with the animal sounds were human voices shouting, some high, some low and angry. We had no idea *what* was going on until another human voice shouted ringingly. *"Shut up, the lot of you!"*

There was instant silence. This was followed by the same voice saying, "Yes, Champ, I love you, too. Just take your paws off my shoulders, please."

Millie shouted, *"Christopher!"* and ran toward the voice.

When I caught her up, she was hanging on to Christopher's hands with both hers, and I think she was crying. Christopher was saying, "It's all right, Millie. I only had a little bother with the changes. Nothing else was wrong. It's all *right*!"

Behind them, looming against the dark sky, was a Traveler's caravan drawn by an irritated-looking white horse. Beyond its twitching ears and flicking tail I could just see a man on the driving seat. His skin was so dark that I never saw him clearly. All I saw were his eyes, looking from me to Millie. The small white dog sitting beside him was much easier to see. Last of all I picked out the faces of a woman and two children looking at us over the man's shoulders.

Here the small white dog decided I was an intruder and started yapping again. Champ, on the ground beside me, took this as a mortal insult and replied. The two yelled abuse at each other, fit to wake the dead.

"*Do* shut them up!" I bawled across the din. "The mansion's full of lawyers and police!"

"And *Gabriel's* here!" Millie yelled. She seemed to be having some kind of reaction to our narrow escapes. Anyway, she was shivering all over.

Christopher said to the dogs, "Shut *up!*" and they did. "I *know* he's here," he said to us. "Gabriel and his merry men were all over the towers and empty castles yesterday, having a good look at the changes. I had an awful job keeping out of sight."

"We *have* to get away," Millie said.

Christopher said, "I know," and looked up at the Traveler driving the caravan. "Is there any chance you can take us all a bit farther?" he asked.

The man gave a sort of mutter and turned to talk with the woman. They spoke quickly together in a language I had never heard before. When the man turned back, he said, "We can take you down to the town, but no farther. We have a rendezvous to make just after dawn."

"I suppose we can get a train there," Christopher said. "Fine. Thank you."

The woman said, "Climb in at the back, then."

So we all scrambled into the caravan, leaving Champ as a melancholy dark hump in the middle of the parkland, and the Traveler clicked to his horse and we drove away.

Twenty

It was strange inside the caravan. I never saw it properly because it was so dark in there, but it seemed much bigger than I would have expected it to be. It was warm—at least it was warm to me, but Millie kept shivering—and full of warm smells of cloth and onions and spiciness, with a sort of tinny, metallic smell behind that. Things I couldn't see kept up a tinkling and chiming from somewhere in the walls. There were what seemed like bunks to sit on, where Christopher and I sat with Millie between us to keep her warm, looking across to the two children, who had hurried inside to stare at us through the dimness as if we were the strangest things on earth. But they wouldn't speak to us whatever we said.

"They've gone shy again. Take no notice," Christopher said. "Why are *you* fleeing Stallery, Grant?"

"I'm a murderer," I said, and told him about the ghost and the camera.

Christopher said, "Oh," very soberly. After a while, he said, "I could really almost believe you *do* have bad karma, Grant, although I know you don't. You certainly have vilely bad luck. Maybe it was the magic— Did you know you were absolutely covered in spells when I first met you? One of them *may* have been a death spell. But I thought I took them all off you while we were walking through the park."

It was my turn to say, "Oh." I explained, rather angrily, "One of those spells was supposed to make Mr. Amos give me a job."

"I know," Christopher said. "That's why I took them off you. I wanted the job. What was Gabriel doing in Stallery—besides looking for me and Millie, that is?"

"Arresting Mr. Amos," I said. "Did you know he was my uncle?"

"Gabriel *can't* be your uncle," said Christopher. "He comes from Series Twelve."

"No, stupid—Mr. Amos," I said. "My mother said

she was married to Mr. Amos's brother."

"That usually does make a person your uncle," Christopher agreed.

"And Mr. Amos is really Count of Stallery," I told him. "Not Count Robert. *His* father was an actor called Mr. Brown. The Countess is really plain Mrs. Brown."

Christopher was delighted. "Tell me all, Grant," he said. So I did.

Millie said, with her teeth chattering, "Did they arrest that witch, too—Lady Mary?"

"I don't think so," I said, "but they may have been going to arrest Mr. Seuly."

"What a pity," Millie said. "Lady Mary *ought* to be arrested. She uses magic in the vilest way. But— No, shut up, Christopher. Stop making clever remarks, and tell me what happened to *you* now. How did you end up with the Travelers?"

"By using my brain," Christopher said, "at last. Before it rotted and fell out of my head. I confess that I got really stuck, out in all those empty towers and mansions. Every time there was a change—and there were plenty of those—I seemed to get farther and farther off from Stallery, and half the time there didn't seem to be a way to get anywhere, even when

I went outside. I got really tired and hungry and confused. I was in a giant building made entirely of glass, when the whole scene suddenly filled with Gabriel's people. Have you ever tried to hide in a glass house? Don't. It can't be done. And they were between me and the way to the roof, so I couldn't go up there to wait for another change. So I panicked. And then I thought, There must be another way! Then I thought of Champ. Champ was never allowed into the house—"

"Just like Mr. Avenloch and Smedley!" I said. "The changes happen out in the park, too!"

"They do, Grant," Christopher said. "The probability fault has two ends, but one is out in the middle of nowhere, and nobody notices it. As soon as I realized that, I dodged out of the beastly greenhouse and went chasing out into the moors to look for the other end. But I don't think I'd ever have found it if the Travelers hadn't come through more or less as I got there. They gave me some food, and I asked them to get me to Stallery—I hoped you were there by then, Millie—and they didn't want to do that at first. They said they would come out in the middle of the park. But I said I'd get them out through the gate-house, so they agreed to take me."

"How *do* we get out through the gate?" I asked.

The words were hardly out of my mouth when the regular clop of the horse's shoes stopped. The Traveler leaned back from the driver's seat and said, "Here is the gatehouse."

"Right." Christopher got up and scrambled to the front of the caravan.

I don't know what he did. The horse started walking again, and after a moment the inside of the caravan went so dark that the kids opposite me gave out little twitters of alarm. The next thing I knew, I was looking out of the back of the van at the tunnel of the gateway, with its gates wide open, and the horse was turning out into the road. I heard its hooves bang and slide on the tramlines as Christopher came crawling back, and then it must have found the space between the rails, because its feet settled into a regular clopping again.

"How did you do that?" Millie asked. It was a professional, enchantress sort of question, even though her teeth were still chattering.

"The gatekeeper wasn't there," Christopher said, "so it was easy to short out the defenses. They must have arrested him, too."

It was a long way down to Stallchester, and the

horse went nothing like so fast as the tram. The slow clopping of its feet was so regular and the inside of the caravan so cozy that I fell asleep and dreamed slow cloves-and-metal-scented dreams. From time to time I woke up, usually on the steep bits, where the horse went slower than ever and the Traveler put on the brake with a long, slurring noise and called out to the horse in his foreign language. Then I went to sleep again.

I woke up finally when white morning light was coming through both ends of the caravan. The clopping hooves seemed louder, with a lot of echo to them. I sat up and saw Stallchester Cathedral going past, very slowly, at the back of the caravan.

A moment later, the Traveler leaned backward to say, "This is where we must put you down."

Christopher jumped awake in a flurry, to say, "Oh. Right. Thanks." I don't think Millie woke up until we were down in the street, watching the caravan swiftly rumbling away from us, jingling and tinkling all over, with the horse now at a smart trot.

Millie started to shiver again. I was not surprised. Her striped Stallery uniform was not at all warm—neither was mine, for that matter. We looked very out of place, in the middle of the wet, slightly foggy street. Christopher's clothes must have been caught in one of the changes. He was wearing wide, baggy garments that could have been made of sackcloth, and he looked even odder than Millie and I did.

"Are you all right?" he said to Millie.

"Just freezing," she said.

"She lived most of her life in a hot country," Christopher explained to me. He looked anxiously around at the touristy boutiques on either side of the street. "It's too early for these shops to be open. I suppose I could conjure you a coat . . . "

Coat, I thought, sweaters, woolen shirts—I know where to find all these things. "Our bookshop is just down the end of this street," I said. "I bet my winter clothes are still there in my room. Let's sneak in and get some sweaters."

"Good idea," Christopher said, looking worriedly at Millie. "And then show us the way to the train station."

I led them down the street and into the alley at the back of our shop. Our yard gate opened in the usual way, with me climbing to the top of it, leaning over to slide the bolt back, and then jumping down and lifting the latch. Inside the yard, the key to the back door was hanging behind the drainpipe, just as usual. I might never have been away, I thought, as we tiptoed through the office. In the shop it was not quite as usual. The cash desk and most of the big bookcases were in different places. I couldn't tell whether this was from one of Uncle Alfred's reorganizations or because of all the changes up at Stallery. The place *smelled* the same, anyway, of book and floor polish and just a whiff of chemicals from Uncle Alfred's workroom.

"You two stay here," I whispered to Christopher and Millie. "I'll creep up and fetch the clothes."

"Will anyone hear?" Millie asked. She settled into the chair behind the cash desk with a weary shiver.

As far as I knew, my mother was still up at Stallery. She had missed the last tram by the time she came into the Grand Saloon, and the first tram in the morning didn't get down to Stallchester until eight-thirty. Uncle Alfred needed two large alarm clocks with double bells the size of teacups in order to wake up in the mornings. "No," I said, and ran up the stairs as lightly as I could.

It was strange. Our stairs seemed small and shabby after Stallery. The fizz of old magics coming from Uncle Alfred's workroom felt small and shabby, too, after the magic I had felt from Christopher and from

Stallery itself. And I had forgotten that the private part of our house smelled so dusty. I hurried through the strangeness up to the very top, to my room.

And I could scarcely believe it when I got there. My mother had taken my room to write in. It was full of her usual piles of papers and copies of her books, and there by the window was her splintery old table with her typewriter on it. For a moment I thought it just might be one of the changes from Stallery, but when I looked closely, I saw the marks where my bed and my chest of drawers had been.

Still scarcely able to believe it, I shot down half a floor to Mum's old writing room. My bed was in there, upside down, and rammed in beside it was my chest of drawers with all its drawers open, empty. All my clothes were gone, and my model aircraft, and my books. They had truly not expected me to come back. I felt—well, *hurt* is the only word for it. Very, dreadfully hurt. But just in case, I went on down and looked into Anthea's room.

That was worse. When I left, there had still been Anthea's furniture in there, along with Mum's papers. Now that was all cleared away. Uncle Alfred had made it into a store for his magical supplies.

There were new shelves full of bottles and packets on three of the walls and a stack of glassware in the middle. I stood and stared at it for a moment, thinking about Anthea. How did she feel at this moment, now they had arrested her new husband for fraud?

I felt quite as bad.

I pulled myself together and tiptoed across the landing to my mother's room. This was better. This room looked and smelled the same as always—though perhaps dustier—and her unmade bed was piled with heaps of her dusty, moth-eaten clothes. There were more clothes puddled in heaps on the floor. Mum had obviously thrown everything out of her cupboards when she hunted out that awful yellow dress to wear at Stallery. I picked up one of her usual mustard-colored sweaters and put it on. It smelled of Mum, which somehow made me feel more hurt than ever. The sweater looked awful over my green and cream uniform, but at least it was warm. I picked up another, thicker sweater for Millie and a jacket for Christopher and hurried away downstairs.

As I went, I thought I heard the shop door open, with its usual muffled tinkle. Oh no! I thought. Christopher is doing something cleverly stupid again! I put on speed and fairly charged out into the shop.

It was empty. I stood in the polished space beside the cash desk and stared around miserably. Christopher and Millie must have left without me.

I was just about to charge on out into the street, waving the clothes, when I heard the flop, flop of slippers hurrying down the stairs behind me. Uncle Alfred bustled out into the shop, tying his dressing gown over his striped pajamas.

"Someone in the shop," he was saying as he came. "I can't turn my back for a moment—never a wink of sleep—" Then he saw me and stopped dead. "What are *you* doing here?" he said. He pushed his spectacles up his nose to make sure it *was* me. When he was certain, he ran his hands through his tousled hair and seemed quite bewildered. "You're supposed to be up at Stallery, Con," he said. "Did your mother send you back here? Does that mean you've killed your Uncle Amos *already?*"

"No," I said. "I haven't." I wanted to tell him that Mr. Amos had been arrested. So there! But I also wanted to tell Uncle Alfred just what I thought of him for putting spells on me and pretending I had an Evil Fate, and I couldn't decide which I wanted to say first. I hesitated, and after that I had lost my chance. Uncle Alfred more or less screamed at me.

"You haven't killed him!" he shrieked. "But I sent you up there with death spells all over you, boy! I sent you to summon a Walker! I sent you with spells to make you *know* it was Amos Tesdinic you had to kill! And you let me down!" He advanced on me in dreadful flopping of slippers and his hands sort of clutching like claws. "You'll pay for this!" he shouted. His face was wild, with strange blotches all over it, and his eyes glared at me through his glasses like big yellow marbles. "I might have had Stallery in my hands—*these* hands—but for you!" he screamed. "With *you* hanged and Amos dead, they'd give the place to your mother, and I can manage *her*."

"No, you're wrong," I said, backing away. "There's Hugo, you see. And Anthea."

He didn't listen to me. He almost never did, of course, unless I forced him to by going on strike about something. *"I could have been pulling the possibilities this moment!"* he howled. "Just let me get my hands on you!"

I could feel the fizz of his magic rising around me. I wanted to turn and run, but I didn't seem to be able to. I didn't know *what* to do.

"Summon the Walker again!" Christopher's voice whispered urgently in my ear. I could feel Christopher's breath tickling the side of my face and the invisible warmth of him beside me. I don't think I have ever been so glad to feel anything. "Summon it *now*, Grant!" The corkscrew key hung around my neck was tugged by invisible fingers and flipped out over Mum's mustard-colored sweater.

I dropped the jacket and the sweater for Millie and grabbed the corkscrew key gratefully. I held it up. The string it was hanging on lengthened helpfully so that I could more or less wave the thing in Uncle Alfred's glaring face. "I hereby summon a Walker!" I screamed. "Come to me and give me what I need!"

The cold, and the feeling of vast open distances, began at once. I could see the immense curving horizon beyond Uncle Alfred's untidy hair, glowing from the light that was out of sight below it. Uncle Alfred whipped around and saw it, too. His mouth opened. He started to back away toward the cash desk, but he did not seem to be able to. I could see dents on the sleeves of his dressing gown where two pairs of hands were hanging on to each of his arms. As the figure of the Walker crossed the huge horizon with its hurried, pattering steps, I could feel Christopher on one side of Uncle Alfred and Millie on the other, both holding on to Uncle Alfred like grappling irons.

Uncle Alfred shouted, "No, no! Let *go*!" and plunged and pulled to get free. His arms heaved as if there were lead weights on him as Christopher and Millie hung on.

The Walker approached with surprising speed, its hair and clothing blown sideways without moving, in the unfelt frozen wind it brought with it. In no time at all, it was towering into the shop and looming among the bookcases, filling the space with its icy smell. Then it was standing over us. Its intent white face and long dark eyes turned from Uncle Alfred to me.

"*No, no!*" Uncle Alfred cried out.

The Walker's long dark eyes turned to Uncle Alfred again. It held out to him the small crimson-stained wine cork labeled *Illary Wines 1893*.

"Don't point that at me!" Uncle Alfred shrieked, pulling away backward. "Point it at Con! It's got a really strong death spell on it!"

The Walker's white face nodded at him. Once. Both its arms swept out. It picked Uncle Alfred up bodily and pattered on past me, carrying Uncle Alfred as easily as if he had been a baby. The last I saw of him were his striped pajama legs kicking frantically as he was carried away beside my right shoulder. As the Walker itself passed me, there was a jerk at my neck, and the corkscrew key flew out of my hands and vanished. The feeling of wind and the horizon of eternity vanished at the same instant.

Millie and Christopher became visible then, staggering away sideways, both looking extremely shaken. Christopher said, in an unusually small, sober voice, "I don't think I like either of your uncles, Grant."

"That," said a deep, dry voice from behind me, "must be the first sensible notion you have had for months, Christopher."

Gabriel de Witt was standing there, gray and severe, and looking tall as the Walker in his black frock coat. He was not alone. All the staff who had come with him into the Grand Saloon were there, too, crowded up against bookcases and standing in the space where the Walker had been. Mr. Prendergast was with them, and the King's solicitor, and one of the Sorceresses Royal—Madame

Dupont, it was—and the dreadful Mrs. Havelok-Harting as well. My mother and Anthea were standing beside Gabriel de Witt, both very weary and tearstained. But I was interested to see, looking around, that every single person there seemed as shaken as I was by the passing of the Walker. Even Gabriel de Witt was a little grayer than he had been in Stallery.

At the sight of him, and of all the other people, Christopher looked as dumbfounded as I had ever seen him. His face went as white as the Walker's. He gulped a bit and tried to straighten the tie he wasn't wearing. "I can explain everything," he said.

"Me, too," Millie whispered. She looked downright ill.

"I shall speak to the two of you later," Gabriel de Witt said. It sounded very ominous. "For now," he said, "I want to talk to Conrad Tesdinic."

This sounded even more ominous. "I can explain everything, too," I said. I was scared stiff. I thought I'd rather talk to Uncle Alfred, any day. "I come of a criminal family, you see," I said. "Both my uncles—and I'm sure I *do* have an Evil Fate, whatever Christopher says."

For some reason, this made Anthea give a weepy little laugh. My mother sighed.

"I need to ask you some questions," Gabriel de Witt said, just as if I had not said anything. He pulled a packet out of an inside pocket of his ink black respectable frock coat and passed it to me. It seemed to be a packet of postcards. "Please look through these pictures and explain to me what you see there."

Though I could not for the life of me see why Gabriel de Witt should be interested in picture postcards, I opened the packet and pulled them out. "Oh," I said. They were prints of the photographs I had taken of the double spiral staircase where we saw Millie. There was one of just the staircase, then two of Millie on the same staircase, shouting across at Christopher, and then one of the same staircase, looking up toward the dirty glass of the tower. But something had gone wrong with all of them. Behind each one, misty but quite distinct, were the insides of other buildings, dozens of them. I could see fuzzy hallways, other stairways, domed rooms in many different styles, ruined stone arches, and, several times, what looked like a giant greenhouse. They were all on top of one another, in layers. "I think I must have loaded a film that someone else had used first," I said.

Gabriel de Witt simply said, "Continue looking, please."

I went on down the pile. Here was the hall the double stairway had led down to, but the other person seemed to have photographed a marble place with a sort of swimming pool in it and somewhere dark, with statues, behind that. The next was the room with the harp, but this had literally dozens of rooms mistily behind it, blurred vistas of ballrooms and dining rooms and huge saloons, and a place with billiard tables on top of what looked like several libraries. The next two photographs showed the kitchens—with dim further kitchens behind them—including the knitting on the chair and the table with the strange magazine on it. The next . . .

I gave a sharp yelp. I couldn't help it. The witch had been even nearer than I'd thought. Her face had come out flat and round and blank, the way faces do when you push a camera right up to them. Her mouth was open in a black and furious crescent, and her eyes glared flatly. She looked like an angry pancake.

"I didn't mean to kill her," I said.

"Oh, you didn't kill her," Gabriel de Witt, to my astonishment, replied. "You merely trapped her soul. We found her body in a coma in one of those kitchens, while we were exploring the alternate buildings, and we returned it to Seven D, where I am pleased to say they promptly put it in prison. She was wanted in that world for killing several enchanters in order to obtain their magical powers."

Millie gave a small gasp at this.

One of Gabriel de Witt's tufty eyebrows twitched toward Millie, but he continued without interrupting himself, "We have of course returned the woman's soul to Seven D now, so that she may stand trial in the proper way. Tell me what *else* you see in those pictures."

I leafed through the pile again. "These two of Millie on the stairs would be quite good," I said, "if it wasn't for all the buildings that have come out behind her."

"They were not there when you took the photographs?" Gabriel de Witt asked me.

"Of course not," I said. "I've never seen them before."

"Ah, but we *have*," said one of Gabriel de Witt's people, a youngish man with a lot of light, curly hair and a brown skin. He came forward and handed me a packet of differently shaped photographs. "I took these while we were searching the probabilities for Millie and Christopher," he said. "What do you think?"

These were photographs of two ruined castles, some marble stairs leading up from a pool, a ballroom, a huge greenhouse, and the double spiral staircase again, and the last one was of the rickety wooden tower where Christopher and I found Champ. All of them, to my shame, were clear and single and precise.

"They're much better than mine," I said.

"Yes, but just look," said the man. He took my first photograph of Millie on the stairway and held it beside four of his. "Look in the background of yours," he said. "You've got both these ruined castles in it and the glass house, and I think that blurred thing behind them is the wooden tower. And if you take yours with the harp, you can see my ballroom at the back of it quite clearly. See?"

The Sorceress Royal said, "In our opinion—and Mrs. Havelok-Harting agrees with me—it's a remarkable talent, Conrad, to be able to photograph alternate probabilities that you can't even see. Isn't this so, Monsignor?" she asked Gabriel de Witt.

Mr. Prendergast added, "Hear, hear."

Gabriel de Witt took my photographs back from me and stood frowning down at them. "Yes, indeed," he said at last. "Master Tesdinic here has an extraordinary degree of untrained magical talent. I would like"—he turned his frown on my mother—"to take the lad back with me to Series Twelve and make sure that he is properly taught."

"Oh no!" Anthea said.

"I believe I must," Gabriel de Witt said. He was still frowning at my mother. "I cannot think what you were doing, madam, neglecting to provide your son with proper tuition."

My mother's hair was down all over the place, like an unstuffed mattress. I could see she had no answer to Gabriel de Witt. So she said tragically, "Now *all* my family is to be taken from me!"

Gabriel de Witt straightened himself, looking grim and dour even for him. "That, madam," he said, "is what tends to happen when one neglects people." And before my mother could think what to say to this, he added, "The same thing can be said to myself, if this is any consolation." He turned his grim face to Millie. "You were quite right about that Swiss school, my dear," he said to her. "I went and inspected it before I came on here. I should have done that before I sent you to it. It's a terrible place. We shall see about a better school as soon as we get home."

Millie's face became one jubilant, shivering smile.

Christopher said, "What did I tell you?"

It was clear that Christopher was still in bad trouble. Gabriel de Witt said to him, "I said I would speak to you later, Christopher," and then turned to Mrs. Havelok-Harting. "May I leave all outstanding matters in your capable hands, Prosecutor? It is more than time that I returned to my own world. Please present my compliments to His Majesty and my thanks to him for allowing me the freedom to investigate here."

"I shall do that," the formidable lady said. "We would have been quite at a stand without you, Monsignor. But," she added rather more doubtfully, "did your magics last night definitely *stop* those dreadful probability changes?"

"Very definitely," Gabriel de Witt said. "Some foolish person appeared to have jammed the shift key to *on*, that was all." I saw Christopher wince at this. Luckily Gabriel de Witt did not notice. He went on, "If you have any further trouble, please send a competent wizard to fetch me back. Now, is everyone ready? We must leave."

Anthea rushed at me and flung her arms around me. "Come back, Conrad, please!"

"Of course he will," Gabriel de Witt said, rather impatiently. "No one can leave his own world forever. Conrad will return to act as my permanent representative in Series Seven."

I have just come back to Series Seven to be Agent for the Chrestomanci here.

Before this I spent six blissfully happy years at Chrestomanci Castle, learning magic I never dreamed existed and making friends with all the other young enchanters being educated there—Elizabeth, Jason, Bernard, Henrietta, and the rest—although the first week or so was a little difficult. Christopher was in such bad trouble—and so annoyed about it—that the castle seemed to be inside a thunderstorm until Gabriel de Witt forgave him. And Millie turned out to have caught flu. This was why she had been feeling so cold. She was so ill with it that she did not go to her new school until after Christmas.

At the end of the six years, when I was eighteen, Gabriel de Witt called me into his study and explained that I must go home to Series Seven now or I would start to fade, not being in my own world. He suggested that the way to get used to my own world again was to attend Ludwich University. He also said he was sorry to lose me, because I seemed to be the only person who could make Christopher see sense. I am not sure anyone can do that, but Christopher seems to think so, too. He has asked me to come back next year to be best man at his wedding. He and Millie are using the gold ring with Christopher's life in it as a wedding ring, which seems a good way to keep it safe.

Anyway, I have enrolled as a student in Ludwich, and I am staying with Mr. Prendergast in his flat opposite the Variety Theater. Though Mr. Prendergast isn't really an actor, he never can stay away from theaters. Anthea wanted me to stay with her. She keeps ringing me up from New Rome to say I must live with her and Robert as soon as she gets back. She is in New Rome supervising her latest fashion show—she has become quite a famous dress designer. And Robert is away, too, filming in Africa. He took up acting as soon as the police let him go. Mrs. Havelok-Harting decided that as Robert only discovered Mr. Amos's fraud when his father died and then refused to be part of it, he could not be said to be guilty. Hugo had a harder time, but they released him, too, in the end. Now—and I could hardly believe this when Mr. Prendergast told me—Hugo and Felice are running the bookshop in Stallchester. My mother is still writing books in their attic. We are driving up to see them next weekend.

Mr. Amos is still in jail. They transferred him to St. Helena Prison Island last year. And the Countess is living in style in Buda-Parich, not wanting to show herself in this country. And—Mr. Prendergast is not sure, but he thinks this is so—Mr. Seuly went there to join her when he got out of prison. Anyway, Stallchester has a new mayor now.

No one has seen or heard of my Uncle Alfred since the Walker took him away. Now I have learned about such things, I am not surprised. The Walkers are messengers of the Lords of Karma, and Uncle Alfred tried to use the Lords of Karma in his schemes.

And Stallery is falling into ruin, Mr. Prendergast told me sadly, and becoming just like all the other deserted probability mansions. I remembered Mrs. Baldock and Miss Semple coming weeping out of the lift and wondered what had become of all the Staff who had lost their jobs there.

"Oh, the King stepped in there," Mr. Prendergast told me cheerfully. "He's always on the lookout for well-trained domestics to man the royal residences. They've all got royal jobs. Except Manfred," Mr. Prendergast added. "He had to give up acting after he fell through the wall in a dungeon scene. I think he's a schoolteacher now."

The King wants to see me tomorrow. I feel very nervous. But Fay Marley has promised to go with me at least as far as the door and hold my hand. She knows the King well, and she says she thinks he may want to make me a Special Investigator like Mr. Prendergast. "You notice things other people don't see, darling," she says. "Don't worry so much. It'll be all right, you'll see."